ROBERT ALLEN

Grimm the Reaper

The Professor's Quota

First edition

ISBN: 979-8-9859619-2-8

Editing by Shayne Robison

*This book was professionally typeset on Reedsy.
Find out more at reedsy.com*

Contents

Foreword

The campus of New Mexico State University was a hallowed place of learning, a sanctuary built on the promise of a better future. But even here, ambition has a price. Some pay with years of toil, with late-night studies and endless debt. Others, like Professor Craig Newman, pay with something more.

Craig made his bargain for a shortcut, a deal struck in a moment of hubris and impatience. He wanted the prestige without the 20-year climb. He got it. Now, the bill has arrived. And the collection agent, Grimm, isn't accepting cash.

In the old legends, the Reaper was a specter of finality. A solitary figure, a force of nature, indifferent and absolute. But myths, like markets, evolve. The simple truths of old have given way to the complex, multi-tiered systems of the new world. Even Hell, it seems, has adapted.

This isn't a story about the grand war between Heaven and Hell. It is an intimate, brutal story of one man's quiet descent. It's about a man who stands in front of a lecture hall filled with hopeful, bright-eyed students, knowing that each one is a potential product, a potential sale. It's about a deal that was never truly over, and a contract that has now turned him into a contractor.

The great myth of the diabolical pact has been rebranded. It's no longer a one-on-one negotiation in a shadowy room, but a sales pitch in a college coffee shop. The endless legions of the damned are no longer recruited; they are enlisted, with quotas and performance reviews.

What happens when the academician becomes a salesman for damnation? When the dreams he's supposed to foster become the very currency of his eternal damnation?

Turn the page to see how a life is built on a lie, and how a legacy can become a ledger of souls.

1

The Deal

Grimm was standing in the Great Hall of the New Mexico State University where Craig Newman was a history professor. He watched as the students walked between classes, most with a friend, chatting about this and that, some were alone, with their heads down, looking at their phones or just counting the floor tiles as they passed over them. They weren't aware of his presence in the least. A few students walked right through the space he was standing in, they felt a cold spot in the air, one even shuddered after going out the other side of Grimm's cloak. His cloak fluttered, waving up, then back down as the student passed through. Grimm was watching for Craig, He could easily transport himself to him with just a thought but today was a little different. His manifest had come to him with a notation next to certain names. **"Optional"** in bold print, highlighted yellow. He pulled the list from within the cloak with his bony, ash colored, skeletal fingers and looked at it again. *'Why optional? What has this one done that would give him a second look? It is not for me to judge a request from the Center Of All That Is Evil. I should be grateful* *that he has allowed me a replacement this far into the year.'* He looked at the photo of Craig next to his name on the list. Craig was a stocky, short statured man, showing only a slight bit of gray at the temples but otherwise a full head of dark brown hair. He wore a full beard but kept it tightly trimmed and always a suit with a tie. Grimm tossed the manifest into the air and it disintegrated into dust, dissipating into a fading cloud. Grimm spun around to face the doors of the hall without moving his feet, he wasn't actually touching the floor, merely hovering a half an inch above it. Through the glass doors he could see the college courtyard, a large grass area with concrete pathways crossing the lawns and leading to a fountain in the center court. Students and staff walked at mostly a hurried pace, squinting in the afternoon sun, trying not to be late for their next class. Grimm spotted his client on the opposite side of the court, walking toward the Great Hall. He didn't appear to be in as much of rush as everyone else was.

Craig had just finished his last class of the day and was strolling across the courtyard toward his office, taking in the afternoon sun of the New Mexico desert town. Craig had been a college professor going on 10 years. He started out of college himself as a high school history teacher. It has always been history for Craig, he actually loved what he taught. He spent only 5 years as a high school teacher then stumbled upon the opportunity to apply for the professor position at NMSU. Craig was, at the time, severely under qualified but thanks to some handshake deals with people he really didn't know, Craig was granted the position and given a salary of that of a professor with a law degree. Craig's dreams had come true in a short period of time if only he made sure a certain few students passed through the system with acceptable grades and little trouble. At first, Craig hadn't liked the idea but he'd wanted the position so badly that he devised a plan to make him feel like he wasn't just passing the students with no effort on their part, but rather he tailored the course materials for those students and they actually earned their grades. He took care of his 'deal' in the first two years that he worked at the college and hadn't thought of the transaction since.

Craig sauntered through the courtyard with his satchel full of history essays he would need to read over this afternoon, slung over his shoulder, enjoying the bright afternoon sun as he neared the center court fountain. The splashing of the fountain waters muted the sound of students talking and laughing at each others anecdotes of the day. Craig enjoyed passing through the center court, seeing students and other staff out in the sun, enjoying life, as well as each others company. Craig was well liked by students and other staff members on campus that he knew but he wasn't a social butterfly so there were plenty of people on campus that he had never met. No one had ever found out about the deal he had arranged to get there. Craig paused at the fountain to watch the streams of water shoot into the air and splash back down into the clear blue pool below. He could barely see the bottom of the tile lined pool, dotted as it was with coins, reflecting in the glaring sun from the turbulence created by the crashing streams of water in the fountain. After a few moments watching the mist reflect in the sun before it evaporated, Craig moved past the fountain, continuing his walk toward the Great Hall. It was nearly 85 degrees outside but as he got closer to the hall he felt a chill in the air. It was slight at first but as he got closer to the steps leading into the building, the temperature seemed to drop even more. Craig went up the five steps to the first landing then stopped and looked up at the sky, wondering if there were clouds moving in for a rare afternoon storm. *'Not a cloud up there.'* He shook off the chill and went up the rest of the steps to the doors of the Great Hall. When Craig pulled open the large glass door to step inside, he was blasted with a cold rush of air. *'Wow! The AC must be on overload.'* He stepped through the doors, walking inside only a few feet when he saw a ghastly dark figure facing the doors. A chill raced up his spine and the cold temperature felt like frozen air. *'It must be 30 degrees in here.'* The figure in front of him stood over six and half feet tall, dressed in an all black robe. Craig thought it must be an art piece as it wasn't moving and there were no recognizable features. It was, after all, nearing Halloween. The head was covered in a long hood, with just a dark shadow where the face should be. *'Ugh, that's kind of creepy. Why is it so cold in here?'* Craig started to walk to the right of the figure but his steps seemed heavy and slow. He couldn't take his eyes off of the black robed giant, like it was drawing him in, some sort of morbid curiosity pulling at Craig's soul. He walked tentatively toward the figure that he now recognized as the Grim Reaper and stopped five or six feet in front of it. Craig stood still in front of Grimm, taking in his presence, pondering the historical origination of the Grim Reaper from the 14th century Black Plague that he had studied when he was an undergrad student. Craig looked past Grimm and around the Great Hall, noticing that no one else seemed to be giving this statue any attention. He hadn't seen it there this morning when he went from his office to the lecture hall for his first class of the day. Grimm stood still, watching Craig look around the hall.

"Craig Newman."

Craig jumped back and took a defensive stance, his arms out in front of him in case he was attacked. Grimm did not move.

"Mr. Newman, I have come to see you." As Grimm stood there in front of Craig he lifted his arm from his side, allowing the sleeve of his black robe to pull away, revealing his skeletal hand. He reached under his cloak and pulled out the manifest with Craig's name and photo. Grimm's voice was low and very clear with a hint of a British accent. "You see here Mr. Newman, you are on my list." Grimm tossed the page toward Craig, it floated easily through the air and hovered in front of his face just long enough that Craig could read his name in bold print, '**CRAIG NEWMAN** (OPTIONAL)'.

Just as Craig finished reading it, the page disintegrated into dusty smoke and was gone. Craig was still not sure of what he was seeing. He adjusted his glasses, rubbed his left eye, then took a hard look at Grimm. He glanced around the Great Hall to see if anyone was seeing what he was seeing. The amount of students in the hall had dwindled as they all found their way to their classes. Craig turned back to Grimm and opened his mouth to speak but nothing would come out. Just then, one of his students walked through Grimm as he approached Mr. Newman.

"Mr. Newman, I wanted to ask you what date was set for our final? I have a trip planned for the holidays and don't want to miss the test."

Craig took a step back after seeing the student walk through the cloaked being. Grimm faded into particles of smoke and drifted toward the ceiling. Craig watched it happen, looking toward the ceiling with his mouth hanging open.

His student stood in front of him with a concerned look on his face. "Are you okay? Mr. Newman? What are you looking at?" He turned around and looked at the ceiling but could see nothing, looking back at Craig, he yelled. "MR. NEWMAN!"

Craig jumped and refocused his eyes on the student in front of him. "I'm sorry, what did you want?" His voice was a bit shaky.

The young man in front of him had a furrowed brow, looking at Craig like he didn't fully trust that Mr. Newman was altogether sane in this moment. "Are you okay? You looked like you were in a trance."

Craig straightened up and adjusted his glasses again. "I was deep in thought and must have gotten carried away with it. Not to worry young man, I'm fine. What can I do for you?"

The young man's expression softened slightly as he adjusted the backpack he was carrying and restated his question. "When is our final? I have a trip over the holidays and don't want to miss it."

"Oh yes." Mr. Newman said, trying to get back to reality. "It will be in three week. I haven't decided if we will have it on Tuesday or Thursday, I believe it will depend on whether we cover all the material I have laid out. It's going to be tight, I suggest not missing any of the classes."

His student looked at his phone for the time. "Thank you, Mr. Newman, have a good day." He turned, with his heavy backpack swinging to the side, making him correct course from the extra weight, and walked toward the Great Hall doors.

Craig stood and watched him go but was thinking about the figure he had just witnessed. *'Did I really just see that?'* He pivoted slowly around, taking note of the students and staff still in the Great Hall. *'No one else seems to have noticed anything unusual.'* Craig started walking farther into the hall, toward the grand curved stairs leading to staff offices on the second and third floors. *'OPTIONAL? What does that mean?'* His hands were clammy and he could feel sweat beading on the back of his neck. He stopped at the bottom of the stairs and looked up at the curved staircase to the second floor. *'Where is this coming from? Was that some creepy hallucination?'* He took a deep breath, wiped a cold sweat from his brow, and climbed the stairway leading to his office, noting that the temperature had returned to normal. Craig's office was on the second floor, down the hall, third door on the right. It was a modest office given his tenure and the salary bestowed him when he started, but he had grown to like it. He'd filled the space with historical artifacts, books, and treasures from all over the world. Each item represented a moment in history that he found interesting. Craig walked in and swung the door closed behind him, the frosted glass in the door rattled when the door struck the jamb. The office was tidy even with the abundant items filling every conceivable spot. Setting the satchel on the edge of the large mahogany desk, Craig sat heavily into his stuffed leather office chair and leaned as far back as he could. Staring at the ceiling, he started to rub his forehead with both hands. *'Maybe I just need some rest.'* Craig put his feet up on the corner of the desk and closed his eyes, it only took a few moments before he was asleep.

Craig's eyes fluttered, eyelids twitching. His eyes moved from side to side and a small tear slipped out from between the lids of his right eye. The room had gotten suddenly cold and vapor came out of his mouth as his breathing got heavier and heavier was he reacted to his dream. Suddenly Craig jolted awake, his feet fell from the desk and his arms flew up in the air to catch his balance. He opened his eyes, looked across the desk, and let out a horrific scream suitable for a movie heroine being surprised by a chainsaw killer. Grimm was sitting with perfect posture in the chair opposite Craig, his skeleton fingers crossed in his lap. Just the lower part of his skeletal jaw could be seen out of the shadows beneath his black cloak hood. Craig jumped, pushing back in his chair in surprise until he hit the wall behind him, his hands gripping the arms of the chair, ready to jump up and run out of the room, losing his balance, he fell over backward, rolling over his head, landing on his hands and knees. Craig scrambled to the edge of his desk and hid there for a moment before slowly rising up so just his eyes were above the edge of the desk. He straightened his glasses and took a hard look at the dark figure in the chair across the desk from him.

Craig's voice came out in a croak. "Who are you?" The air in the office was bitter cold. He could see his breath as he heaved air in and out.

"I think you know who I am. You've always known this day would come."

Craig's eyes got huge. "You've come for me? That can't be, it's not my time!" Craig, on the verge of panic, ducked down behind the desk again. *'Is there a way out of here? This can't be happening.'*

Grimm stood up and leaned over the desk, his bony hands propped in the middle of it. "Don't be pathetic. Come out from behind your desk."

Craig looked up but remained in his crouched position. "I don't think I want to do that."

Grimm's voice boomed like Darth Vader, "STAND!"

Flinching, Craig slowly began to get to his feet. He backed up as he got off his knees but was cornered against the wall of his office. His face was turning bright red from the chill in the air. "Who sent you?"

Grimm was standing now and Craig could see the bony structure of his lower jaw and his weathered fingers protruding from his sleeves. Waiving off the question, Grimm spoke slowly, in a deep voice, drawing out his words. "You made a deal over a decade ago, the time has come to settle your end of the contract."

In Shock Craig's his mouth dropped open and he looked at Grimm with astonishment. "You must have the wrong person, I haven't made any deals."

Grimm pulled a dark, weathered piece of paper from his cloak and let it float to the desk. "You most certainly did make a deal, to gain the position you hold here in this office."

Craig moved slowly to his desk and looked down at the paper. "This is the contract I signed when I became a professor at the college." He leaned over the desk, reaching out to pick up the paper to examine it closer. As he touched it, the paper crumbled to dust and blew off the desk. Craig looked at Grimm. "How is that a deal with…. who Sent you?"

Grimm crossed his arms in front of his chest. "Your deal was made with the Devil. You signed a contract to give him your soul, at any time he so chooses to take it after a decade has passed from the date of the signature."

Craig stood up straight, summoning his confidence, and spoke with arrogance in his voice. "I most certainly did not sign a deal with the Devil. I have never met the Devil, therefore, this cannot be happening." Craig then crossed his arms and faced Grimm as if to say, 'HA! Take that.'

Grimm reached inside his cloak and pulled out yet another paper, tossing it in the air. On it was a video playing the day he signed and shook hands with the hiring officer of the university. "This is you, is it not?"

Craig was astonished at the sight of the paper floating in front of him showing what looked like a silent black and white film clip. "It appears to be," he said slowly, reaching out to touch the paper. "But that isn't the Devil, that's James Lucky, he works for the university as the hiring manager." Craig watched the image as it floated at eye level, replaying the interaction between himself and Mr. Lucky. He was just about to touch the paper when Grimm waved his emaciated hand through the paper and it poofed into smoke and vanished.

"What did you think he should look like? Mr. Lucky is an agent of the Most Evil One himself, working to sign clients into his service. You see, Mr. Newman, you should always read the fine print of a contract. By accepting the deal to work here and let those few students slide through the system, you were given the position you desired and left alone for over a decade until your services were requested by the Center of All that is Evil. I am sure you still have a copy of your contract somewhere in this stuffy little office, why don't you take some time to pull it out and read it. I will return in two days time to have a discussion about your new assignment."

Craig was standing with his arms folded across his chest trying to fend off the cold, rubbing his hands on his arms to create some friction. "Why is it so cold? I thought the Devil was all fire and brimstone."

Grimm looked at Craig, his eyes beginning to glow red from beneath his hood and spoke slowly in a menacing tone. "My being requires all the energy from around me in order to survive. Energy is heat, therefore all that is left for you is the absence of heat." Grimm turned around elegantly and strode from the room, straight through the door without opening it.

The heat slowly returned to the room, Craig leaned against the desk, with both hands exhausted by the encounter, hanging his head with his eyes closed. *'What on earth just happened? The contract!'* Remembering this, he rushed to an old file cabinet against the wall and pulled open the bottom drawer. He started rummaging through the old papers, looking for the contract he signed when he was hired. He found it tightly crammed in the back deep in a file marked 'Personal.' Taking it to his desk he flopped it down, stumbling over his overturned chair. After picking up the chair and sliding it back into position, Craig sat at his desk reading his hiring contract page by page. Finally, under section 5 Presence, subsection 4.A. Appearance and Dress Code. Was a long winded paragraph about suitable clothing, personal upkeep and care.

'B. Signer of contract shall submit soul to the Controller of All That is Dark at such time that he calls upon signer for service, no sooner than one decade from date of signature. The Controller of Evil will call upon signer for services of his design and choosing for all eternity or until the execution of a secondary contract, nullifying this agreement, is set in place and agreed upon by both parties in writing. Should the signer not preform to the satisfaction of the Center of All Darkness, Harbinger of Hate and Evil, said signer's soul will be taken and tortured for all of eternity.'

Section C. goes on about code of conduct when interacting with students.

Craig stopped reading and sat back in his leather chair. He stared at the pages on his desk, dumbfounded that he had missed this in the contract, but also not surprised, as he barely skimmed it once it got to mundane things like dress code. Those things were a given in this line of work and not surprising at all in a contract like this.

'I have to go see James, he must have known what he was doing when he gave me this contact.' Craig glanced at the clock on his desk, *'3:10, he may have left already.'* He gathered his contract paperwork, stuffing it back in order and into the file as he stood up at his desk. Craig marched across his office, determined to go have a talk with Mr. James Lucky. He reached for the door handle but stopped with his hand hovering just above it. *'He went right through the door when he left.'* Slowly, he grasped the handle and turned it, pulling the door open, he peaked his head into the hallway, looking both directions. *'I guess it really doesn't matter, he can go through walls. WHAT AM I SAYING!? GO THROUGH WALLS? THIS IS CRAZY!'* He stepped into the hall closing and locked the door behind him.

Craig climbed the stairs to the third floor. In the front hiring office, Rita was packing her things, getting ready to leave for the day.

"Hello Rita, I wonder, would you know if James Lucky is in his office? I rather need to speak to him."

Rita looked up at Craig from her seat, a bewildered look on her face. "Mr. Newman, Mr. Lucky died several years ago. Well, we presume that he died, he just stopped showing up one day. I think there was a fairly large search for him but I never heard what came of it. I believe that there was never anything found so the searching stopped."

Craig had to remind himself to close his mouth as he stood there, in awe at what he was hearing. "I do seem to remember

12

seeing some sort of posters for a missing person. I can't believe I didn't realize it was James."

Rita was looking at Craig with wonder. "I take it you two weren't friends."

Craig looked down at the desk in front of Rita. "Well, no, I didn't know him other than him being the one that hired me on, and I would occasionally say hello when seeing him in the building. Thank you, Rita."

"Sure thing. Do you want to talk to Matt Reid? He is the new hiring administrator."

Craig shook his head slowly as he thought about it. "No, not right now. I'll come back if I change my mind."

'I wonder if Matt is still having people sign the same paperwork that I did.' Craig turned and walked out of the office, out to the main staircase. He stood at the rail over looking the Great Hall from 30 feet above the main entrances. He watched as more students started filling the area from the classes on the first floor. *'How many of you have already struck a deal with the Devil and don't know it? What do I do now?'* He turned and walked slowly down the stairs, returning to his office, looking over his shoulder several times, feeling a bit jumpy.

2

Consultation

Craig was on edge over the next two days, waiting for the return of the ghost in the black cloak. He couldn't bring himself to call him the Grim Reaper. *Why didn't he just finish me off right then? Isn't that what the Grim Reaper does? I guess I should feel lucky to still be alive.'* Craig was sitting in his office, he had tried not to spend much time in it over the last day and a half, he felt an eeriness about it after being confronted by the Grim Reaper the day before. He was trying to eat his lunch that he had brought from home, but was finding he didn't have much of an appetite. The contract he had signed was sitting on his desk in the manila folder, Craig flipped it open again for what seemed like the hundredth time, reading the same paragraph over and over. He had questions now that he had some time to consider its contents, but wasn't sure he would have the nerve to ask them even given the opportunity. *'The Devil owns my soul for all eternity unless there is a secondary contract. What kind of secondary contract? How does that come about? Can I propose a contract? What would I have to do for it to be acceptable?'* Craig sat slumped in his leather chair, his sandwich laying on the desk with two bites taken out of it. He had a blank look on his face, his eyes were empty of life, his mind was numb with the idea that he would no longer be living his life, but rather living for evil. *'What does that look like? What will I have to do?'* At that moment, he realized the office had gotten bitterly cold.

"You don't look well."

The voice startled him. Craig looked up toward the door and jumped to his feet. The giant figure stood in front of him, cloaked in black, having just materialized through the closed door, with his arms behind him and only a deep dark shadow under the hood where his face should be.

Craig shifted his feet to move backward slightly and gathered his thoughts quickly, stammering over the first word. "Wha... What should I call you?"

Grimm replied with a calm tone, as if he was having a conversation with an old friend. "I am Grimm, with two m's. As luck would have it, that was my name before becoming a Reaper."

Craig surprised himself with how calm his next words were. "As you can imagine, I have been a little freaked out since I last saw you. I reviewed the contract with the buried terms giving my soul to the Devil or The Controller of Evil as I believe it reads in the contract."

Grimm stood motionless in front of Craig. "The terms were there for you to read, you just didn't do your due diligence. Had you taken the time to read it, you most certainly could have refrained from signing the contract and we would not be here having this conversation."

Craig looked down at his uneaten sandwich. "You can't be serious, those terms had nothing to do with the contract that

I was signing."

Grimm stiffened, his voice slightly more stern, which made Craig step back. "Those terms had everything to do with the deal that you made when you agreed to move those students through the program."

Craig looked down at the floor, ashamed. "Oh, that."

Grimm remarked dryly back at him. "Yes, that."

Craig stood still, thinking about how he had gotten into this mess to begin with. "Is there anything I can do to nullify the contract?"

Grimm didn't speak for a few moments, as if he were thinking of something Craig could do. "No. The contract is very specific, and the Lord of Darkness does not bend when it comes to contracts."

Craig cleared his throat slightly. "In the contract it states that a secondary contract can be used to nullify the original contract, how does that work?"

Grimm moved forward in the room, hovering just above the floor toward the chair he had sat in during the last visit. "Please be seated, lets discuss your options."

Craig backed into his chair, careful not to fall into it. Grimm sat across from him, folding his bony fingers in his lap.

"In short, your options are as follows: One; you can choose not to believe what I am telling you, or not take part in the recruitment process and I will arrange for your untimely death, after which your soul will spend eternity tortured in hell. This happens quite often as people somehow don't believe that I am serious. Look at me, do I not look serious?"

Craig wasn't sure if he was supposed to answer so he just shook his head and Grimm continued.

"Two; you can take part in the recruitment process, if

16

you are successful, you will move up the ranks of Recruits, eventually overseeing other Recruiters and not having to do the dirty work yourself, all while living a somewhat normal existence until you pass on naturally, at which time you will become a Reaper.

Three; your final option is to take on the Challenge. The Challenge sets forth an allotment of recruiting that you must complete in a short period of time. If you are successful you will be released from your binding and allowed to live out the rest of your existence free from The Controller of Evil. But be warned, if you should fail, you will not have the option to go back to option two. Your soul will be harvested and tortured in hell for all eternity."

Craig was in shock. *'These aren't very good options.'* "It sounds a little like a Pyramid Scheme."

Grimm's cloaked head cocked to the side slightly. "Where do you think Pyramid Schemes came from? Recruitment has been low lately, we are looking to pick things up a bit, so the Evil One has been making these offers as of late instead of harvesting souls directly."

Craig buried his face in his hands with his elbows on the desk, he could feel how cold his hands were on his face. *'This is an impossible decision. I can't believe my time is up.'* He looked up at Grimm. "How long do I have to decide?"

Grimm waved his ashy hand through the air. "I should have taken you already. Time is short but I will give you another 48 hours to decide which option you will move forward with."

Craig had lost all color in his face and was feeling as if he might puke. "Can you tell me more about option three? How many people would I need to recruit and how long do I have to do it?"

Grimm stood up, towering over Craig at his desk, "NO! You either choose to be challenged or you don't."

Craig slid his chair back and craned his neck to look up at Grimm, he could see the lower part of his jaw, gray, with fine ridges running the length of the bone. He paused for a moment, stunned at what he was seeing, he mouthed words and nothing came out at first. After clearing his throat he was then able to speak roughly. "How am I supposed to make a good decision without knowing about the options?"

Grimm tilted his head toward Craig and leaned down close. Craig felt even colder when Grimm got close, as all of his energy was pulled away. He felt weak, like he was going to faint. Grimm whispered very clearly in a low menacing tone. "The same way you made the first decision and signed the original contract." Grimm stood up straight again and turned to leave.

Craig quickly got to his feet, wanting more, almost passing out from the close encounter. "Mr. Grimm, wait! I need more information!"

It was too late, Craig watched Grimm pass through the door in a dusty cloud. He sat with a thump in his office chair, feeling dizzy. His mind blanked for a moment. *I don't know what to do.*' He sat motionless for several minutes before reaching for his laptop. His search began with, 'How to break deals with the devil.' He sat staring at the screen, waiting for the search to complete. The screen turned blue, then went black. He could smell a hint of burnt electronics. Craig started pressing the enter key frantically, then the power button. Nothing.

"Oh shit! No, no, NO! Oh this can't be happening!"

Exasperated, he slammed the computer closed. '*48 hours to figure out what to do. What if this is all in my head? Maybe I should go see a shrink... I could see that conversation. "Hey doc the grim reaper came to visit me and wants my soul. No, no one else can see him, he goes through doors and I saw a student walk right through him." Yeah that wouldn't go over well, I would get locked up right away, they would send me straight to the loony bin, that's as good as doing nothing. But if I do nothing and it isn't just in my head, I could be tortured for eternity. That doesn't seem worth the risk, I have to do something, I have to try. If I take the Challenge and lose, again I will be tortured for eternity. If I become a Recruiter, I could theoretically, live my life in a pyramid scheme working for the Devil.'*

Craig buried his face in his hands, his elbows on the desk. He wanted to cry and puke at the same time. The whole ordeal was happening so fast. *'I would almost rather have had him just put me to death so I don't have to make this decision.'* Craig opened his eyes with his head still in his hands. His partly eaten sandwich was under his face, he could smell the bread, turkey and lettuce. He jerked away and leaned toward the trash can, feeling like he was going to vomit for sure. Nothing came out but he stayed over the trash can for a few moments just to make sure. *'Get yourself together man! There's no time to waste.'* He stood up and swept the sandwich into the trash. *'I need to talk to someone about this ordeal. Someone that will listen to me without judgment, someone that wont think I'm crazy. someone that could help me process the options and choose the best one since it appears that I don't have any choice but to go along with one of them.'* Craig's first thought was his father, he had always had a good relationship with him. The problem was that his father was in a nursing home and most days he couldn't remember who Craig was, let alone be able to help him get through a problem of this magnitude. *'I need to go see*

19

him anyway, maybe we can talk it out.'

Craig looked at the time and realized he would have to hustle to make it to his next class on time. His thoughts weren't all together and he wasn't even sure what he would talk about in today's class. He gathered the student's papers and crammed them into his satchel, snatching it up before he hurried toward the door. Craig half trotted from his office and down the stairs, out of the Great Hall, across the open courtyard to the other side of the campus where his classroom was located. He made it with a few minutes to spare, not all of the students were in their seats as he arranged his notes and set them on his desk, his mind wandering in half panic. *'If I am thinking about my options correctly, I will have to recruit others to work for the devil so that I can keep living.'* He stood at the front of the class with 20 some students in front of him and he started to wonder about them, *'How many of these students would sign away their lives knowingly, or unknowingly, to get where they ultimately want to be? Can I do that to them? I'm going to have to do that to someone just to try and save myself.'* The students, mostly first year, were sitting fairly quietly, looking at Mr. Newman, waiting for him to start the class with some historical knowledge that was interesting to him and not always interesting to them. Craig was just staring at them, not saying a word, the look on his face somewhat blank. He glanced from face to face, not sure what he was looking for as he read each one individually.

Finally, from the back of the room, "Mr. Newman, is everything okay?" It took a moment for it to register before Craig looked at the student in the back row. "Uh, yes, yes, I think so. I have a lot on my mind today. Sorry for going blank there for a moment." He broke a weak smile just to make light of himself.

He found it very hard to focus but dove into the lesson for the day and the historical reading that he had the class cover previously. Just as Craig was about to dismiss the class for the day, recruiting popped into his head again with an idea.

"Before you go today I have a new assignment for you. This assignment will make the final for the semester easier for you so please take it seriously. I want you all to consider how you want your lives to impact history. Not the history we are covering but the history that will come after you. Where do you want to be at the end? What do you want to be remembered for? It doesn't have to be earth shattering, it just has to be important to you. Anything from career aspirations to making a difference in the community, volunteer work, art, movies, music, politics. Whatever it is that is important to you, tell me how you want to be remembered in your history. Please keep it to 1000 words, due next Tuesday. Thank you, all."

The idea had just come to him at the end of class. If he was going to need Recruits, he would need to know what they wanted. The students filed out of the class as Craig gathered his papers and books rather hurriedly.

"Mr. Newman?"

Craig turned to find one of his students, Brandon Wells, behind him. "Yes, Brandon. How can I help you?"

"Mr. Newman, it struck me that this assignment is a little off from what we usually study or report on. I was just curious what brought this up?"

Craig slowly picked his satchel off the desk, putting the strap over his shoulder, searching for something to tell him other than, *'I need to recruit you for the Grim Reaper.'*

"Mr. Wells, I have been thinking of my father lately, he is getting fairly old and probably wont live too many more years. It has made me think of the impact that everyone has in history. Not very many people think of the history they will leave behind. I considered it an opportunity to have you, as young adults, think about what your impacts might be."

Brandon nodded in understanding with a thoughtful look on his face. "Thank you, Mr. Newman, I was just curious. See you next week."

Craig took a deep breath and let it out slow as Brandon left the room. *'Good cover. I'll have to give this assignment to my other classes as well.'*

3

Mike Newman

Craig drove his C-Class Mercedes the 20 minutes to the Winding Tree care facility that his father lived in with the windows down, trying to clear his head. He was feeling on the verge of panic knowing he needed to make a decision that would ultimately define his eternal ever after. *'If I play my cards right I could be around forever. That might not be so bad. Though Grimm doesn't seem to be the happiest demon around. Like I have met so many demons. What if I have? How many demons have I met and don't even know it.'* Craig smiled at his own ridiculous conversation with himself. *'I wonder if there are demons doing this recruiting thing that are happy with it. Oh, man! I wonder if there are people that knew what was in that contract and signed it anyway. Is there a support group for this? That would be amazing, Devil Recruiters Anonymous.'* Craig relaxed as he parked his car, laughing at himself for coming up with DRA. *'If that's not a thing, I'm going to start it.'*

As he walked through the entry of Winding Tree, he noticed areas in the building that were cooler than others. *'That's kind of weird, feels like the Reaper is close by. Well... I guess that's not all that surprising for an elderly facility.'*

He knocked lightly on the door to his fathers room and went inside. He welcomed the warmth of the unit and found relief at the same time.

"Hello, Dad. How are you today?"

Mike Newman was sitting in his recliner, chuckling at something goofy Barney Fife had done on his favorite TV show. The sound was down low, Mike had incredibly good hearing for a man in his 90s. "Hello, Craig! It's good to see you. Come on in and sit down."

Craig was happy to be recognized, it always made the visits more enjoyable. "How are you today, Dad?"

Mike swiveled his chair around so he could face Craig on the sofa, his voice sounding wrinkly like his skin, but strong. "I'm doing well, all things considered."

Craig relaxed a little into the sofa, trying not to seem like he had a specific agenda to the visit. "That's good, did your prescription come through last week?"

Mike nodded and pointed up at the counter where several bottles of pills were lined up. "It sure did, the nurses brought it in a few days ago. Those new pills have me feeling 70 again."

Craig laughed a little. "You've been chasing the nurses around again haven't you?"

Both Mike and Craig laughed. "Sometimes I think I would like to but then I realize I couldn't do anything with them if I caught them so, it's pointless."

They laughed some more at the thought of it. Craig didn't know how to bring up what he wanted to talk about and figured there might not be a way to ease into it. "I wanted to ask you about something that happened to me and see what your take on it is."

Mike folded his hands in his lap, much like Craig had seen Grimm do at their last meeting. "Okay, what is it?"

Craig felt a little uneasy but charged ahead anyway. "I had a visitor come to me the other day, someone completely unexpected. Someone that I haven't ever met. Well, I suppose he's someone most people hope to never meet."

Mike's brow was furrowed a bit and his voice became quieter. "Was this meeting bad?"

Craig took a slow breath. "It wasn't good Dad. It most definitely wasn't good."

Mike's brow stayed down and his voice stayed low. "Have you done something wrong and now it's come back to haunt you?"

Craig was a little surprised at Mike's choice of words, he felt like Mike knew what he was talking about. "I didn't think I was doing anything wrong at the time. Do you recall when I took the position at the university? Do you remember I told you what they wanted me to do?"

Mike's face relaxed but his voice stayed low. "I do remember that, you needed to make sure some certain students got through the program without issues as I recall. Is it time to pay the piper, so to speak?"

Craig hung his head for a moment, then looked back at his dad. "It appears that it is. I thought once I held up my end of the deal that it was over. It's been over ten years since I signed that contract. I had no idea this would happen."

Mike was staring into Craig's eyes. "Who came to see you and what do they want?"

Craig couldn't sit any longer. He stood and found some space to pace back and forth for a moment. "Dad, it was the Grim Reaper. All dressed in the black cloak with the hood

25

and everything."

The expression on Mike's face didn't change, he sat looking up at Craig as his son paced the room. "Did he have his scythe?"

Craig squinted his eyes a little as he thought about it. "No, none of the times I've seen him."

Mike nodded knowingly. "He has been seen around here as you could imagine. There are plenty of folks on their way out. He almost always has his scythe. We talk about the times we have seen him in the hall, going into rooms, and the next day someone has always passed on. There have been days that we see him without his scythe, no one is dead on those days. I guess that's a good thing. You're not dead."

Craig was standing with his arms folded on his chest, listening to what Mike was telling him. "Have you seen him yourself?"

Mike nodded slowly. "I have, many times."

Craig turned and took three steps, then turned back again. "Who do you talk to about seeing The Reaper?"

Mike pointed at the wall to his right. "Jim Freeman, next door. He and I talk fairly often."

Craig's heart was racing a little. "Have you spoken to him? The Reaper?"

Mike looked away from Craig. "Not yet, but I fear that my time is coming soon. Why else would I be able to see him? I've seen the staff walk right past the Reaper and seemingly, they don't see him, but I can. It makes me a little uneasy."

Craig paced back and forth again, three steps one way, turn around, three steps back the other way before Mike broke his concentration.

"What does he want from you?"

Craig stopped mid stride and looked Mike in the face. "He wants me to work for him. At least that's what it comes down to. It's like a pyramid scheme, he recruits others to recruit more souls and eventually everyone has made a deal with the Devil."

Mike sat back in his chair and stared at the ceiling. "This has to do with the contract you signed at the university?"

Craig hung his head and let out an exasperated sigh. "There was a paragraph in the contract that gave me a decade to go about my normal life, after which time my soul could be called upon to do whatever the Evil One wants me to do. If I choose not to accept his instructions then my soul will be harvested and tortured for eternity. When I spoke to the Reaper, he gave me some options to consider." Craig held up a finger. "Become a Recruiter, getting more people to sign a contract like mine I am guessing," he held up a second finger. "Take some sort of challenge to recruit some number of souls in a limited amount of time." Craig held up a third finger. "Or refuse to do either and be tortured for eternity. Actually I think that was the first option he gave me, but you get the idea."

Craig went back to pacing the floor and both of them were silent for a while.

Mike rocked lightly in his recliner with a serious look on his face. "What's the challenge?"

Craig stopped pacing and sat on the sofa across from his father. "He wouldn't lay out the details, he just said I either accept the challenge or I don't. Basically I would have to recruit some number of people to make deals in a short amount of time, if I succeed then I am released from my contract. My fear is that the challenge will be unattainable.

I am dealing with the Devil here, so I don't feel like fairness is his top priority. If I fail, he takes and tortures my soul for eternity."

Mike stopped rocking his chair and nodded agreement. "Why did you say it's like a pyramid scheme? What does that have to do with loosing your soul to the Devil?"

Craig leaned his elbows on his knees, his hands clasped in front of him. "He called it the recruitment process. The way I understand it, I would have to get other people to agree to similar terms as I agreed to and once those people's contracts expire, I believe they will have to start recruiting and they work for me, which allows me to not have to recruit as long as the other people are doing the recruiting. He said that I could live a somewhat normal life at that point until I die, then I become a Reaper."

Mike was processing the information with a questioning look on his face. "How long are the contracts?"

Craig sat back on the sofa. "Oh, I hadn't thought about that. They could be ten years like mine. So I would have to be recruiting for ten years before the others start to take over for me."

Mike sat motionless in his recliner, looking at Craig's face. "Yes, I suppose it could be ten years, it could also be more I suppose. But considering that, it could also be less. I don't know that it matters given the options that are in front of you."

Craig nodded his head slightly. "Yes, I suppose you're right. I really don't have much in the way of options here. It feels to me like becoming a Recruiter allows me to stay alive, at least for now, and possibly for a normal lifespan."

Mike leaned forward with another question. "Don't you

think you are up for a challenge?"

Craig got a sinking feeling in his stomach that made his face wince with distress. "It seems to be the quickest way out of this mess. However, it is a deal with the Devil, I really don't trust that the challenge would be fair. Best not to go that direction. I know myself and I don't do well under pressure. My best option at a somewhat normal life is to become a Recruiter. That's actually the option that I am leaning toward."

Mike reached for his phone on the table next to his recliner, "I think you should talk with Jim, he had a run in with the man in the black cloak."

Mike dialed the phone and waited for Jim to answer. Craig got up and went for a glass of water while Mike invited Jim over to talk. Moments later there was a slight knock and Jim, a slender fellow that was once at least six feet tall, now slightly less as he struggled to stand up straight, opened the door.

Mike got up from his recliner as a show of respect when Jim came in. "Good to see you friend, please come in. Jim, this is my son Craig."

"Hello Jim, nice to meet you." Craig stepped toward him and shook his hand.

"Nice to meet you too. Mike, what might I be able to help you with today?"

Mike sat back down. "Please, make yourselves comfortable, I can't stand too long. Jim, my son has had an encounter with the man in the black cloak."

Jim's face went pale and his mouth dropped open. "Oh, goodness. Well, you're still alive, so things must have gone well for you?"

Craig grimaced a little. "Well, I still have a decision to make."

Jim nodded in response. "That's unfortunate. How can I

help?"

Craig shook his head. "I'm not sure that you can at this point. I think I am just trying to make an informed decision. What do you know?"

Jim looked from Craig, to Mike, then back at Craig again. "I confronted him when I saw him come out of one of the rooms down by the recreation hall. I asked him why he was here and why I can see him but it seems like not everyone else can. He said that my time was getting close and that's why I am able to see him. He asked me if I was interested in becoming a Recruiter, I declined."

Craig was listening intently. "So you're choosing the option to be tortured for eternity?"

Jim shook his head. "No, not at all. I haven't made any deals with the devil so he can't take my soul unless I agree to it. At least, that's what my research has led me to believe. I found a few books about going to the ever after and that's what those books explained. Seemed like it worked, he hasn't said anything to me since."

Craig leaned in close and spoke in a quiet voice just above a whisper. "Did you get his name? Did he have an accent?"

Jim looked into Craig's eyes through squinted lids. "No, I didn't think to ask for a name. His voice was rough but I couldn't put an accent to it. Why do you ask?"

Craig relaxed a bit and took another drink of his water. "I asked the Reaper that I was talking to what I should call him and his name is Grimm with two m's. He has a bit of a British accent. From talking with Grimm it sounds like there are multiple Reapers. It isn't just one Reaper that harvests all the souls."

Jim raised his head and his eyebrows went up, "Oh, I didn't

even consider that there might be more than one Reaper. Those books only go into it just so far and really, who knows if anything they write in there is real or not, its all based on myth and legend. I didn't even think that the Grim Reaper was a real thing until I saw him. If I may ask, what is the deal he offered you?"

Craig's face turned slightly red. "Well, the three options I have in front of me are; do nothing and my soul is reaped then tortured for eternity. Become a Recruiter of others, or take a challenge where, if I pass, I am let out of my contract. If I fail, spend eternity tortured."

Jim slumped back in his seat, first, looking at Craig dumbfounded, then, at Mike. "Those aren't great options. From my reading, again, based on myth, I learned that the Grim Reaper would come to visit someone when it was their time to go to the ever after, but they were just a guide. The way the myth is written, it would have you believe that you could be going either to Heaven or to Hell but that the Reaper himself didn't make that decision."

Craig let out a deep breath that he didn't realize he was holding. "I seem to remember something about that as well from reading I did ages ago, but my Reaper for certain works for the Evil One."

Jim shook his head with a look of disbelief on his face. "Have you decided what you will do?"

Craig joined him in shaking his head. "I don't have a choice but to make some decision. I am leaning toward becoming a Recruiter just because, if done right, it seems to have the best possible outcome for a normal life until I die."

Mike looked at Jim. "Sorry to hear that you might be coming close to the end. I suppose that goes the same for me since

I can see him as well. Good to know that I can just tell him I'm not interested. I am a little bit curious as to what others here are doing, I wonder how many of them had already made deals that they couldn't get out of."

Jim stood up with a groan looking toward Mike. "I am a bit curious about that myself, I haven't been asking around since you and I saw him together that day. I think that I will, just to see if there are others that can see the man in the black cloak. My guess is we aren't the only ones that can see him."

Craig stood and shook hands with Jim. "If you discover anything interesting, I would really like to hear about it."

Jim moved toward the door slowly, then turned around just as he reached the door. "Let me know the next time you come to visit and I'll fill you in. Besides, I want to know how your next meeting goes."

Craig felt a stabbing pain in his chest as Jim closed the door behind himself. "I have to say Dad, I'm more than a little concerned about how this is going to turn out."

Mike gave him a look that was part pity and part concern. "Can't say that I blame you. Unfortunately, you have gotten yourself into a mess that no one could see coming."

Craig helped Mike to his feet and gave him a long hug. "Thanks for being here for me to dump out my problems. Somehow it feels better knowing that someone else knows what I'm going through."

Mike looked him in the eyes. "I wish I could help more. Let me know how that conversation goes with that black cloaked man, what was his name?"

"Grimm." Craig said quietly.

Mike nodded. "Yes, Grimm the Reaper."

As Craig left his Dad's unit, making his way down the hall

toward the exit, he felt that cold blast of air. He spun around, looking up and down the hall for a Reaper, not sure how close he would have to be to feel the cold. He hurried to the intersection of the next hall and caught a glimpse of the black cloak as it went through a door. *'Oh, that probably isn't good for someone.'* He stood at the intersection of the hallways for a moment. *'Should I go see if I can talk to him? Or let it go?'* Craig started walking toward the door the Reaper had gone through, he made it ten paces, then had second thoughts. *'I wouldn't want to meddle with things I don't know about. What if a different Reaper could just take me now, then I wouldn't have a chance at all.'* He turned around and walked through the lobby, feeling the warmth return as he got farther away from the Reaper, then was hit with a hot blast of New Mexico heat as he left the building on his way to his car.

4

The Contract

Craig woke up early, after a not so restful night of sleep. He rolled out of bed feeling tired and stressed already, there was an awful, giant knot in his stomach. *'I don't think I ate anything yesterday. Maybe that would help.'*

Craig lived in a small, two bedroom home in the park district, 15 minutes from the university. His house was small, in a very well kept part of town, perfect for a bachelor. All the homes had perfectly manicured landscaping, most owners hired out the same landscape company to keep the uniform look from house to house. Each one on the street had perfectly green grass, trimmed hedges, and spotless flower beds. Trees lined the streets and not a leaf was out of place. Craig's home was white with light blue shutters and trim, a large front porch area with a hanging swing to the side of the entry that never got used. There was a detached garage on the right hand side with narrow cement paths for the tires to follow, where he parked his Mercedes. Inside Craig's home were hardwood floors stained a light maple color, ivory painted walls, and white trim and crown moldings. The home was built in the 30's and the interior remodeled in the 90's, adding some modern touches to the kitchen and bath areas like stone counters and built in appliances. Craig had an interior decorator help with furnishing his home. He hadn't had the first clue what to furnish it with that would feel right for the architecture of the space. However, he had been sure to have his input adding touches of his treasured historical artifacts so they were neatly displayed throughout the space.

Craig wandered into the kitchen where the coffee had already brewed and poured himself a mug to get his day started. He managed to eat some toast with his coffee before returning to his room to get ready for the day, but it did little to untie the knot in his gut.

Craig normally reserved mornings for grading papers and reading over documents he might want to use in coming classes. This morning however, he would have a meeting that would change the rest of his life, and he didn't feel prepared for it. It was a bright sunny day, already 75 degrees as Craig drove to the university. *I wonder when Grimm will come by to pay his visit.* His chest got tight with the thought of what was to come. *I wish there was a way out of this. This can't be real.* He parked in the staff lot and sat in his car for a couple of minutes with the engine off, just staring out the window across the campus toward the Great Hall where his office was. *This is what happens when I make bad choices. Or don't read a contract.* He smiled soberly to himself, knowing this whole thing was his fault and his fault alone, then took a deep breath and let it out slowly trying to calm his nerves. *I'm going to try to make the best of this.* He popped open the car door, grabbed his satchel as he got out, then started the five minute walk to his office. There were very few people on campus at 8 AM.

The class load was lighter early in the day, most classes didn't start until after 9 AM. Craig walked extra slow as if showing up late to his office would put off the inevitable.

As he walked through the courtyard, past the fountain, it seemed cooler than usual, even at 75 degrees. *'Is he already nearby? It feels cold.'* Craig looked around the courtyard as he meandered past the fountain, feeling sure he would see Grimm watching him. Stopping at the top of the steps before entering the Great Hall, he and turned to face the fountain. *'Where are you? I feel your presence already, and it doesn't feel good... I hope he can't read my thoughts.'* This made him shiver along with the cold air surrounding him. Craig turned and went into the hall, he glanced left and right as he entered, only seeing a few students sitting at tables with textbooks open, using the morning quiet time to finish what would presumably be an assignment due today.

He walked directly up the stairs, the click of his dress shoes on the stone tiled floor echoing in the Great Hall as he went to his office. When he grabbed the handle to open his door, it was icy cold. *'He's already here.'* Craig's heart raced in his chest, he hung his head and stared at the floor for a moment, trying to gather the courage to go inside. Slowly he pushed the door open and entered the room.

Grimm was seated, his hands in his lap. "I trust you already knew I was here."

Craig closed the door behind himself and went behind his desk, setting his satchel on the edge. "I could feel it, yes."

Grimm nodded slightly. "You will notice more things in the future, more 'paranormal' things, as you would call it, that others won't be able to differentiate. You mustn't let those things bother you."

Craig eased into his chair, his pulse still quick, but speech slow. "Okay, good to know. Can I ask you something about Reapers?"

Grimm stood and turned toward the door, moving a few feet away from the desk without taking a step with his legs. "Given the situation, you being committed to the duty of the Mighty Being of Darkness, I don't see why not."

Craig's eyes widened at hearing the description of him being committed. "I have done some research about Grim Reapers. I have read that a Reaper is sent here to help souls pass from the living to the ever after, whether they are going to Heaven or Hell is not decided by the Reaper, they are only there to help in the transition. Is that really how it works?"

Grimm stood silently, facing Craig for a long moment. "Myths." He followed this with quite a long pause. "Those are myths put forward by souls that only have parts of the information. Each Reaper is a 'contractor,' lets say, that works for either the Light or for the Darkness. Now, in your case, you committed an act below yourself and agreed to do something set forth by a Recruiter of Darkness. Hence, you are now under the control of the Evil One by way of his Reaper. Do you understand? There are other Reapers out there that you will be able to see and communicate with who are under the control and guidance from another level which I will not speak of. It will do you no good to communicate with them, they will not help you. Further more, if you were to try to make a deal with one of them, your contract would be terminated effective immediately, ending in eternal torture." Grimm stood motionless and silent, letting Craig process this information for some time. "Have you made your decision?"

Craig felt his throat close up and go dry. He cleared his

throat and tried to swallow but there was nothing there. "I have, yes." His words came out as a croak.

Grimm turned around to face Craig, he looked elegant and mysterious in his flowing black cloak with his hands clasped behind his back. "What will it be?"

Craig's heart raced even faster, his mouth was still dry and his throat completely closed off. He tried again to clear his throat so that he could speak and not appear to be a complete idiot. "I…. I choose to be a Recruiter." Craig's voice trailed off at the end.

Grimm approached the desk slowly while reaching into his cloak, he pulled out a tattered document with calligraphy printed on very old parchment paper and let it float in the air, just in front of Craig.

"The term of this agreement is eternity. You will be allowed to live out the remainder of your natural life as long as the quota of recruitment is being met. Once your natural life has expired, you will then become a Reaper and move into another avenue of recruitment.

"Now that you have made your decision we must cover what can and can't be done while you are under contract to recruit souls. There are only a few things you cannot promise," Grimm waved his hand and the document disintegrated into nothing and was gone.

"The promise that the soul you are recruiting will be sent to Heaven, or the Light, once the contract is complete, is not allowed. This usually only comes up if your recruit knows this is a deal with the Center of All That is Evil. The promise of eternal life is not allowed. The promise of magical powers is not allowed. The statement, 'This is NOT a deal with the Devil,' is not allowed. You are allowed to tell someone directly that they are making a deal with the Devil, if they are still willing to sign, then that is on them. This can be a useful tactic, as most people don't believe it and laugh it off. You are allowed to be as deceitful as you like, again, as long as you don't say that it isn't a deal with the Devil. There will always be a written contract. If your potential client reads the entire contract and decides not to sign, you are required to let them go, however, you may still pursue them and try to sweeten the deal until they agree, but they must sign of their own free will. You can promise anything you want outside of the things we have discussed, usually the deal is an exchange for something that is of much less value, just like the contract that you signed. Lastly, there must always be a signature. Without it, there is no contract. The Evil One will make the rest happen. Do you understand everything so far?"

Craig had an overwhelmed look on his face. "Yes, I think so. May I ask a question?"

Grimm placed his hands behind his back and faced Craig. "Yes, you may."

Craig cleared his throat. "Say I know what someone desires, a career for instance, there are usually other people involved that require some kind of input. Someone that will do the hiring for example. I can recommend that someone go apply for a job that would end up being the career they desire but how do I make sure the contract has the language in it in order to recruit for the Dark One? For instance, when I signed my contract, I desired a job at a university. It just happened that this position came open and was put in front of me knowing that I would take it?"

Grimm was motionless except his fingers, still behind his back. Craig could hear Grimm's harsh, cold fingers rubbing together, gently clicking over the joints. "Mr. Lucky was in a position that he could hire whomever he saw fit. It was relatively easy for him to put a contract in front of you, he had already discussed with you his need to push certain students through the program. That part of the deal had nothing to do with being recruited by the Evil One, that was Mr. Lucky's own doings. Once you signed the contract, the deal was done. For you, since you are not in a position to hand out contracts, you will need to be present when the contract is signed. Just pick up the paperwork, have a look at it, when you set it down the language will be present. There is no need for extra immoral activity, just the contract. If you find yourself in a situation that extra immoral activity is on the table, feel free to take advantage of that, use the contract in your satchel. You will know what to do when it comes time."

Craig had a confused look on his face. "I'm sorry, where do the contracts come from?"

Grimm didn't move but continued to click his finger joints together. "The contract will be automatically generated, keep several blank sheets of paper stapled in threes in your satchel at all times. When you reach into your bag and retrieve the contract it will be complete and ready for signature by the time you lay it on the table. This is a special power that you will be armed with, it is to be used for evil purposes only."

Craig smirked at what he thought was a joke about the special power, then let out a puff of air, visible in the frigid room. "Another question please."

Grimm nodded. "Proceed."

Craig shuffled uncomfortably behind his desk. "What is my quota? How long do I have to wait for each Recruit to start recruiting others? What happens if a Recruit defaults on their agreement?"

Grimm was still completely motionless. "You will need to recruit five souls per calendar year. It doesn't seem like much, however it is more difficult than it sounds. You will need to be in the right place at the right time and know what the Recruit is after in order to even have a chance at getting a signature. As far as the terms of each contract length, that will be up to you. Keep in mind that short term contracts look good at first and can start the process of the Recruits working for you sooner. However, when you collect on those contracts and each Recruit starts recruiting others, word gets around to mortals that the contracts you are offering may not have good endings. Longer contracts allow people to move on and go their separate ways before the term is up. Often over a longer contract people will forget they even made a deal. This keeps people from putting your contracts or dealings together with bad deals so that you are able to continue to make arrangements without getting a bad name."

Craig was taking it all in, trying to understand everything he was being told, not sure that there would be any way for him to refer back to this in the future. "I see. That's why I had ten years on my contract?"

Grimm gave a slight nod. "If someone defaults, it is turned over to a Reaper. However you will be required to back fill any missing Recruits position, usually within 90 days."

Craig was rubbing his hands together, trying to warm his fingers without thought. "I have a year to recruit five souls, starting the day I sign the contract?"

Grimm shook his head slowly. "This year started in January, you have roughly three months to recruit your five required souls for this year."

Craig's eyes widened in disbelief. "What happens if I don't get a Recruit in the specified time?"

Grimm folded his arms across his chest. "You would be in breach of contract, at which point I will arrange for your demise and the harvesting of your soul."

Craig broke into a cold sweat, he could feel it on his forehead and under his arms. "Why did I end up with you, Grimm? Since I signed a contract with James Lucky, I am assuming that he was the Recruiter and I should be working under him, correct?"

Grimm lifted his head as if he were looking to the sky or stretching his neck just for a moment. Craig got a good look at most of his skeletal face. His empty eye sockets were deep and black, there were cracks in the bone at the left cheek. His teeth seemed mostly in tact from the quick look he had but there was damage to the jaw on the right side.

"Mr. Lucky was unable to fulfill his recruitment requirements, therefore I have taken over the remaining souls that he was able to recruit as their contracts expire."

Craig nodded. "That's what happened to James."

Grimm waved a hand through the air. "Indeed. Now you know what will happen if you are unable to keep up with the requirements of the contract. We have spent long enough with these questions. It is time."

Grimm reached into his cloak and pulled out the tattered document again, letting it float above Craig's desk. Craig stood up so that the document was in front of his face.

"These are the terms of our agreement, we have discussed each of these terms at length and what should happen if you default on your side of the agreement. Feel free to read it over before signing."

Craig looked at the page floating in front of his face. He had gone ash white. *'This is it, I am signing my life away.'* He began to read but was having a hard time focusing on the words. He blinked several times to try and get focus but it wasn't working. Craig lifted his left arm and wiped sweat away from his eyes and forehead, then tried again to make out the words.

Grimm was losing patience. "Let me help you." Grimm waived his hand and the words on the document became larger as if increasing the font size on a computer screen.

Craig refocused on the page and was able to read the document. Sure enough, it outlined all of the details they had discussed. "Okay, I'm ready."

Grimm motioned with his hand to Craig. "Hold out your hand."

Craig slowly held out his right hand with his palm up. Grimm lifted his arm, exposing the skeleton of his right hand, extending his index finger, which seemed to Craig to be brighter white than it had been before. The tip of his finger was extremely sharp.

Grimm reached over to Craig's hand and punctured his pointer finger. "Now sign."

Craig saw the blood from the puncture start to run over the edge of his finger. He held up his index finger and signed the document floating in front of him. As he lowered his arm, the blood ran down from his signature to the bottom of the page, but didn't drip to the floor.

Grimm waived his hand through the air, the document rolled up as he reached for it, and he put it in his cloak. "The contract is now executed. You have limited time, only a week to produce your first Recruit and each one there after can be any time before December 31st. Don't delay, there is no forgiveness for being late."

Grimm turned toward the door to leave but Craig interrupted. "Only a week for the first Recruit? You didn't tell me that before I signed!"

Grimm turned back toward Craig. "Would it have changed your mind about what option you would choose?"

Craig looked at the floor, then back to the dark space in Grimm's hood. "No," he said quietly.

Grimm shook his head. "I didn't think so."

Craig shifted on his feet and blurted, "I saw another Reaper yesterday."

Grimm moved toward the door, then faced Craig again. "You will notice more of them from now on. Where was it that you saw this Reaper?"

Craig was standing but wanted to sit down. He backed up until his legs touched his chair but didn't sit. "I was at the elderly care facility that my father lives at. It's called Winding Tree."

Grimm nodded. "Oh yes, that would be Glen the Reaper. He has been at that facility, and others like it, since they were built. He was elderly when he signed his contract over a hundred years ago, now he helps the elderly move on when it's their time. I will check in with you from time to time to answer any questions you may have." Without taking a single step Grimm moved silently backward and faded into a dusty cloud disappearing in a light puff of smoke. The heat slowly came back into the room, Craig eased himself into his leather chair, feeling exhausted from the experience and the energy suck that happened every time he met with Grimm. *'Well that's that then. I best figure out how to find the people that want something and figure out how to get it to them.'* He leaned back with his hands clasped together across his belly and spun the chair around to gaze out the window. He could see a few students walking the path along the side of the building, in and out of the shaded areas. His eyes grew heavy and he soon fell asleep in his chair.

* * *

Craig woke up an hour later with a terrible kink in his neck. He grimaced in pain as he worked his head side to side, trying to relieve the tension as he massaged his neck as best as he could. *'Oh that feels awful. Crap!'* He stood up and braced himself against the desk as he looked at the time. *'Class starts in 30 minutes.'* He gathered his satchel with what he would need for the days class and swung it over his shoulder. He thought of the contracts he would need to keep with him. *'I better put some in my bag just in case an opportunity presents itself.'* He set his satchel back on the desk and went to the printer sitting on top of the filing cabinet, grabbed some blank paper from the tray and stapled the sheets in threes, then stuffed them into his satchel. He slung it onto his shoulder, realized he hadn't put on his sport coat, and set it back down to grab his coat and start the process over again. He hustled out the door, letting it slam behind him. He ducked his head a little and his step hesitated when he heard the window rattle in the door as it slammed shut, half expecting to hear the glass hit the floor. Craig felt winded and out of sorts when he got to the classroom, some of his students were already seated and waiting for him to arrive, others were still coming in. Craig managed to focus on the history lesson enough to get through the class and remind everyone that the papers of how they wanted their history to turn out were due next Tuesday.

"I hope you all have a great weekend."

Craig gathered his things stuffing them into his satchel without care for organization, crumpling some of the blank contracts in the process. Craig was just as anxious to be done with the day's class as any of the students. He left the class with many other things on his mind, he wasn't thinking of the students or history lessons. Craig was thinking of Reapers, still in disbelief that he had not only been meeting with a Reaper but now was, for all intents and purposes, working for a Reaper. Beyond that, he was working for the Devil! Chills came over him as he walked away from the classroom, he stopped quickly, looking all around, afraid he would see Grimm watching him. There was nothing to be seen, but the chill hung on. He held his head down and walked hurriedly to the edge of campus where the staff parking area is located, nearly stumbling over raised edges in the sidewalk, having a hard time focusing and an even harder time breathing. He wasn't sure he would be able to make it to his car.

At the edge of the lot, next to the sidewalk, stood several trees and a concrete bench in the shade. Craig stumbled to it, bent at the waist, gasping for air. He dropped his satchel and collapsed onto the bench, frantically grasping at his tie in order to loosen its stronghold on his windpipe. Once the tie was sufficiently loosened, he laid back onto the flat bench and closed his eyes as tightly as he could, bringing his arm over them to wipe them dry. Craig was having a panic attack and he knew it, he had only had a few in his lifetime but after the first he had understood what it was. He laid there for several minutes as he regained his composure, feeling the desperate need to go see his father.

5

Glen

Craig left directly after his last class and his slight panic attack Thursday. He drove to Winding Tree to visit his father. The 20 minute drive was a blur, when he pulled into the parking lot he sat in his car with the AC blowing for several minutes, before realizing he wasn't sure how he had gotten there, not remembering a single minute of the drive over. It was time for the afternoon meal when Craig walked through the front doors of the home. He could hear the bustling in the cafeteria where all the residents gathered at least twice a day to eat and converse. He walked toward the noise, taking in the scene as he got closer, looking for his father a midst all the residents. Craig stood at the open doors to the dining area, he felt a cold blast of air that made him shiver and he didn't think he would ever get used to that feeling. He spun on his heel and checked his surroundings. Glen the Reaper was moving about the hallways and Craig saw the tail of his cloak as he vanished through a door down the hall to his right. Craig turned back to the dining hall and spotted his father, Mike, and Jim Freeman, sitting with two other residents toward the back of the room. He started making his way to the table when Mike caught his eye and shook his head. Craig stopped, locked eyes with Mike, and waited. Mike excused himself from the table, whispering something to Jim as he left. Jim looked toward Craig and seemed to understand, nodding his head. Craig turned around and walked to the exit of the room, waiting just outside the doors for Mike to catch up.

"Hello, Dad. Good to see you."

Mike approached slowly and gave Craig a hug. "It's good to see you too. Glad you stopped by. Let's go to my room where we can talk."

Craig hesitated and motioned to the dining hall. "Are you sure? I don't want you to miss your meal."

Mike had started walking to his room already. "Yes, I'm sure. I can afford to miss a meal. There will be snacks later anyway."

They walked down the hall outside of the dining area at Mike's pace, Craig looking down other hallways as they passed them. "Do you feel that cold air?"

Mike glanced at Craig, "Yes, I feel that happen pretty often."

Craig nodded at him. "That's a Reaper. More specifically, that's Glen the Reaper. I asked Grimm what his name is."

Mike's face brightened with a smirk. "Glen? Really? Interesting. I always thought they didn't have names, or that they would be more sinister." Mike opened the door to his apartment and they stepped inside where they both made themselves comfortable. "What was your final decision? I am guessing you're here because you met with Grimm again."

Craig nodded and nervously rubbed his hands on his pants. "I did have my meeting with him. I decided to go ahead with the Recruiter option. I think I can live out a pretty normal life as long as I can keep up with the recruiting schedule."

Mike took a deep breath, a look of concern on his face. "What are the requirements? How many Recruits do you need to get?"

Craig looked around the room as if avoiding the subject, but he couldn't. "I am required to recruit five souls per year. Grimm said it is harder than it sounds, plus I have to get five for this year and there are only three months left. I guess that's the catch for this year, it's not exactly pro rated." Craig broke a weak smile at his attempt at lightening the mood.

Mike's expression hadn't changed. "Have you started recruiting?"

Craig shook his head, then stopped and held up a hand. "Kind of. I have some ideas. I have put some feelers out there to try and have a direction to go. I hope that I can get a system figured out quickly."

Mike got a sad look on his face and turned away. "I'm sorry that you are in this situation. It's going to lead to more heartbreak and despair to those that you will eventually recruit."

Craig had been ignoring this fact, he knew inside that in order to save himself, others would be hurt in the process. "It really isn't an ideal situation. I have to look at it from the angle that anyone that will sign a contract that I put in front of them, would sign the same contract from someone else, I may as well reap the benefits of getting their signature."

Mike nodded and looked back at Craig. "It is, at this point, what you have to do."

They sat in silence for a few moments, weighing the gravity of the situation, when they heard a light knock on the door. Craig went and opened it.

"Hello, Jim. Good to see you."

Jim Freeman entered the room and shook hands with Craig. "Good to see you as well. I wanted to stop by and ask you what you had found out about that Reaper you were meeting with. Did you find out if the Reapers will take you to heaven or hell depending on your status?"

Craig smiled and nodded. "I actually did ask him about that. Turns out there is a bit of misinformation out there about Reapers. He told me Reapers are sort of like contractors. Some work for the dark side while others work for the light side, if you know what I mean."

Jim looked astonished. "Really? Now, I wouldn't have thought of that. So it's their job to move souls from the living to the other side, depending on which side they're on then?"

Craig nodded, affirming Jim's assessment. "Also, the Reaper that is here at Winding Tree, his name is Glen, Glen the Reaper. Grimm told me he has been a Reaper for over a hundred years and started coming to retirement facilities as they were built."

Both Mike and Jim chuckled, making Craig laugh at the absurdity of it all. Jim looked at Mike with a big smile on his face. "I can't wait to see him again so I can talk to him by name. I have some question for that one."

Mike laughed at the thought of Jim confronting the Reaper. "You let me know how that turns out. Maybe you'll get to be on first name basis with him and we can learn his deep dark secrets."

Jim's smile faded. "I'll bet he has secrets that we don't want to know about."

They were silent for a moment before Craig chimed in. "He has been around for a long time, probably seen some amazing things, good and bad."

Both Jim and Mike nodded their agreement. Jim turned and faced Craig. "What was it like, meeting with the Reaper?"

Craig looked at the floor, he could feel his face getting hot with shame. "It was scary, he is very intimidating. He materializes through doorways, he floats across the room, he looms over me with an imposing stature that makes me want to run and hide. It is not pleasant. This whole situation is extremely upsetting and frightening."

Jim's eyes squinted down, with his brow pushing low. "I'm sure it is, I can't really imagine what you're going through. What was it like, talking to him?"

Craig took a slow breath. "It wasn't so bad to ask him questions, he answered like you or I would answer any question. However, I did notice that when he is done talking or gets a little irritated with me that his evil tendencies show up, his tone changes, his posture gets aggressive, and that is scary."

Jim stood up to go. "Craig, please keep me posted on your meetings with Grimm, I am very interested in how this works out."

Craig stood up and shook hands with Jim. "I will let you know next time I come in for a visit, and I can't wait to hear how your conversation with Glen goes."

They all let out a nervous, relieved laugh at that as Jim left.

Mike got up from his chair and motioned to Craig. "Come give me a hug, then I'm going to ask you to go. I'm tired, going to sit and watch a show and probably fall asleep in front of the TV."

Craig gave him a hug. "Thanks for talking, I'll keep you posted."

Craig left as his dad sat back down, TV remote in hand,

starting to flip through the channels. As he walked the hallway toward the exit, Craig felt the now familiar blast of cold air whip past him as if blown from the end of the hall. Craig looked up and down the intersecting hallways but didn't see any sign of a Reaper. He stood motionless for a moment, not sure which way to turn. He wanted to talk with Glen. He turned back toward his fathers room and walked down the hall. The air was getting colder the farther down the hall he went. He stopped outside his fathers room, he could just barely hear the TV through the door. Across the hall he heard voices behind the door, but couldn't make out what was being said. He leaned in close, trying to hear what was happening, but it went quiet. Craig stood there for a moment, waiting for another sound. He tapped lightly on the door.

"Glen?" He held his breath waiting for a response. "Glen, are you in there?"

An inquisitive voice came from the other side of the door. "Who is asking?"

Craig stood up straight, surprised that he got an answer. "It's Craig Newman. Can you come out and speak with me?"

There was no response. Craig looked up and down the hall, verifying he was still alone. "Glen, are you there?"

Glen materialized through the door in a granular cloud of smoke. "How is it that you knew I was here?"

Craig took a step back, keeping his voice low. "I could feel your presence."

Glen floated backward from Craig a few feet, as if to allow a comfortable distance between the two of them. His black robe flowed elegantly at his sides, the hood dark covering his skull. "You're a Recruiter are you? Who is your Reaper?"

Craig was intrigued but also slightly scared. "I am a

recruiter, Grimm issued my contract. I just wanted to ask you a question, if that's okay."

Glen was motionless and didn't respond right away. "What question do you have?"

Craig hesitated, trying to formulate what he wanted to ask. "Are there a lot of people to Recruit here, or are you leading people that have already made deals?"

Glen's tone went lower and he spoke quieter. "Many of the resident here have made deals in the past. Some of them have paid their price in order to wait until the end for their souls to be harvested. Some of them were lucky and their services were never called upon after they signed their deals. Those individuals won't feel so lucky when their souls are tortured for eternity."

That was shocking news to Craig. "What? That can happen? Their turn never comes to pay the price for making a deal?"

Glen waived a bony hand through the air. "They were never asked to pay the price while they were alive. They will pay the price in the ever after." Glen hesitated for a moment then said slowly, "It's in the fine print."

Glen started drifting backward, he'd had enough of this chance meeting. He moved away from Craig accelerating down the hall dissipating into a smokey cloud until he was gone. Craig stood still, thinking about what Glen had told him. *'It really doesn't matter for me, I guess I would prefer it this way so at least I think I know what my destiny is.'*

"Excuse me, sir, is everything okay?" A staff member had walked up behind Craig while he was standing in the hall, reviewing his conversation with Glen.

"Oh, yeah, sorry. I was on my way out and got a little distracted. Have a nice day."

He could feel the heat in his face, embarrassed that he was caught standing in a hallway, so deep in his thoughts that he didn't see anyone coming. Craig turned back toward the entrance and walked slowly out to his car, considering that he may be able to ask Glen other questions if he were to come up with any.

6

Slump Friday

Feeling refreshed, Craig started the next morning in his office, looking over student assignments. He thought he would feel stressed, trying to figure out who he would approach to sign a contract with the Evil One, but for some reason, his mood was light and he felt positive that he wouldn't have any troubles at all, even though he didn't yet have a solid plan.

Craig tried his best to focus on moving forward, acting as if nothing had changed. He sat at his desk, looking over the assignments for over an hour, trying his best to read and analyze the papers that had been turned in. Nothing would stick in his brain. After reading a page, he would realize that he couldn't remember anything he had just read, then he would read it again, only to be distracted by other thoughts.

'How am I going to go about this? How will I make contacts and get someone to believe I can get them where they want to be in life. Then, of all things, I stab them in the back! Send them to work for the Devil without them even knowing that's what is happening.' Craig slumped back into his chair, his feeling from just an hour ago, that everything would be okay, had faded. Now,

he was feeling a heavy dread that he may not be able to go through with his part of the contract.

He stood up from his desk and his body felt heavy. The stress of the situation had set in, but he hadn't noticed until now. He looked down at his tan slacks, they were wrinkled, and the arm pits of his dress shirt were stained dark with sweat. He lifted his left arm and sniffed, just to test his deodorant. *'I can't go to class like this. Students are getting lucky today, I'm calling it off.'* Craig picked his sport coat off the hanger and slid it on as he left the office, leaving the pile of assignments in the middle of his desk. He took one sheet of paper with him before walking out the door and scribbled across it: CLASS IS CANCELED SEE YOU NEXT WEEK.

He walked slowly to the entrance of the Great Hall, feeling dazed, not really sure what he was doing or where he was going. He pushed through the heavy doors and stepped out of the hall, onto the landing above the stairs, stopping at the top to gaze across the courtyard. The heat of the day hit him in the face, the sun was high, glaring down directly where he stood. It stung his face and made him think again about the Evil One, the legends of burning in Hell for all of your sins committed over a lifetime. *'Is it true? Is that what happens when you're sent to spend eternity being tortured by the Controller of All That is Evil? Or is it more mundane? I hope to never find out.'* He raised a hand to shade his eyes and looked across the courtyard at the fountain, showering down into the pool below, sending spray into the air. He could see arched rainbow colors through the mist as the sun refracted through the water droplets. Normally, a scene like this would have made him relax and feel happy about where he was in life, but at this point in time, Craig didn't know where to go.

He walked down the steps, proceeding across the campus to his classroom. He nodded casually to students that he recognized as he walked, passing many others without making eye contact, staring at the sidewalk in front of his feet. As Craig neared his classroom he noticed several of his students waiting outside the locked door.

"Sorry, everyone, class is canceled today. See you next week. Have a good weekend."

Most of them scattered like mice when a cat comes in the room, hoping if they got away quickly he wouldn't have time to change his mind.

"Mr. Newman?" A female student in her early 20s stood near the door with a questioning look on her face.

"Yes, Miss Turner, what can I do for you?"

Haley Turner stood with her backpack over one shoulder and a history book clutched in both hands, against her waist. "I've been thinking about the assignment you gave us the other day, about what we want our history to be. I have relatives that have placed themselves in history, I have read about them, studied their lives some. I don't want to be like them, but I am afraid that I will become like them just because of who my family is."

Craig put the note he had made to cancel class in the clip on the door so everyone could see it, while listening to Haley come out with her story. "I'm sorry Miss Turner, I didn't realize your family had that kind of historical background. May I ask who your family is? What background that would be?"

Haley looked at the ground and hesitated. "Yes, well, my family is in politics. They were heavily into politics in the civil war era and much of what you might read about them, isn't good. My family has been in politics since that time and many of their beliefs have been carried over generations. It's not something i believe they should be proud of, and yet, it continues." Haley stopped and glanced at Craig's face, looking for a reaction.

He wasn't letting it show, but he was processing where he may have read about the Turner name in his studies of the Civil War era. He could vaguely recall some Turners in his reading, but they didn't stand out in any big way.

"Did they use the name Turner back then?"

Haley looked down again, feeling ashamed. "No, but if you don't mind, I don't want to get into that right now. What I wanted to ask is about *my history*, I think I know what I want my history to be, but I'm afraid my reality might be completely different. What should I write about?"

Craig shuffled his feet slightly, then crossed his arms in front of his chest. "Miss Turner, you should most certainly write what you want your history to be. I believe that is the only way to move forward. If you don't like where the history of your family has been, or where your family may be going, the only way to change it is to press on with what you want to make out of your own life."

Haley stood still for a few moments, a smile spreading across her face but still looking down at the sidewalk, the embarrassment wearing off. "Thank you, Mr. Newman." She looked up to see Craig smiling back at her.

"You're most welcome, I look forward to reading about your direction in history."

Haley gave a small wave and turned to walk away. "See you next week."

Craig stood for a moment and watched her go, then

proceeded to walk toward the staff lot where his car was baking in the sun. He opened the door and threw his satchel in the passenger seat, then plopped down in the driver seat, feeling the seat burn through his pants. He wanted to help Haley realize her dream of not being the same as the rest of her family, but he could only do so much for her, the rest would be in her hands. Craig sat in the drivers seat for a few minutes, pondering how to go about offering her a scholarship, then realized he was starting to sweat, the sun heating the inside of the car to well over 100 degrees. He keyed the ignition on, then powered down the windows until the AC started to to cool off. Craig backed out of his parking spot and started the drive home. He circled the campus once before leaving, watching students walk from one building to the next on the cement paths, noticing the brick buildings reflecting the mid day heat in stark contrast to the green grass surrounding the campus. He turned from the campus onto the neighboring streets, a few commercial buildings surrounding the campus, along with towering dorms. Just beyond the dorms were apartments that housed thousands of students every year. The dorms were well kept by campus staff, the apartments, in various levels of disrepair, being privately owned. A person could almost tell what the rent was just by looking at the building. The area beyond the apartments was mostly residential housing. Again, many of the homes were rented by students for the year, rent split by room mates, or more likely, parents paying their way.

Craig liked to drive the neighborhoods from time to time, just to take in the area, to see what was new. He circled several blocks, getting farther away from campus with each pass and soon he was far enough away that all the homes were owned by their occupants. As he neared the Park District where he lived, Craig rolled the windows down and let the warm air circulate through his car. He could smell fresh cut grass as he passed the park, the giant riding mowers gliding across open fields, getting the park ready for weekend activities. He took in the sight of the sun peaking through the leaves of giant maples lining the park, people walking their dogs on the path, enjoying what life had to offer.

Craig was trying his hardest to not think about his ultimate fate. He glanced at the houses as he passed them, nearing his own. Each one perfectly kept, each one with it's own occupant, each occupant with their own secrets. Craig was keeping his secret as he pulled into his driveway, wondering if any of his neighbors had a secret as big as his, wondering if he could find a neighbor that had a need big enough for him to help with.

Craig only knew his neighbors from sight, he didn't know all of their names. Two that he did know, lived in the house directly to the left of him. Tom Downy was a retired police captain, his wife, Sue, worked at city hall, part-time. Craig wasn't sure if they had any needs that he would be able to fulfill, they traveled fairly often, mostly within the U.S. They would go see their kids in other states once in a while, but it was mostly just leisure travel. *'I'll have to think about that for a bit, maybe talk with Tom. I should find out if there is anything they could use.'*

George Write and his wife Megan lived to the right of Craig's house. Megan was an attorney and George worked for some mega-chain, superstore, corporate office, downtown.

'Megan probably already sold her soul to the devil,' Craig thought with a smirk, *'but if she hasn't, maybe that's an opening*

that I should consider.' Craig got out of his car and walked up the four steps to his front porch, then turned around to look at his yard and the neighborhood. The landscapers had been by that morning, the lawn was freshly mowed and the beds raked, everything in perfect order. He turned and looked at the swing that never got used and considered sitting for a moment, something that, up to that point in his life he had never taken time to do. Now that he was faced with the possible end of his road, he was feeling melancholy about the time he had wasted not appreciating every aspect of life. Craig turned back to the front door, unlocked it, and went inside, feeling frustrated. *'Now I feel like it's too late to enjoy the little things in life.'* He went to his refrigerator and pulled out a beer, then returned to the front porch, sat on his swing, and watched as the neighborhood went about its every day events. Watching cars pass, some very slowly, as the occupants admired the neighborhood, some whizzing past, as if they were late for a very important date. Couple after couple walked past, some pushing strollers with one, and sometimes two, little ones on board. Other couples with dogs towing them down the sidewalk, even one with a dog in the stroller. He watched and admired each person going by, wondering where they were in life, if they were happy, if they were taking advantage of every moment. Craig sat on the front porch until it was dark out, thinking about different paths that he could have taken in his life, considering whether he should have tried harder to find his soulmate. It made him feel sad, but then the next person would walk by and his focus would shift again. His mind wandered from this to that, never fully focusing on one thing for too long. The only constant was that he always came back to Grimm and what he had to do in order to keep living. He had to ruin other people's lives. Not up front, but eventually.

Craig was mentally exhausted, it was time to try and put this out of his head for the night and turn in. He was constantly thinking about this person or that person, what do they want that they would be willing to make a deal with the Evil One to get? *'Sell your soul to the devil they said, it will be fine they said. Now I can't sleep, I said. I feel dirty, I am an awful person, what I have become in order to continue to live.'*

Craig had gotten ready for bed and laid back on his pillows, propping himself up in bed to read about lost Mayan history, trying to unwind, trying to calm his brain from the racing thoughts that would almost certainly keep him awake. He set his eyes on the words of the first chapter describing the cultural background of the ancient people. Chapter two began describing the burial rituals of the Mayans, graves facing North or West, directed at their heavens, some located in caves, cold and dark, scary to enter. Craig's eyes were getting heavy, thoughts of dark caverns, with crypts lining the walls, dashed in his mind as his eyes darted back and forth behind his closed eyelids.

The mummified bodies lay stacked in their tombs, one on top of the other. Craig walked into the darkness, reaching out to his left and right with each hand, dragging his fingertips across the dusty stone of caskets that had laid untouched, and unseen for centuries. He could smell the musty, damp cotton bandages the bodies were wrapped in. The smell made him gag, but he couldn't turn back, he took one step after another as if he couldn't control himself. He had no idea what he was doing here or what he was looking for. It got cooler as he moved farther into the darkness, the air thick with humidity and dust near the entrance. The darkness surrounded him, pulling him farther into the cave, still he dragged his fingertips on casket after casket on each side of the path. The silence was oppressive, only the soft sound of his footsteps on the damp path reached his ears. Step by step, he felt pulled into the darkness. He struck his foot sharply on a stone protruding from the ground, until then the path had been perfectly smooth, as if it had been worn smooth by millions of feet following the same invisible gravity, pulling them deeper and deeper into the darkness. He stumbled over the stone but didn't fall completely to the ground, his right knee touched the floor of the cave, the dampness soaking through his pants immediately. He braced his hands harder on the caskets to his sides and stood upright once again, pausing to listen to his surroundings. Craig could hear his heart in his ears, beyond the slight ringing that always existed there. The longer he listened and tried to control his breathing, the quieter it became. In the distance, he could hear a shushing sound but he couldn't tell from what direction it was coming. Was it ahead? Or was it behind? Was it wind from the opening of the cave 200 yards back? Or something that lay beyond, waiting for him to arrive?

Craig put his hands together and rubbed them, feeling the grit of the dust he had touched on the caskets. Some of the dust floated into the air, entered his nose, and made it itch. The smell of a thousand years worth of aged remains exploded in his senses. The air in the cave had gotten very cold, heavy, and damp the deeper he was pulled into the darkness. He reached down and touched his pants where his knee had hit the floor, it was cold and wet but not muddy. Reaching out to the caskets at his sides again he started walking ahead, this time with caution in his footsteps in case there was another stone in his path, only to stop after four or five steps forward. He turned around and looked back toward the opening, it was a straight shot out but it was so far away now that the entrance was just a golf ball sized dot. He wondered how many caskets he had passed, he wished he had counted them along the way. *'There must be hundreds of them, stacked two high on each side of the cave. I'll count them when I leave.'* Craig slid his hand over the top of one of the stone caskets to the opposite side, then beyond it. His fingers touched something else just past the lid. It was flat on top, like the first. He stretched his body over the closest casket and slid his had across the next object. *'Another one! They're stacked two deep side by side.'* He pulled his hand back to him and reached across the casket on the opposite side of the cave, finding a second row on that side as well.

Craig hesitated, his consciousness started to swirl, he stood motionless for a few moments, then turned away from the light at the end of the tunnel. *'I should go back. I shouldn't be here. How do I go back?'* Regardless, Craig started walking farther into the blackness, feeling as if there was a hand in the middle of his back pushing him down the path. Still, he dragged his fingertips along each casket, the rough stone scraping at his skin, making it raw. He looked over his shoulder, trying again to see the light, unable to stop moving farther into the darkness. The shushing sounds seemed to be getting louder, drawing him farther into the black abyss.

Step after step he went, until his right hand came to the end of the row of caskets. Craig stopped with a lurching motion as if the invisible hand was still trying to push him forward. He reached farther forward with his right hand, brushing it through the air, feeling for the nearest object. Keeping his left hand on the stone casket he moved forward, still holding his right hand out, waiting to feel another stone. He took three more steps and there it was, yet another dusty stone under his right hand. He turned to the right and felt his way forward to the gap between caskets. He had reached a change, an intersection. Craig waved his hand through the air, searching for anything within arms reach and finding the caskets continued in another direction, stacked two by two on each side of this new pathway.

Craig walked down the new path, 10, then 15 steps, and stopped. He listened intently, the silence had a heavy pressure to it, like he was under water. All the weight of the world was sitting on him, closing in around him, he could feel the pressure like a lead blanket holding him down, he had never been anywhere that the silence was so heavy. He couldn't hear the shushing any longer, he wasn't sure if it had stopped or if he had gotten far enough from the entrance that he could no longer hear the outside air. The pressure was starting to make him panic. *'What if I get lost? What if I can't find my way out of here? It's so incredibly dark.'* Craig took another six steps forward. *'No, that's the wrong way! I want to go out!'* He took another six steps forward. *'No! Turn around!'* Six more steps forward and his foot ran into something solid. Craig stumbled forward, dragging his shin across the jagged edge of a casket. *'OOH ouch!'* He fell forward on top of it, scraping his hands across the stone, pushing the centuries of dust into piles where his hand came to a stop. Searing pain raced from his shin, then from his scrapped palms. Craig recoiled, turning around quickly to grab at his shin and try to ease the pain. He sat on the casket and reached down to where blood was starting to soak through his pants. As he leaned forward, putting pressure on the lid of the casket it moved, teetering from side to side, unbalanced on the box where it was placed. Craig jumped away from the lid, fearing it might collapse and he would fall into the casket. He crumpled onto the ground instead, still trying to grasp at his shin, the searing pain not giving in.

He pushed himself backward a few feet before grabbing at his shin again, still reacting to the pain. Craig sat there for a few moments, gripping his leg, trying not to panic. He could feel the damp floor soaking into the seat of his pants as he sat with his leg pulled to his chest. His hands were now covered with muck from blood and dirt. They hurt too, from the scraping they had taken from sliding across the stone casket lid. His shin throbbed under his bloody pant leg but the pain was starting to subside.

Craig sat in the silence with his face pressed against his leg, holding his shin, regaining his composure. He lifted his head and opened his eyes, still unable to see anything, not even the slightest hint of light. He reached to his sides and found one of the caskets nearby, grasping at the top, he pulled himself to his feet. The pain shot back through his leg once again, making him wince and gasp. The sound of his gasp died out quickly under the pressure of the earth surrounding him. He felt his way forward again to the edge of the low casket that he'd hit his leg on, running his hands over the edges of it once more. *'Why is this one out of place?'* He traced its outline, feeling the edges and discovered it was actually across the path, seeming to have been removed from the stack of two on the left side of the walkway. The lid was slightly ajar, it had been slid off center, maybe when it was removed from the stack, but there was no way to know for sure. The lid teetered when he pushed on it, he could hear it rock back and forth. It was balanced on raised edges of the rough stone. Craig stepped over the casket blocking the path, careful not to harm himself further while doing so, balancing himself with the next casket in the line.

Craig stopped to listen once again, his hearing getting more acute, the ringing had died down but now there were no other sounds. He wanted to turn back, only now that he was on the other side of the casket blocking the path it made sense to move on. The open casket was calling him, he was curious and afraid at the same time. *'What could be in there? Human Remains? Treasures? Why is it open? Why is it off the stack? No, I should leave it alone.'* He turned in a small circle with his hands out for balance, kicking his toe at the casket he had just stepped over to get his orientation, then turned around to take a step when something suddenly brushed across his face. Craig flailed an arm through the air, trying to brush away whatever it was, letting out a panicked wail. He stepped back to get away from this unknown attacker that brushed his face and he accidentally backed into the casket on the path, its lid rocked in, then out, and started to slide. The sound was intense, it hurt Craig's ears, the scraping and screeching like fingernails on a chalkboard happening in slow motion. At last the lid fell to the side with a tremendous thud. As Craig spun around and stepped forward his toe caught the edge of the giant stone lid and he couldn't stop his momentum falling forward into the casket. Terrified that he would land on the remains of an ancient Mayan he held his hands in front of himself to brace for impact, but there was nothing. It was just darkness, weightless falling, sinking, the pressure getting greater with every passing second. He struggled to breath through the musty air, his body rolling weightless through the nothingness, struggling to catch himself, his chest tight like he was holding his breath but the dust was in his lungs, he could taste it in his mouth, it hurt his nose. He was holding his breath waiting to hit the bottom, whatever the bottom was.

BLAM!!!

Craig jumped, nearly bouncing himself out of bed, covered in sweat, his arms and legs splayed across the bed, waiting to hit the ground or to catch himself from falling into nothingness. He sicked in a huge gasp, then gulped at the air to try and breath. He had indeed been holding his breath, waiting for the impact that would surely be the end of his life. It was a relief that he was still in bed, the book about the Mayans had thumped onto the floor, waking him from his hellish dream. *'All of those caskets!'* He sat up, dripping with sweat, his nose itching with the dust he had dreamt about breathing in. He leaned his elbows onto his knees, still trying to catch his breath, his head still spinning with the thought of falling. It was several minutes before he could breath properly. Eventually, Craig stood and went into the bathroom to dry himself off, but decided he wouldn't want to go back to sleep and he took a shower to wash off the nightmare and try to collect his nerves instead.

7

Second Thoughts

Nearly a week had passed since Craig had finalized the contract with Grimm, he knew that he was cutting it close getting his first recruit to sign a contract. He had been sitting at his office desk reading about the history each of his students wanted to leave behind for several hours. On his desk were three stacks of papers, one stack was unread, the second stack were papers to consider again, the third was set far to the corner of the desk, just above the waste basket, not to be looked at again. Some of the papers in the second stack had very interesting ideas about what the future would bring, for themselves, their families and the overall history of the world. The third stack, not so much. *Some of these students don't have a clue what they want in life and can barely blunder their way through this assignment with generalities. Wanting to be a good father or mother is fine and something every mother and father should want, but not noteworthy in the scheme of history for themselves, as if someone would look back on them and that would be the only thing they could find to say about them in their obituary. "He was a good father." Okay, that's great. Did he do anything else?'*

Craig set another two page paper aside in the third stack, shaking his head, wondering what some of these students were even here for. *'They don't have a purpose yet. No goals. Don't waste the time and money going to school if you don't know why you're here.'* He was getting flustered with the nonsense he was seeing, hoping somewhere in the pile of student history papers there would be something he could use to get his first contract signed for the Evil Prince. He recalled the conversation he'd had Friday with Miss Turner and flipped through the remaining papers, searching for her history. He found it mid way down the stack, it was no longer than any of the others, not surprisingly, students didn't often take the initiative to write overly long essays when it wasn't a requirement. Miss Turner's paper was vague about the past, just like when she had spoken to Craig. She included just enough detail to say that she didn't want to follow the footsteps of her ancestors, and that she wanted to break away from the political path. Instead, she was interested in going into journalism. She preferably wanted to become a writer, expose political misconduct, uncover the wrongdoings of so many politicians in the past, possibly even expose the history of her own family and stop the cycle of abusing the system. *'Noble cause. She actually wants to make the world a better place and wants to start with her own family. That would be a history worth writing about. I can help her go down the right path, I can help her get where she wants to be.'* Craig set her paper in a fourth spot on the desk, now reserved for the extraordinarily good essays worth following up on. Craig reached for the number two stack of papers and flipped through them. He had read a history of one of his students that he now decided was worth putting in the extraordinary pile. The essay was from Mr. Brandon Wells. Brandon was not a stand out student, but at this point, Craig didn't care. He was looking for anything he could possibly exploit in order to recruit the required number of souls in the shortest amount of time possible.

Brandon wanted to be a professional athlete. Craig almost put this paper in the third pile, above the trash can. *'Every fit young athletic boy wants to be a professional athlete, and most don't likely have a shot at it.'* He reconsidered, and now pulled it out of that pile with a little more interest in what he had seen. Brandon had a promising high school football career but failed to get the attention of any Division 1 university athletic Recruiter. *'I'll bet I can get him on the football team and get a contract from him at the same time.'* Craig was starting to get into a flow, finding little things in each paper that he could potentially exploit. A singer in one paper, an aviation major in another, while yet a different student wanted to become an engineer and help send people to space. Each of the students had a common theme, trouble finding the resources or contacts to achieve their goals. *'Now I can see how each of these students have a path they want to pursue, yet it seems a little out of reach. Nothing like a scholarship to help them on their way.'* He read through the remaining essays, setting several in the 'trash can' pile and only a few in the 'worth looking into' pile.

Craig looked at the time, it was late in the day already on Tuesday. *'I have until Thursday to get the first signature. Hmm, possibly Haley. I can get her a scholarship easily.'* He gathered up the papers and stuffed them into his satchel, along with the stapled blank forms that he intended to use as recruitment contracts. Craig left his office feeling like he had a plan, anxious to get that first signature. He walked confidently down the steps to the front of the Great Hall, looking around at the students, trying to put names to faces and tie them back to the papers he had just read. There were so many students that he didn't recognize, he hadn't ever noticed how many students on the campus he'd never made contact with. The realization was a bit overwhelming. Craig snapped out of it, realizing he was standing in the middle of the Great Hall staring at students walking past. *'I must look insane. Get it together.'* He moved on, walking across campus toward the staff lot. Just past the fountain he spotted Miss Turner sitting on one of the concrete benches, she looked his way and he nodded, giving a small wave, then diverted his direction to have a word.

"Hello, Miss Turner, how are you today?"

She was less shy than in their previous meeting and stood to greet him.

"I'm well. How are you, Mr. Newman?"

Craig broke a weak smile. "I too, am doing well, thank you. I just finished reading your history paper. I liked it very much. I am intrigued to know, are you on track to be a journalist?"

Haley looked down and started to blush slightly. "No, I'm in political science right now. As you could imagine what with my family background."

Craig folded his arms in front of his chest, trying to remain calm and act casual. "Yes indeed, I can see how that would be something your family would want you to pursue. I was thinking after I read your paper that I might be able to help. What would you say if I could get you into the Journalism program, perhaps with a scholarship. Would you be interested?"

Haley's face shot up to look directly into Craig's eyes. She broke a weak smile in disbelief. "I would very much be interested. However, I don't think my family would be behind me making that move."

Craig nodded his head. "I thought about that, I am sure that money is not an issue with a political family, however with a scholarship you wouldn't need to rely on the family money to get the degree that you actually want."

Haley glanced around nervously to see if anyone was nearby. "I'm not sure I can do it. I am sure it would cause a huge falling out within my family."

Craig nodded again. "I understand, I am not asking you to make a decision today. Please consider it, however. I have a small window of opportunity to work with. I would need to have a decision by Thursday."

Haley looked back at the ground with a strained sort of grimace on her face that Craig could see when she looked back at him. "I will think about it. It would mean a lot to me to be able to change my course of history."

Craig dropped his arms and started to turn away. "Miss Turner, you are a bright young woman. It would be a waste for you to pursue something you're not passionate about. I will see you in class Thursday."

Craig left Haley standing in the courtyard. *'I may have laid that on a little thick, but I think it went well.'* He walked slowly back across the courtyard, past the fountain, feeling the mist on his face as the sun burned the back of his neck. The fountain drowned out the sound of his dress shoes on the concrete until he was out of the center court.

Craig clicked his way down the sidewalk in the afternoon sun, deciding he would go visit his father for a short time.

73

Craig drove out of the lot headed to Winding Tree Home to visit his dad, his mind wandering as he drove. Before long, he had passed the entrance to Winding Tree and merged onto the highway, headed east on Highway 70. Craig wasn't thinking about where he was going, just driving in silence, letting the hum of the road blur his mind and distract him from what he was going to do to innocent people. He could feel a lump swelling in his throat as he thought about turning Haley's dream of changing her family's history into an unspeakable hell, just so that he could live longer and *possibly* not be tortured for eternity. Tears started to trickle down his face, stinging in his eyes, making his nose run slightly. *'Why should I take advantage of someone else's dreams just to stay alive? I should just end it with Grimm, tell him I can't move forward with this scheme he has presented me with.'* Craig rolled the windows down in his Mercedes, letting the warm wind fill the cabin of the car, drying the tears on his cheeks. The sun was getting lower on the horizon, Craig had been driving for an hour and a half. The sun started to blind him in the rear view mirror as he headed east up the pass. He glanced at the speedometer, seeing it read 72, he let off the throttle to slow his pace. Looking farther ahead, he saw a pull out at the peak of the mountain he was driving up and pulled over, gently gliding the C Class into a parking spot that allowed him to see out across the desert. Craig put it in park and sat motionless, with the engine off, staring out the front window while the warm wind blew through the car. He didn't blink or move a muscle for 10 minutes. He was breathing shallow, short breaths, with only one thought going through his mind. *'I can't do this.'* A picture of Haley would come to his mind, *'I can't do this,'* a picture of Brandon Wells came to his mind, *'I can't do this,'* a picture of James Lucky, *'How it turned out for him, I can't do that.'*

A couple, in what Craig thought was their mid 30s, walked past his car from one of the hiking trails nearby, they were chatting and getting ready to get back in their car. Craig watched them pass, then looked back at where they came from. He looked around the parking lot, they were the only other people in the lot. Craig reached for the door handle and popped the door open but waited to push it open until the other people had backed out of their parking space and started to drive away. He stepped out of his car with an old man groan, stiff from not moving at all the last two hours. He stretched his back after standing up and glanced around the road side pull-out for signs of anyone else he may not have seen from inside the car. Feeling assured that he was alone, he bent back into the car and reached under the driver's seat, tapping his fingers around on the floor. He pulled a heavy, soft sided case from under the seat and set it on the roof, again glancing over his shoulder to the right, then the left. He stood there, looking at the case, then looking across the desert at the mountains in the distance. He leaned on the side of the car with his hands over the top of the case, pressing on it, spinning it around on the slippery surface of the car. Craig grasped the zipper and wound it from one side to the other, unfolding the case to reveal his PT92, 9mm pistol, that he had purchased for what turned out to be protection from nothing but stories he had made up in his head. He lived in a nice neighborhood, in a nice town, and had never in the 12 years that he had owned it, even thought about pulling it out from under the seat of his car for protection. He had pulled it out to learn how to use it shortly after purchasing it, taking it to a gun range and firing 30 or so rounds through it. He had even pulled the case out of his Camry when he purchased the Mercedes, only to tuck it under the seat and not move it again for another 8 years, until now.

Craig stood in the setting sun, staring at the pistol sitting on the roof of his car, contemplating again if he would be able to go through with being a Recruiter for the devil, or if a bullet in the head would be a better end to this nightmare. He picked the pistol up from its soft resting place and felt the heft of the metal in his hand. It was warm from being under the seat near the exhaust and the hot road he had been traveling on. He moved it from one hand to the other for a moment, then dropped the clip out with a press from his thumb. The clip was full and heavy, it carried 30 percent of the weight of the gun. Craig slid the clip back in and pushed it until it clicked into place, then pulled the slide back and allowed a bullet to enter the chamber. He carefully put his thumb on the hammer and released it, lowering it back into its resting place, and flipped the safety on. *'Wouldn't want to shoot my leg before my head.'*

He placed the pistol into his sport coat pocket, feeling the weight pull his jacket down on the right side, then threw the case into the passenger seat of his car, along with his keys. Craig stood up straight and pulled his shoulders back as he looked around the lot, only three cars had passed on the road since the other people had left the lot. He started to walk toward the trail he had seen the others come back to the lot from, as he got to the stone wall that lined the visitor information area he stopped and looked over the expanse of desert scenery before him. It was all shades of brown, from the tall desert grass to the sand, and even the sandstone was a shade of brown. Far in the distance, the New Mexico Organ Mountains loomed dark with the evening shadows and the sharp rocky edges cutting into the sky. Heat radiated from the stone wall as well as the sandy path in front of him, his shoes seemed too hot at this moment as he stepped off the sidewalk onto the firm sandy path. Craig walked with his head up, looking at the scenery as he passed, not watching his footing even though he was wearing dress shoes. He stumbled on occasion, slipped here and there, but was not concerned about it. His mind had wandered again to Haley and Brandon and the others in his classes, deep inside he wanted the best for his students, he hadn't realized it until now, as he was faced with using them for his own benefit, and he couldn't help but feel distressed about it.

He had been walking in the desert landscape for nearly 40 minutes, it was starting to get chilly, the wind was picking up as it always did in the evening when the sun was setting. At some point, Craig had veered off the worn path and taken his own direction through the scrub trees and dried grasses, he had spotted a hill from far away with a rocky flat top and wanted to go stand on top of it just to see the view, before ending it all. The hill was much taller then it had seemed when he first saw it, but Craig was able to climb to the top and take in the glorious views of the valley below, as well as the mountains in the distance. He stood on the little peak facing west, watching the sun descend on the horizon, turning a different direction every so often to see the contrast of colors, from the bright orange of the sun, to the dark blues of the sky in the east. The shadows grew longer and the air got colder. Craig turned back to the sun and decided it was time. He pulled the gun from his pocket and held it by his side as he watched the sun, still close to an hour before it would fully set below the horizon. Craig's hand was starting to sweat, he could feel the gun's handle getting slippery in his palm, he was very aware of his body at that moment, sweat running down his back and under his arms, his heart racing in his chest, his pulse in his neck. His right arm tensed and brought the pistol up, he didn't look at it, he didn't want to see the end coming. He felt the muzzle press against his right temple, he trembled slightly, banging the barrel against his head, causing a wince in pain. Holding his breath, he squeezed the trigger hard, with a jerking motion.

Nothing happened, the trigger didn't move. He let out a gasp and dropped his right arm, looking at the gun in his hand, sweat dripping now from the end of his nose after running off his forehead. *'Ahhh, the safety is on!'* He fumbled with the safety and heard the slight click as it was disengaged.

"Yes, you could go ahead and end it now. My how I do love a good splattered soul, there isn't one better to spend eternity being tortured. I'm sure you have thought of that though, haven't you Craig?"

Craig was standing bewildered at how Grimm just showed up out of thin air. Tears and sweat stained Craig's fear wracked face, the pain and anguish showing in every wrinkled line, from his forehead to his chin. His words came out rough and choppy. "I feel as if the torture has already begun, the torture of sending other souls to spend their lives working for the Devil or the Reaper or whomever oversees this pyramid scheme! I don't think I can do it!"

Craig, still holding the gun, pointed it back at his head and started to sob again, deep from his stomach, uncontrollable convulsions of sobbing causing him to double over at the waist, yet still with the gun to his temple. Grimm stood still, hands clasped behind his back, ever so elegantly, the wind lightly blowing his robe to the side. Somehow, he didn't cast a shadow to the dry sand, even in the glaring evening sun the robe was void of any light or reflection, as if it were a black hole devouring all the light with his incredible gravity. "Come now. Stop your hemorrhaging. Either pull the trigger and be tortured forever, or live up to the contract that you agreed upon. Though, I guarantee you that the latter is the better choice."

Craig finally let the pistol drop away from his head and stood up part way, putting his hands on his knees for support, the gun still in his right hand, he gasped out a few words. "Yes, I am sure the latter is a better choice for me. However, I have had a bit of a conscience about recruiting others to walk this same path."

Grimm moved to within just a few feet of Craig. "That is not for you to be concerned with, every soul that signs that agreement has done so on their own accord. Should they read the contract and discover it is not what they thought it was, then they are not required to sign, yet, so many do. You are merely a facilitator, allowing these people to get what they want from their otherwise dull, inconsequential lives. They will be happy, at least for the amount of time before their contracts come due. Now stand up and pull yourself together, carry on with your day, you won't find any Recruits out here."

Craig pushed himself up with his hands on his knees, standing upright, his body shaking, he wasn't sure if it was from the cold air that was surrounding him or from the absolute trauma of trying to pull the trigger of a gun that was pointed at his head. After taking a few deep breaths, he straightened himself up and looked back at the sunset and all of its glorious colors streaming across the sky, the sun nearing the horizon, sending blinding waves of light across the land. Craig turned around, looking straight at Grimm, his face wracked with anger, contorted in ways that made him look deeply deranged. He pulled the gun up from his side, pointing it again at his temple, tears streaming from his eyes, feeling tortured by the emotional decision of whether to live or die. Craig's arm shook as he let out a horrendous, mournful, screaming wail. He leveled the sights of the gun at Grimm and pulled the trigger.

CRACK!

The gun went off, sending the lead hurtling through Grimm, slamming into the sandstone 30 yards behind him, sending sand and rock flying into the air, the dust catching the wind blowing to the south. Grimm hesitated, letting the gravity of what Craig had just done sink in, then let out a booming laugh that seemed to shake the nearby mountains as it echoed off the rock walls.

"You can't kill me! 'A' for effort though. I will not hold your anger and distress against you. Now, it is time to return to your home, become the Recruiter you are contracted to be."

Craig had let the gun hang in his right hand down at his side, his jaw clenched, his face still somewhat contorted as he looked at Grimm with hateful disdain through the tops of his eyes. Craig relented and started walking back to his car, this time more careful of his footing, trying not to slip in his dress shoes on the sandy stones underfoot. He watched as Grimm hovered backward for several yards, then disintegrated into wind blown sand and disappeared. Craig hadn't planned on returning to his car so he hadn't payed attention to his surroundings while he had walked out into the desert. Now it was getting dark and the fear that he might not be able to find his way was starting to sink in. He did recall that he had walked mostly straight toward the setting sun, so now he kept the sun to his back and picked his way across the desert, through the bushes and around rocks, until he came to a path that looked as if it could be one of the nature trails. After another 10 minutes on the trail, he found a wooden sign that pointed him back to the visitor area at the lookout where he had parked his car. The wind picked up and pelted sand on his exposed skin, it stung his face and he could feel the grit in his mouth, he had to squint his eyes to keep sand from blinding him. 15 minutes more of trying not to trip on the dark dusty trail, his feet sinking into soft spots, filling his shoes with sand and he was back at his car, cold, tired and dusty, but alive.

He sat heavily into the seat and reached over to the passenger seat. Picking up the soft case, he slid the gun into it and zipped it closed then tucked it back under the driver side seat once again. He leaned back in the seat, resting his head on the headrest, he closed his eyes and could feel tears welling behind his closed eyelids. He had given up, ready to put an end to his life and not have to deal with Grimm and the contract. Now he was going to have to find a way to cope with a life of working for the actual worst boss ever, the Evil One himself. He opened his eyes as tears rolled down his cheeks, the last of the sunlight had gone below the horizon, leaving the giant black silhouette of the jagged mountain tops looming over the valley floor. A cold blast of wind blew through his open car windows, sending a shiver down Craig's spine, making him think again, of Grimm. It made him angry to think of Grimm coming out into the desert to save him from himself but he knew taking his own life was not really an easy way out.

He was exhausted as he drove home, the yellow lines of the highway flying by as he blinked slowly, trying not to fall asleep at the wheel. The rumble strip at the edge of the highway woke him before he ran off the road, his heart raced for a few minutes, then he settled into the seat again and the slow blinks returned. When Craig opened his eyes he was sitting at a stop light only a mile from his home. The light turned green and he sat there for a few seconds, looking all around. No other cars were on the road, but what really struck him was, he wasn't sure how he got there. He was sure he had slept the last several miles, only remembering hitting the rumble strips and swerving back onto the road, but that felt like hours before.

He finally made it home, stumbled in, left his dusty shoes at the door, his clothes piled on the floor, and collapsed into bed.

8

The First Recruit

Tuesdays meltdown was a distant memory only two days later, it bubbled to the surface on occasion, then was pushed back with effort and clinched teeth. Thursday seemed to take forever to come, Craig was getting anxious, he had relied on Haley saying yes to the proposal of a scholarship to change her major to journalism. If she declined, Craig was in jeopardy of missing a contract deadline. He had pulled several papers out of the stack that were very promising but he had not yet approached any of the students regarding their "opportunities."

Craig was preparing to dismiss class for the day. "Remember the final is next Thursday. I feel that everyone here is prepared but if you have any questions before then please bring them to me by Tuesdays class and we will review. Thank you, all."

The students started gathering their belongings and filing out the door.

"Mr. Wells."

Brandon had just stood up and pulled his backpack onto his shoulder. "Yes, sir."

Craig waved him to the front of the class before speaking. "I would like to have a meeting with you in private. Would you please come to my office before noon tomorrow?"

Brandon got a wary look on his face. "Did I do something wrong? Am I failing?"

Craig smiled wide. "No, not at all. You are doing quite well actually. I have an opportunity I would like to present to you if you have time."

The worry dropped and Brandon's face brightened. "Oh, excellent! Yes, I can come after my morning class, maybe about 10, if that works."

Craig reached out his hand to shake with Brandon. "That would be perfect, see you then."

Brandon left the room and Craig looked into the mostly empty seats to see that Haley had stayed behind, still seated in the second row, waiting to speak with Craig.

"Mr. Newman, I would like to talk about the Journalism program."

Craig smiled to himself and leaned against his desk, preparing to listen. "Yes, Miss Turner, I was hoping that we would have this opportunity today."

Haley fidgeted in her seat with a sheepish look on her face. "I have been giving it a lot of thought, I really want this opportunity. I was very concerned about tarnishing my relationship with my family, so I had to speak with my father about it before making a decision."

Craig's stomach churned on the coffee and bagel he had before class. He didn't like the way this was sounding, small beads a sweat started forming at his hairline.

"I hope the conversation went well for you." He managed to say without sounding too anxious.

Haley smiled and glanced at Craig. "It did, actually. I was surprised that he was receptive to my desire to change majors, though he doesn't want me to quit the political program completely."

Craig shifted, sliding a little farther onto the desk, using it as a better seat, with one foot still on the floor. "I can see how that could be advantageous, having a background in politics as a journalist."

Haley nodded in agreement. "I think it would be advantageous as well. It will take a fair bit longer to complete my studies, but I can see how it would be worth it in the long run. I would like to take you up on the offer of a scholarship, if it is still an option."

Craig's heart jumped in his chest, then he felt tension and thought for a split second that he might be having a heart attack. He realized quickly that it was a panic attack as he thought of Tuesdays episode in the desert. *'Push it back, bury it, you must bury it.'* Craig stood up as casually as he could and turned to reach for his satchel, concealing the pained look on his face, pulling it across the desk and flipping open the leather flap. Inside, he sorted through several history papers until he came to a set of three pages stapled together which Grim had told him to carry with him. His hands started to get clammy as he pulled the papers out into the light for the first time.

"I brought a contract with me today hoping that you would say yes to the scholarship. Today is the deadline. Sorry it's a little wrinkled, I got in a hurry this morning putting things in my bag."

He held the contract in front of his face to have a look at the blank pages, inspecting the wrinkled papers. They were no longer blank, NMSU letterhead, perfectly professional looking type set, with Journalism Program Scholarship sub heading made out; presented to Haley Turner. Craig was trying to hide his astonishment that just pulling the document from his satchel had actually worked.

"I will need you to sign this right away so that I can turn it into the admissions office before closing." He took two steps forward and set the papers on the desk in front of Haley, along with a pen. "Just a signature at the bottom, with a date, will do. I will get it turned in and you can start selecting classes next semester as you desire, the tuition will be covered."

Haley slid the papers closer to her and read through the first page, then turned to the second page and started reading. Craig got a little nervous and started to fidget with the other papers in his satchel, trying to come up with something else to talk to Haley about.

"Have you given any thought to how you will go about finishing school, with this new direction?"

Haley didn't look up right away, making Craig hold his breath for a moment. She reached the end of the second page and turned to the third, glancing through the paragraphs and headings. "I have thought about it. I should have most of my per-requisite courses out of the way for this program, so I will combine as many classes as possible, then alternate some depending on my interest level in the course." Haley let the pages fall closed and picked up the pen. "Honestly, I am more interested in the journalism classes, so I think it will be hard to continue on the political route, but I will have to find a way to keep motivated." She smiled at him, then looked back at the paperwork. Haley quickly signed her name and put the date next to it. "Here you go." She held out the forms by the very edge of the paper.

Craig hesitated before taking a step forward and taking them from her. "I will get these turned in today, thank you."

Haley smiled and seemed excited about the new adventure she was about to start. "Oh! Thank you, if it weren't for you I would never have taken this step toward doing what I really want to do." Haley stood up gathering her books getting ready to leave. "Thanks, again. Could you please get a copy of the scholarship paperwork that I could keep?"

Craig nodded and stood awkwardly at the front of the room. "Yes, of course, I will have admissions send you a copy as soon as it's processed."

Haley left the room and Craig let out a big sigh, having not realized he was holding his breath. He was slightly stunned that he actually had his first signed recruitment paperwork in his hands. He finished putting his belongings into his satchel, the scholarship paperwork last, double checking that it was actually signed, and threw the bag onto his shoulder. Craig wasn't sure how it would go when he delivered the contract to admissions, they weren't expecting it, and he was sure there weren't any scholarships available at this time. He was just going to trust the process and turn it in, after all, what he really needed was for Haley to sign it, and she did.

The admissions office was next to the Great Hall, Craig took the long route around the building to stay in the shade, even though his favorite part of the campus was the fountain courtyard, but it allowed him to go in through the staff entrance at the back of the building. Janine Jesper was at her desk typing away at her computer when Craig came to her office.

"Hello, Janine, how are you today?"

Janine glanced over the top of her computer screen and gave Craig a half smile, half smirk. "I could complain, but I don't think it would do any good. Besides, no one would listen."

Craig gave a cursory chuckle, *I just want to get this over with.* "I have some student scholarship paperwork to turn in, should I give it to you?"

Janine gave him a confused sideways look. "I didn't know we had any scholarships open right now, and what are you doing with that paperwork anyway? That should be handled by counselors."

Craig panicked. "Yes, it was a holdover from the first semester. I have a student that is changing her major and I was just helping out."

That seemed to satisfy Janine, she nodded and her expression eased back to neutral. "Okay, you can put it in that basket in front of you, I'll get to it tomorrow."

Craig dropped it in the basket with 20 or so other documents, hoping it would get lost in the shuffle and that no one would look too deeply at the fine print. "Thank you, Janine, have a great night." He turned and walked out before she could respond.

Craig went to his office even though he was done with classes for the day. He decided that he would look over Mr. Wells' history paper again to make sure he had the details correct. He wanted to make an offer that would allow Brandon to join the football team the following year. He may have to have a conversation with the athletic director in order to set it up. It could be a contract allowing him to work out with the team but not actually be on the squad until tryouts come around again next summer, but ultimately, if he was able, he would like to get Brandon a firm spot on the team.

Having no in depth knowledge of the sport, Craig was going to have to do some research to find out if he would actually be able to sell Brandon to the athletic director, Gavin Scott.

9

In A Daze

Craig went to see his father after leaving campus, he was having mixed emotions about getting his first Recruit. Haley had signed willingly, but, just like Craig, she didn't read the entire document and would someday be stuck with a life serving the Evil Lord. He felt bad for her, remorseful for what he had done, but there was nothing he could do now to change it. As he pulled into the lot at Winding Tree, Craig thought about trying to pull the trigger with the gun pressed to his head and cringed. He looked down at the steering wheel of his Mercedes and drew in a deep but ragged breath. *'What have I done to her? I should have pulled the trigger even after Grimm stopped me.'* Craig parked his car in front of the building and sat quietly for a few minutes, staring blankly at the white exterior walls, the sun reflecting like a laser into his eyes off the front of the building. He wasn't sure if he wanted to go in and visit with Mike or not. *'Will he feel different about me now, knowing that I have done such a despicable thing?'* Craig swallowed his fears and opened the door, stepping out into the heat of the afternoon, he took his sport coat off and laid it across the passenger seat, then walked to the front doors. Once inside, Craig glanced through the foyer, then into the cafeteria as he walked past. Meal time was over, only a handful of residents sat at a few tables, having a chat. The air conditioning was working well, it was a comfortable 70 degrees in the common areas of the building. Glen came to mind when Craig felt a cold blast of air before realizing it was a ceiling vent blowing cold air from the AC that he had just walked past.

Something felt different while he moved down the hall toward his fathers room. The building seemed quieter than usual, there wasn't the same amount of bustling noise in the building. There were usually more residents moving about the foyer and in the halls. Craig looked at his watch, it was only 5:30, not late enough that everyone had turned in already. He stopped and looked back at the foyer, it didn't seem out of place, just quieter. He shrugged and kept going to Mike Newman's room.

Craig tapped on the door and opened it slowly. "Hello, Dad, how are you today?"

Mike was napping in his chair with the TV on, wearing his jeans and a flannel shirt that Craig had gotten him for his birthday the year before. The local news was showing the weather forecast. Craig walked in quietly and watched the end of the forecast. *'Sunny again, what a surprise.'*

"Dad, hello." Craig reached out and tapped him on the shoulder.

Mike stirred, slowly coming into consciousness, opening his eyes. Craig could see some confusion on his face as Mike woke up.

"Hi, Dad, how are you doing today?"

Mike didn't say anything, he was still trying to process the fact that someone was in his room, now standing over him. Confusion at first. "What are you doing in my room?"

Craig took a step back to give him some space. "Dad, I just came to visit. I wanted to talk to you about the last couple of days."

Now Mike was getting a little angry that this man had barged into his room. "Why are you in my room? Who are you?"

It was then that Craig realized what was happening. Mike wasn't himself today, so he did what he had done in the past when the Alzheimer's acted up.

"Mike, I'm your son Craig. I just wanted to talk. Can we talk some?"

Mike seemed more determined than Craig had seen him in the past. He started getting up from his chair, shouting. "What are you doing in my room!? Who are you!?" Mike was standing now, moving toward Craig, when he looked up into Craig's eyes and stopped in his tracks. Mike's expression changed, his face went from stern to worried in the blink of an eye. Craig saw the change happen. "What's wrong? Dad, what happened?"

Mike took an awkward step back, his eyes glued to Craig's, his express growing more scared with every passing moment. He took another feeble step back, away from Craig and pointed at him, his voice shaky, "Those eyes! I've seen those evil eyes before! You're evil! Leave! Leave! You need to leave!" Mike screamed with all the power he had in his lungs, everything he could muster was pure fear in his shaky voice.

Craig was shocked at the outburst, he knew it was the Alzheimer's talking, but the fear in his dad's voice and on his face was more than Craig had seen before, more than he had ever expected as a reaction. Craig held his hands out as if trying to calm Mike down and started backing his way to the door. "Okay, Dad, I'm going. Don't worry, I'm going."

Craig hurried out the door, closing it behind him. He took a few steps away, then leaned against the wall, letting his nerves settle for a moment. *'He said I'm evil. What's wrong with my eyes?'* Craig looked down the hall toward the exit. At the intersection of another hallway stood a credenza with a vase filled with silk flowers, a mirror hung behind it on the wall. Craig walked toward it, stopping just a few feet in front of where it stood. He didn't look into the mirror right away, instead he looked at the silk flowers placed directly in the center of the credenza, no other decorations sat near the flowers. Craig looked closer at the flowers, some of them half faded from pink to white, they were lightly covered in dust and had small webs strewn from petal to petal, flower to flower. Craig blew on them, the dust poofed and floated towards the ceiling, making him think of Grimm leaving a room. As he watched the dust rise into the air the mirror on the wall came into view. Craig stopped watching the dust and his eyes looked into the mirror where his face came into focus, he was sobered by his own image. He didn't see what he thought his father saw, he wasn't sure how his father saw evil in his eyes, but he did see fear, and ghostly pale skin that looked as though he himself had seen the devil. He nearly chuckled to himself thinking about this. He had not seen the devil, but he had seen someone who worked for him. As if that weren't bad enough, Craig, in essence, was now working for the devil as well. *'He can see it in me. He knows there is evil controlling my actions.'* Craig looked away from the person

93

staring back at him in the mirror, then down the hall toward the exit. He heard some commotion behind him and spun around, ready to engage, but it was just someone from house keeping struggling with a cart, trying to pull it from a storage room. *'Calm yourself, good grief, not everyone is out to get you.'* He turned and walked to the exit, nodding politely to the receptionist as he passed the front desk. The sun was hot as it hit his face. Craig stopped at the edge of the sidewalk before crossing the parking lot to his car. He stood with his eyes closed, letting the sun sting the skin on his face and burn into his closed eyes. *'He can see that I have turned evil, that contract with Haley has solidified evil in my soul.'* Craig's shoulders slumped with the weight of his wrongdoing. He felt the crushing weight of the world sitting on him, smashing him, pushing the life out of him. *'How am I going to cope with this feeling? How am I going to keep moving forward knowing what I need to do to survive is ruining the lives of others?'*

Craig stepped off the sidewalk with his shoulders sagging and his head hanging down, watching the pavement as he walked to his car. The drive home was mostly a blur until he got to his neighborhood. Craig's attention was drawn once again to the park and the neighbors' homes, all of them manicured and perfect. *'This used to make me happy, this used to be my restful place of peace. Will I ever be able to have that feeling again?'* Craig pulled into the drive next to his house, then slowly walked to his front porch and stood at the bottom step looking at his home, the porch, the swing, the large window looking out to the park across the street. The swing. He walked up the steps and stood at the swing for a moment, he nudged at the chain that suspended it from the beams in the ceiling of the covered porch. He watched it glide forward and back with a slight creak of the chain rubbing on the hook at the top. He turned around and sat down right in the middle, then slowly started to push his feet on the floor, moving him back, then released and glided forward. He let the swing slow on its own, then repeated, push back and release, then glide. It was calming, the rhythmic motion, the slight creak of the chain and otherwise silent action. The feeling of no other distractions. He had missed out on this his entire life, even as a child Craig could not remember just sitting on a swing, gliding back and forth, not thinking about anything, just letting it happen. The anxiety of all that had been happening to him was melting away, fading with the motion and the creak. His mind was freeing itself from panic. Craig sat on the swing for an hour, gently gliding forward and back as he stared across the street, into the park and through the trees. The occasional car went past on the street in front of his house but he barely noticed. He was in a trance, forward and back, forward and back.

* * *

Tom Downy slowed in front of Craig's house before he turned into his own driveway. He waved at Craig, a friendly, neighborly wave that Craig didn't see. Craig wasn't trying to be rude, he was simply lost in thought, staring far off into the trees of the park across the street. Tom exited his vehicle and walked across the lawn in front of Craig's house.

"Hi, Craig." He raised his hand with a friendly wave. "How have you been? I haven't seen you in quite some time."

Craig snapped out of his daze and focused in on Tom standing at the bottom of the steps of Craig's porch wearing khakis and a blue polo style golf shirt. "Hello, Tom." Craig managed to speak without sounding too out of it. "I'm doing pretty well, how have you and Sue been?"

Tom smiled and came up the stairs and stood against the rail. "I'm doing okay." Tom hesitated and was suddenly somber. "Sue hasn't been doing well, seems she has an infection in her lungs that the doctors can't figure out."

Craig's attention became a little more acute. "Really? That is unfortunate news. Is she able to go to work still and get around?"

Tom looked off into the distance, not sure if he could hold it together. "Well, no. She hasn't been able to get out of bed much, let alone get out of the house. It's been tough getting her to go to doctor visits, she gets winded just standing up. We brought home one of those oxygen tanks and she has to wear that mask most of the day."

Craig shook his head. "I'm really sorry to hear that. Where have you been going for medical?"

Tom looked back in Craig's direction after a quick glance down the street and into the park. "We finally got our insurance to clear us to go to Mountain View Regional but we are having a hard time getting cleared to see the right doctors. Damn insurance blocks everything, they really don't care who lives or dies as long as they don't have to pay the bill."

Craig nodded. "That's terrible, I suppose they wont let you go out of state either?"

Tom looked at the floor shaking his head. "No way, I didn't realize how restrictive our insurance is, we haven't ever needed anything major before so it wasn't a problem and now we can't change coverage because of pre existing condition clauses."

Craig took a long deep breath and gazed out across the street again, looking at the park. "Tom, that's terrible, is there anything I can do to help?"

Tom forced a painful smile. "No, I don't think so. I might bug you once in a while to sit down and have a talk though if you don't mind. All of this has piled up on me and I can't leave the house for too long at a time."

Craig nodded, looking up at Tom. "Would you like a beer or a lemonade?"

Tom straightened up his stance, feeling like he was slouching with the weight of the conversation. "That does sound really good, I will take you up on that, but I need to go check on Sue first, just need to make sure she is doing okay and see if she needs anything. I could be back over in 15 minutes, if that's okay?"

Craig nodded agreement. "That sounds good, I'll see you then."

Tom turned and went back down the stairs and across Craig's perfectly manicured lawn, back to his house to check on Sue. When he arrived he found that Sue was sleeping with the oxygen mask on, she seemed to be resting comfortably enough. He checked her cell phone on the bedside table for messages, there was one from her sister, but it could wait. He made sure her phone was on silent, then texted a message to her letting her know that he was next door visiting with Craig. He changed his clothes into jeans and a t-shirt so he wouldn't feel too formal to have a beer with a friend, then went back outside. Craig had gone in the house while Tom was away and made sure he actually had a few beers in the fridge since he had made the offer without actually knowing. He was in luck, there were four bottles from his favorite local brewery, chilled and ready to drink. He picked up two, and a bottle opener, and returned to the porch. A few minutes later, Tom returned looking more casual than when he left.

"She's resting, I left her a message so she knows I'm just right next door."

Craig handed Tom a beer and they both sat on the swing. "I haven't ever really spent any time out here on this swing. I think today is the longest I have ever used it."

Tom leaned back and the swing rocked, floating forward and back once more. "It's nice, actually, very relaxing." Tom popped the top of his beer and held it toward Craig. Craig returned the gesture and tapped the bottles together. "Thanks for the beer and suggesting we do it now. My stress level has been through the roof lately."

Craig took a drink before responding. "I can imagine so, that can't be easy to deal with."

Tom shook his head, then took a long drink of his beer as well. "I just don't know where to turn next. This came on so suddenly a month ago, it seemed like it was a cold or something but she thought it felt more like allergies because her respiratory system was irritated. But when it wasn't getting better, actually getting harder for her to breath, we started seeing doctors and getting passed around from one to the next, some would see her and some wouldn't because of the insurance, and now she can't even get out of bed most of the time. I am at a loss."

Craig was feeling his pain, the feeling of being at a loss for what to do or where to turn. His next thoughts made him mad at himself. *I can fix this for them, I can get them into a healing program at the university, it would be easy, just whip out one of those blank sheets of paper and tell them they can go in and get healed by the university teaching hospital, that they would be able to get taken care of wouldn't even have to use their insurance.'* Craig was frustrated with his own thoughts, using Tom and his wife for his own gain. Sure it would help them in their time of need but the price they would have to pay in the end could be greater than they would want. Craig was staring at the park as the swing rocked slowly. *'I could tell them they are actually making a deal with the Devil before having them sign it, then at least they would know going into it. I wouldn't feel as responsible for them if they chose to continue.'*

Tom noticed that Craig had a far off look in his eyes, staring across the street into the park. "What are you thinking, Craig?"

Craig slowly came back to the present. "I was trying to think of a way I could help you. Wondering if there was something I could do to help get you into the university's medical treatment program. They are a teaching hospital and often have programs that can help with those sorts of things. Uh, what do they call that? A medical study? I believe they focus on whole body healing."

Tom looked disappointed. "We thought about that but our insurance denied it. We can't get in there."

Craig nodded. "Yes, I figured you had looked there, but I may be able to help get you in without insurance, sort of a scholarship program. Would you mind if I looked into that on your behalf?"

Tom stopped the swing rather abruptly, clomping his feet to the porch. "Craig, I would owe you the world if you could get us that kind of help. Of course I wouldn't mind."

Craig nodded his head and took another drink of his beer. "Good then, I will look into it and get back to you in a couple of days."

Tom leaned back in the swing again and lifted his feet, the swing glided easily forward and back, forward and back. He took another drink of his beer and felt a relaxing wave wash over him as he sat in silence on the swing, looking out across the park, through the green leaves and over the grass, letting his mind wander with the possibilities of a cure on the horizon.

Craig, however, felt uneasy about it, the beer making his stomach turn over. Or was it knowing that the offer he was considering for Tom was a deal too good to be true. He couldn't tell.

10

Athletics

Craig went to speak with the athletic director first thing in the morning, before any of the students arrived. Gavin Cross was in his office just down the hall from Craig's office in the Great Hall, though the two men rarely crossed paths. Not surprisingly, Craig led a very non athletic life, he wasn't interested in attending the school's team events or even watching them on TV. Gavin, on the other hand, was, as you would expect, a full on sports guy. Football, baseball, basketball, and just about any other sport they offered on campus, he was into all of them.

Craig knocked firmly on Gavin's open office door, looking into the cluttered space, sports memorabilia strewn about, not in an organized fashion.

"Good morning, Mr. Cross, how are you this morning?"

Gavin looked up from a sports journal and what looked like a statistical spread sheet on his desk. "Oh. Good morning, Mr. Newman. What can I do for you this morning?"

Gavin stood up behind his desk and reached out his hand to greet Craig. Craig stepped in and grasped hands with him, feeling more welcomed than he anticipated. Gavin had a firm handshake as expected, but not to the point that he was trying to prove a point by crushing your hand. He was a well built man, about five foot ten inches, and maybe 190 pounds of mostly muscle, dark hair and green eyes, with a neatly trimmed two week beard. His build showed that he worked out daily, a perk of his job.

"Mr. Cross, you can call me Craig. I know that we don't interact all too often, but I have someone I want to talk to you about." Craig eased into a chair across the desk from Gavin.

"Well, Craig, you've come to the right place if you want to talk about an athlete."

Craig was a little tense, sitting on the edge of his seat like he was interviewing for a job. "Yes, he is an athlete. His name is Brandon Wells, have you heard of him?"

Gavin gave a squinted look across the desk as he thought about the name. "Hmm. I don't recognize the name off the top of my head, should I?"

Craig nodded his head, then immediately shook it back and forth. "Maybe. I believe he came out for football early in the summer. I don't know if he just didn't make the cut or if he was too late to get on the team. Either way, he isn't on the team."

Gavin raised a hand to stop Craig. "Wait a minute. If he didn't make the team early in the year, right off the get go, don't be bringing him to me now."

Craig smiled. "No, of course not. That's not my intention. I would like to see him given a shot for next season. Just wanted you to keep an eye out for him. Is there anything he can do in the mean time that would give him a better chance at a spot for next year?"

Craig could tell he was losing Gavin's interest before he really got going. He had stumbled right out of the gate and would need to recover.

Gavin pressed his lips together and leaned back in his chair, staring at Craig, trying to size him up and figure out where this is all going. "Who is this kid? What's his background? And mostly, why do you care?"

Craig moved to the back of his chair and leaned back. "His name is Brandon Wells, I told you that already. I had my students write a paper recently that gave me some background on where they have been, but mostly where they want to go. Brandon had an impressive high school football career and would like to continue playing football for this school. Let me show you his paper."

Craig pulled the paper out of his satchel and slid it across the desk to Gavin. Gavin picked it up and glanced over it. Brandon had listed some of his high school stats before going into his projected history, wanting to become a professional athlete.

"Well, his stats aren't that great. I can see that there might be some potential, but if he was late for tryouts and practice, I can see why we passed over him." Gavin dropped the paper on his desk and leaned back in his chair, looking at Craig across the desk, waiting for his response.

Craig took note of his posture, recognizing that Gavin was trying to put an end to the conversation. "I believe he has potential, I would like to see him given a serious shot at the team, I would even hazard a bet that he would be a starter next season."

Gavin's eyes got wide with surprise. "Wow! That's a lofty statement. How much do you know about football, Mr.

Newman?"

Craig paused, then had to concede. "Admittedly, very little, but what I do know is people and determination. Brandon is that person that is determined to do whatever it takes to be the best." Craig was blowing smoke at this point, he needed Mr. Scott to see it his way and let Brandon on the team.

"Mr. Newman, Brandon is welcome to come out for tryouts again next fall, but I won't be giving him any special attention."

Craig's face started to burn, he could feel the redness in his cheeks, the air in the office got bitterly cold and Craig's face became stern. Their exchange didn't warrant the anger he was feeling but he couldn't control it. He hammered his fists on the desk and stood up abruptly, causing his chair to slide across the floor and tip over, slamming against the file cabinet near the door. Gavin jumped in his seat and pushed back away from his desk, he let out a gasp of air and could see the condensation rise as he did it.

Craig's eyes went completely black, dilated to the point that only the pupil was visible, his voice was massive, as if it surrounded the entire room and pressed down on Gavin from every angle. "You will put Brandon on the team, there is no other discussion needed!"

Gavin was frozen with fear, not sure what to make of this sudden aggression. He responded politely trying not to further upset Craig. "Mr. Newman, I don't think this outburst is called for. You admitted that you don't have the best grasp on football yet you believe you've found someone that should be on our team? Let's take a step back here and calm down."

Craig's face was burning red. Gavin could only see Craig's black pupils burning into his own eyes. "Mr. Scott, I will provide the necessary paperwork to secure a spot on your football program and you will accept Brandon Wells as the newest member of your team as if this whole idea was your own. Do you understand?"

Gavin became mesmerized looking into Craig's eyes and didn't put up any more argument. "Yes, I understand."

Craig relaxed slightly. "I will have Mr. Wells come see you soon, make sure he feels welcome."

Gavin submitted completely. "Okay, I'll do that." Gavin stuttered out the words before thinking them through, not sure what else to say and completely surprised by the anger coming from Craig. "Have him report to the team facilities for workouts starting next semester."

Craig straightened his tie, then picked up his satchel before turning to walk out of the office, speaking casually as he left. "I'm sure you won't regret your decision, thank you for your time."

As Craig left Gavin's office, walking down the hall towards his own, his eyes returned to normal and the temperature came back up in the room. Gavin moved slowly around his desk to the door, and peeked out into the hall to watch Craig unlock his office and step inside. Gavin's heart rate was elevated and his mind was swirling, not knowing what to make of the interaction. After picking up the toppled chair, he went back around his desk and settled back to work, checking athlete stats, writing Brandon Wells's name into his log book. Before long, Gavin Scott had forgotten the interaction with Craig, believing Brandon joining the team was completely his idea, already making plans with him in mind as a crucial part of the team.

Craig unlocked the door to his office and stepped inside. He was smiling to himself, he had never felt that type of exhilaration before. He stood up to Gavin and got what he wanted. He didn't realize that the temperature in Gavin's office had dropped or that his eyes had become black, he only knew that he was about to sign a contract with Mr. Wells, putting him on the team where he wanted to be.

Craig hung his coat and sat at his desk, flipping through another pile of student papers, trying to make a decision on which student to accept into the recruitment process next. Brandon would be along in a few hours to discuss his future football career, giving Craig time to consider other options. A paper written by Karina Duncan was at the bottom of the pile, and the name jumped out at him for no apparent reason. He picked it up and started to read, refreshing his memory as to why he'd set it aside.

* * *

Just after 10am, as Craig was reading history papers and making corrective notes, a knock on the open door of his office made him look up. It was Brandon Wells filling the open doorway.

"Brandon! Please come in, happy that you came to see me."

Brandon walked in and reached out his hand across Craig's desk. "Thank you for having me, I admittedly am a bit nervous. Not sure why I'm here."

Craig reached out and shook hands. "Please take a seat and I will explain." Brandon set his backpack down next to the same chair that Grimm had sat in and made himself comfortable. "Mr. Wells, in short, I read your history paper and felt compelled to try and help you realize your dreams. Now, I do admit that I don't know a lot about sports, that is not my forte; however, I could tell just from your essay that you are passionate about football and just the fact that you have stats to fall back on tells me that you must have had a successful high school career."

Brandon shifted in his seat, crossing his legs. "I was an above average player in high school, I know that in D1 sports you really need to be WAY above average, but I am motivated to be that person. I know I can work hard and progress fast enough to be a starter."

Craig leaned forward on his desk, clasping his fingers in front of him as he listened to Brandon. "I believe you Brandon, I really do. You know it's going to take a lot of work, you're going to have to work in the off season like no one ever has in order to shine above all those other guys that want that same spot on the team." Craig was talking out his ass, he had no idea what it meant to work hard in the off season, it was just some expression he had heard on TV while flipping channels, but it seemed to fit. Craig was feeling in over his head, he wasn't even sure what position Brandon played, a wide tight end? Maybe? Not sure. "I took it upon myself to speak with Gavin Scott, the athletic director here at NMSU, on your behalf." Brandon sat up straight and put both feet on the floor, his expression changing from inquisitive and unsure, to surprise and possible excitement. "Really? Just from my history paper?"

Craig nodded his head and continued. "Yes, sir, your paper made me believe in you. It took some convincing, but I was able to secure a spot on the team for you. You will need to report to the training facility starting next semester to start work outs with the team."

Brandon couldn't contain himself, he jumped to his feet

and reached across the desk to shake Craig's hand vigorously. "Thank you! Thank you so much! This is amazing!"

Craig couldn't help but smile at Brandon's enthusiasm. "You're going to have to really work for this Brandon, it could be your big break."

Brandon sat back down, nodding his head. "Yeah, of course, I'll work harder than I ever have at anything to make this work."

Craig smiled again, knowing that Brandon meant what he said and believed that he would no doubt put in the work that he needed to in order to make this chance of a lifetime pay off. "I will need you to sign a contract putting you on the team, it merely states that you won't give out team secrets and has code of conduct language in it, language that says you will keep your grades up and stay enrolled in school in order to be on the team. Things like that. Are you willing to sign that?"

Brandon nodded his head emphatically. "Yes, for sure, when can I sign?"

Craig straightened up his posture and reached for his satchel. "I have the contract right here."

He reached into the bag, shuffled through a few other papers, looking for the blank stapled sheets. He saw the edge of one of the stapled papers and pinched it between his fingers and thumb. There was a feeling he hadn't noticed the first time he pulled the papers from his bag, they were warm, as if they had just come out of the copy machine. He pulled it slowly from between other papers and held them up in front of his eyes. Again, he was astounded that what he knew were blank pages when he put them into his bag, now had full letter head for NMSU, with Brandon Wells filled into all the appropriate spots, for a division of athletics football player contract.

Craig smiled slightly before sliding the contract across the desk toward Brandon, followed by a pen. "Feel free to read it over, if you like."

Brandon grabbed the pen and barely glanced at the first page, just long enough to find the line that asked for his signature. The pen flew across the page, leaving Brandon's name barely legible, with the date next to it. He shoved the papers back across the desk in an excited hurry.

"Wow! I can't believe it. Thank you so much, this is amazing!"

Craig reached out and pickup up the contract. "You're welcome Brandon, I am sure you will make the best of this opportunity. I will turn this in this afternoon and you will belong to the New Mexico State University Football program. Congratulations." Craig stood up behind his desk and reached his hand out to congratulate Brandon. "Mr. Scott's office is just down the hall on the left. You should stop in and thank him for the opportunity before you leave."

Brandon stood and shook Craig's hand. "Thanks again, Mr. Newman. I'll see you in class next week."

Brandon turned and walked out the door after picking up his backpack. Instead turning toward the exit, when he left Craig's office, he turned toward Gavin Scott's door. Seeing that Brandon went that direction, Craig was curious what would happen. He stepped out from behind his desk and went to the door to try and listen to the interaction.

"Hello, Mr. Scott, I want to thank you for the opportunity to play football for NMSU."

Gavin was looking at Brandon with a furrowed brow for a moment. "Oh! You're Brandon Wells. I've heard good things about you. I'm excited to see what you can bring to the program. Come in for a moment, lets talk."

Brandon disappeared into the office and Craig could no longer hear what was being said, as their voices were lowered, but he had a feeling it was working out fine. Craig stood in the doorway with the contract in his hand, looking at it with a tinge of guilt. He had done it again to yet another person that was unsuspecting of the future implications. Two people within the last two weeks. *At this rate I will meet my quota way before December 31st.* Craig stepped out into the hall and walked to the third floor to turn in the contract Brandon had just signed. Janine had gone to lunch as indicated by the *'out to lunch'* sign on her desk. Craig dropped the contract in the same box stacked with papers that he had put Haley's contract in, feeling pretty sure that Haley's was still in the pile as well. He left the office feeling disgusted with himself, yet accomplished at the same time. *'Not sure how I'm supposed to deal with these conflicting feelings.'*

Craig spotted Brandon leaving the Great Hall as he came down the stairs back to his office. He stopped to watch him leave, wondering how long the contract would take to execute. *'I never looked to see what the timeline was.'* He stopped before going all the way down the stairs, looking at his watch. Janine would return in 15 minutes. Craig went back to Janine's office and grabbed the contract he had just dropped on the top of the pile. He flipped through it to the last page, scanning for the Evil language. It was there, halfway down the page, in a similar section as his had been, buried in dress code verbiage. *'For a term of 5 years.' 'Oh that's short, that poor kid.'* Craig's heart sank with the thought of Brandon barely making it out of college when his term would end. *'That's going to be rough.'* He put the contract back on the pile and walked slowly back to his office, considering whether or not he could vary the length of contracts and how to go about it. *'Maybe I can ask Grimm or Glen.'*

11

Clinical Trial

At the end of most weeks, Craig usually spent his time studying history lessons that he would eventually pass on to his students as assignments. Keeping history *new* could be a full time job in itself, the history didn't change but what he teaches did. Not every student would be subjected to the same history lesson. This morning, Craig sat at his desk in casual attire, no tie, with the same Mayan history book that had given him nightmares on the desk in front of him. He fully planned on developing a lesson plan for the following semester based on the burial rituals of the culture. At the moment though, he couldn't focus on it, his mind kept going back to Tom and Sue Downy, they needed his help. Craig felt the same guilt that he'd had when he first spoken with Tom a week ago, telling him that he might be able to get him into the clinical trials at the University Medical Center. He was doing it for his own benefit more than the benefit of Tom and Sue. *'I need to do some research on this one, I don't think I can BS good enough to get them into a trial without knowing a little about the inner workings and the admitting process.'* Craig set the Mayan book aside and pulled his new laptop toward him, flipping open the top. His first search was the campus directory that only staff had access to. Scrolling through the registry on the medical center site, looking for names he might recognize, he wanted to make contact with someone and be able to ask questions without raising suspicion over why he was asking. As he reached the bottom of the list, he was dismayed to discover that he didn't recognize a single name on it. Next stop was the admissions site for the University Hospital, then the clinical trials site. *'I'll bet Tom has already looked at all of these.'* Craig discovered that there were a ton of hoops to jump through, not just to get admitted to the hospital, but to get into one of the trials. Usually, it had to do with getting a referral from another physician, followed by an application, followed by interviews. *'People aren't trying to get a job here, they just need help.'* Then Craig found it the other way around, where a physician actually applied on their behalf. *'Good grief, how do people ever get help?'*

His head was starting to spin with the back and forth of searching for information. *'I just need to go talk to someone.'* He glanced at his watch, just after 12:30. *'Good time to go pay the admissions office a visit.'* He closed his laptop and tidied the files on his desk in case he didn't make it back to the office the rest of the day. He slid the Mayan book into his satchel and threw the strap over his shoulder As he left the office, closing the door behind him, he felt a chill in the air. Craig stopped abruptly, looking down the empty hallway, slowly turning around, checking the hall behind him, all empty. He carried on toward the stairs, the temperature seeming normal as he walked down the hall. *'That's was strange, if Grimm is here I'm sure he would show himself.'* Craig stopped at the top of the stairs and looked over the edge into the empty Great Hall below. He couldn't see or hear anyone and the chill was gone. He shrugged his shoulders to himself and continued on his way out to his Mercedes, baking in the sun. 15 minutes later, he found himself struggling to find a parking spot at the medical center, he circled the lot twice before finding one in the far corner that may not have actually been a parking spot, but it would due. Craig started sweating as he walked to the main building with his satchel over his shoulder. It was nearly 95 degrees with no wind, the pavement absorbing the heat and pushing it back up at him as he walked over it, his feet burning through his dress shoes with each step. Craig was sure he could feel the tar from the asphalt sticking to the soles of his shoes. He was relieved to finally make it to the main path leading to the building's front entrance, it was lined with trees providing a shaded walkway for the last 100 yards. Once inside, the relief of the air conditioned space was very welcoming, the building was hushed, though there were people moving about. Craig looked for a directory as he walked into the main lobby. To his right, not far from the entrance, there was an information desk. As Craig approached, a man stood up from behind his computer screen.

"Hello, sir, how can I help you today?"

Craig wasn't sure how to phrase what he wanted to ask so he went with a general inquiry. "I need information on how to get someone admitted into this hospital for treatment."

The man at the desk who's name tag was blank, looked at Craig, expecting more information. "Do you know what department you will be admitting to?"

Craig raised his eyebrows. "Oh, no, I don't, uh, we don't

know what's wrong."

Blank Tag pointed past Craig, behind him. "Down that hallway, follow the 'General Admitting' signs."

Craig took a step back, gave a half wave. "Thank you."

He looked for the general admitting signs as he walked the hallway he was directed to, he thought the signs would be easier to see, they were just small two inch lettering signs every so often at hallway intersections. Eventually, after seven or eight minutes of walking, he came across the admitting / receiving office, which made it sound like a warehouse loading dock. As he stepped inside he saw several cubicles with office staff talking with people Craig presumed to be patients, or future patients, as well as several people in the waiting area, with multiple chairs lined back to back. Craig took a number from the pull tab station and found a place to wait. Number 39 showing on the reader board, number 45 in his hand. *'This could take a while.'* At that moment, a gentleman came out and called number 40, Craig looked around the room, as did everyone else in the waiting area.

"No number 40?" said the man. "Okay then, 41?"

A woman on the far end of Craig's row of seats stood up, with what seemed to be a great effort, and followed the man into his cubicle. After looking around the room, Craig sat back in his seat, preparing for the wait.

Craig sat silently, watching other people come and go from the room, his right leg bouncing nervously up and down. 50 minutes had passed when number 44 had been called. He'd watched an older gentleman, with silver gray hair and a scruffy beard, get up slowly from his chair, appearing to be stiff from sitting for so long. This made Craig realize his back was hurting and stiff from sitting still for nearly an hour, waiting his turn to speak to someone, and also realize he may not get the answers he was looking for and that he may have wasted his time. *'I'm coming into this blind, I don't even know what questions to ask.'*

"45!" Came a voice from a young lady standing at the front of the room with an expectant look on her face, "45, anyone?"

It clicked in Craig's head, *'Oh, that's me.'* He raised his hand a little to acknowledge it was him as he struggled to stand up. Craig stretched his back a bit as he followed her to a cubicle at the back of the office.

"Hello, I'm Jacky, I'll be helping you today. Please, have a seat." She pointed to a chair that looked just as uncomfortable as the one in the lobby, but he gave in and sat across from her. "What is your name?" Jacky asked as she seated herself at her desk.

"I'm Craig, and before we get started, I work here at the university, I'm a history professor."

Jacky smiled. "Wonderful to meet you, what can I do for you today?"

Craig shifted uncomfortably to the edge of his seat. "I am looking for some information. Basically, how can I get someone into the hospital for diagnosis. I have a friend that has been bounced around from one hospital to the next and she has not been able to get a solid diagnosis. I am aware that there are clinical trials that happen here, not sure if any of them would pertain to what she is going through, but I would like to find some help for her."

Jacky reached into her desk, flipped through a few files, and pulled a stack of paperwork out, setting it in front of her. She flipped through it, then reached back into the drawer and searched for something else. Unsuccessful, she spun around in her chair and pulled open the middle drawer of a file cabinet, flipped through more files and found what she was looking for towards the middle of the drawer. Turning back around to face Craig, she set the papers on the desk.

"This is what you need currently to apply. You... I mean, she, would need to apply to be accepted for diagnostics or research and discovery. Here are the forms that need to be completed to apply for the program, admitting is done once a quarter." She handed Craig a stapled packet of forms that must have been 65 pages. "The bottom half of that stack of papers need to be filled out by the current referring physician."

Craig was not pleased with the stack he was just handed and got a perturbed look on his face . "What if there is no referring physician?"

Jacky looked back at him, dumbfounded that he would even be asking the question. "There has to be a referral or they can't get into the program, since this is a teaching facility we don't take walk in patients."

Craig looked at the stack of paper, picking it up, it seemed overwhelming. "Where do the papers go after that?"

Jacky folded her hands on the desk. "There are a couple of ways to file them with our applications office. You can scan them all and submit them online after building a profile, or you can deliver them by hand to the applications office, which is not on this campus, or you can mail them to the applications office at the address on the first page."

Craig grimaced again, scrunching his nose and furrowing his brow. "Which is the most likely to have fewer problems?"

Jacky grimaced back at him and laughed at the question. "Really it's all in how the paperwork is filled out, I don't think any of them go through the system without some kind of hiccup."

Craig shoulders dropped and his head hung to the floor. "Okay, well, is there any chance, since I work for the University, that I can bypass some of the red tape?"

Jacky pressed her lips together, making them thin red lines and squinted her eyes at Craig. "I'm not coming up with anything in your situation, since she isn't directly employed by the University and she's not related to you, I don't think there is anything that would help."

Craig sat up straight again and pulled his shoulders back. "Well, I will just have to push through this like everyone else. Can you give me directions to the application office where this would all be turned in when its done?"

Jacky nodded and pulled a sheet of paper from the desk. "Here is the address and a pin on the map where its located."

Craig stood up and reached his hand across the desk. "Thank you for the information."

Jacky stood and shook his hand. "I hope everything works out for you, please call me if you need any other information."

Craig left the office with mixed emotions, on the one hand he had known he might not get information that would help, but on the other hand, at least now he had a direction to turn. In the back of his mind he knew the whole time that he would use the Evil One's powers to get the paperwork complete and turned in, hoping that no one would notice.

12

Oh, The Dreams

Craig's head started to throb on the drive home from the university hospital. Everything Jacky had told him was swirling in his mind, all the paperwork, the different ways to submit it. *'No one gets their paperwork through without a hiccup of some kind.'* He wanted to talk with Tom this evening but wasn't sure what he would say. It had been a week since they'd sat on the porch and had a beer. Craig said he would get back to him in a couple of days and didn't follow through on his word.

Driving was becoming difficult with the searing pain behind his eyes. Just a couple more blocks and he would be able to rest his head and take something for the pain. He didn't remember driving the last ten minutes home but he was in the driveway with his eyes closed and the car shut off when he came back to consciousness. Craig opened his eyes and looked from side to side out the windows, looking to see if anyone had spotted him. There wasn't anyone around, he was alone in the driveway, sitting in his car with his eyes closed, not entirely sure how long he had been there. His head had stopped hurting so it may have been a long time. He looked at his watch. *'6:30. Maybe I've been sitting here 20 minutes? That was strange. My head stopped hurting though.'* He shook his head a little bit and shrugged off the strange feelings he was having, then got out of the Mercedes and went to the house. There was a slight breeze blowing across the porch, the swing was rocking awkwardly side to side. Craig stopped at the top step and looked at it, then moved to it and sat down. *'Why not, it was so nice last week to just watch the neighborhood go by, to soak it in and act like I have no cares in the world.'* He pushed back with his foot and heard the moan of the chain on the hook, then released and let the swing glide back and forth. Again, push and release. He looked across the street at the park. Only a few people out in the grass this late in the day, enjoying the evening's cool breeze. The wind rustled through the leaves of the maple trees, Craig could hear them from his swing. The rhythmic feeling and the creaking with every motion was calming. The gentle breeze across the porch felt good, a relief from the heat of the fall. Craig's eyes got heavy as he rocked back and forth, he laid his head on the back of the swing, listening to the leaves rustle in the distance, still pushing with his foot, back and forth.

Hearing birds in the distance, he looked to the sky to see a swirling flock moving in a rhythmic dance led by an unknown leader, rising high to the clouds then darting left and right, before dipping low to the tree tops. It seemed like hundreds of birds moving in unison, somehow communicating a choreographed pattern only they could understand. As Craig watched the sky, the clouds started to darken in the distance, rain on the horizon streaked the skyline, flanked by blue from above. The birds were getting closer and tree limbs started to bend farther with the wind. The birds were bigger than he originally thought and much louder now. Large black birds, crows or ravens a hybrid maybe, he couldn't tell. *"Am I in a movie? Is this 'Birds'? What is happening?"* They were darting this way and that but generally heading his direction. There seemed to be a couple birds leading the flock, he saw them look his way and change course, directing the others toward his porch, toward him, on the swing. They swirled around his front yard, flying between the pillars, directing their path right at him, coming uncomfortably close to his head. Dark clouds started to form in front of his house, spinning menacingly high above, then a funnel started to form, stretching from the center of the darkest cloud, reaching for the ground. The birds got louder still, there were more of them swarming the front yard, flying past his face as he tried to swat them away. He could feel their wings brush against his forehead and cheeks. The wind picked up, he could feel it blowing at his hair, he watched the birds fight against it as leaves and branches flew past his porch. Some of the giant black birds struggled to stand their ground in the front yard, leaning into the gail. Craig fought off several as they whipped their wings over his head, flogging him with wicked black feathers. He looked through squinted eyes from the debris blown through the air, out at the yard as the funnel stretched from the epicenter of the storm like a long wicked finger from the sky. Color had drained from his surroundings, the rain streaks were gray but the sky was sepia toned and the clouds ran together, except for the funnel that seemed to have a life of it's own, darker gray than the rest, with black streaks twisting throughout the long finger reaching to the ground. Some of the birds in the yard tried to fly away against the wind, but disintegrated into black speckled dust and blew across the grass. Craig's squinted eyes bulged when he saw it happen. *"Grimm!! What are you doing to me?!"* He thought for sure it had to be related to the Evil Master. *"Are you testing me?!"*

More birds attacked from the sky, their talons outstretched as they dove under the roof line of the porch, sharp claws tearing at Craig's shirt and thighs, tearing his pants to shreds. Craig could feel the wetness of blood running down his arms and legs as he tried uselessly to swat the birds away. He reached for his legs to try and stop the bleeding and felt things moving and crawling quickly up his hands and arms. Craig looked down to see that spiders had engulfed his legs from the floor, he couldn't see his feet anywhere in the sea of spiders racing over each other up his legs, covering his hands and arms now, running toward his face. In a panic, he jumped up from the swing, swatting at the birds and trying to swipe away the spiders as he moved and danced across the porch to escape. Craig was getting dizzy, spinning out of control, the relentless attack from the birds and spiders making him panic and fall down the stairs toward the yard.

The twisting funnel of clouds had reached the ground, spinning wildly across the yard, out into the street, then back again. Somehow, the birds could withstand the howling wind, still flapping madly around Craig's head as he sprawled across the yard. Rain started beating down, adding to the discomfort of spiders and panic, it was hard to see what was happening around him. Craig tried to see where the next attack was coming from but the rain and wind mixed into a washy whirl in front of his face. He was unable to make out more than a blur of black movement, the birds still flapping around the yard and diving at him from all angles. Darkness was closing in from the sides, he was loosing consciousness, or was this the end of the line?

* * *

Tom Downy was just arriving home, the rain pelting his windshield, his wipers on high, barely keeping up. Tom glanced at Craig's house as he passed and turned into his driveway, noticing that Craig was sitting on the porch, but it didn't look natural the way he was slumped over on the swing. *'What is he doing? He has to be getting wet out there.'* Tom got out of his car and quickly ran across the yard, trying not to get soaked in the process. As he ran up the porch steps he noticed Craig looked to be sleeping. *'Oh, poor guy must have fallen asleep before it started raining.'*

Tom reached over and nudged Craig on the shoulder. "Hey, buddy! Wake up! You're getting soaked!"

Craig's eyes twitched beneath his closed eyelids, his brow furrowed and the corners of his mouth turned down, one eye crunched together as he reacted to something in his sleep, pulling his head that direction. Craig's hands were twitching in his sleep.

Tom nudged harder. "Craig! Wake up!"

Craig jolted and lurched back, pushing his feet on the floor, causing the swing to rock violently. He slid back and the swing went out from under him, causing Craig to fall on the wet porch floor.

"AH! Grimm stop!!" Craig went flat on the floor and covered his head with his hands. "Stop! Stop!"

Tom stepped back quickly. "Craig, it's okay! It's me, Tom!" He reached down and touched Craig's leg to try and calm his reaction. Craig pulled away and rolled on his side, peering through his arms over his face, heaving and out of breath. Tom pulled back again. "It's okay, just me your neighbor, Tom. You must have been having one hell of a dream. It started raining and I saw you on the swing. Thought I should wake you up before you got a bad chill."

Craig was tense, not yet sure what had happened. Craig looked out to the yard and up toward the sky. It was raining hard but there was no funnel cloud, no birds, no spiders on his legs. He pushed his elbows on the floor and started to sit up.

Tom reached a hand out to help him to his feet. "Wow! What was that about?"

Craig stood up, pants and shirt soaked through. "That was some bad dream, there were birds coming at me and a tornado, then spiders everywhere. I couldn't get away from them, they just kept coming at me."

Tom stood there with a dumbfounded look on his face. "That sounds awful. I hate spiders. That would freak me out. Are you okay?"

Craig looked at his legs and arms, remembering vividly the talons ripping into his skin and the blood pouring out. "I think so, a little cold now but I seem to be okay."

Tom stepped back as if to turn to leave. "Who's Grimm?"

Craig reacted quickly, jerking his head up to look at Tom's face. "Why do you ask about Grimm?"

Tom looked back at Craig with a questioning stare. "You asked Grimm to stop. Yelled it actually."

Craig's face started to burn with embarrassment. "Oh." Craig paused for a moment, searching for something to say. *'Would now be a good time to tell Tom about Grimm? The door is opened.'* "I was doing some reading today, about the Grim Reaper, must have been in my subconscious."

Tom smiled at him, almost laughed. "That explains the bad dreams, that sort of stuff will get to ya." He chuckled again as he turned to go. "You going to be okay?"

Craig waved him off. "Yes, I'll be fine. Thanks for coming to check on me. Oh, by the way, I did some checking on the process for applying to the medical program at the university. It isn't for sure, but I think we will be able to get you in. I'll talk to you about it in a few days, I still have some paperwork to fill out."

Tom had a look of disbelief on his face. "Are you serious? That is amazing news. Thank you so much, I don't know how I'll ever repay you."

Craig blushed and hoped that Tom couldn't see it in the low light. "Don't thank me yet, we have some hoops to jump through. Like I said, we can talk more about it later."

Tom nodded approval. "Well, even with hoops to jump through, I want you to know I appreciate it tremendously."

Craig waved him off. "Don't mention it. Have a good night."

Tom waved and trotted across the lawn towards home through the rain. Craig tried to dry his hands on his pants that were also wet and glanced at the porch nervously, checking for spiders. He shivered and went inside to clean up and get warm.

13

Losing Time

A week had passed since Craig's unsuccessful visit with his father Mike. There was so much that he wanted to share with his dad and get his take on. He couldn't tell anyone else about recruiting people for the Devil, he couldn't tell anyone else that he had personally met the Grim Reaper. Craig didn't have a best friend or even a close acquaintance that wouldn't think he was absolutely bat shit crazy for believing any of this was even remotely true. Except his dad. But for it to be meaningful he wanted his dad to know who he was when he talked to him. There may be an argument for telling someone these things knowing that they would forget them right away, but that wasn't what Craig wanted.

Craig had a high level of apprehension as he knocked on Mike's door. He listened for a response for a moment but didn't get one. He tapped again, a little harder this time.

"Hello, who's there?"

Craig cleared his throat. "It's Craig, can I come in?"

It took a moment for Mike to respond. "Yes, come in."

Craig opened the door to find Mike standing halfway

between his favorite chair and the door. "Oh Craig, I didn't recognize your voice. How are you?"

Craig was relieved at the recognition and welcoming smile on Mike's face. "I'm doing okay. How are you doing?"

Mike got an unhappy look on his face. "I don't know. I feel okay right now but I have been losing time. I go to sleep and the next time I wake up it's two days later. I don't like whats happening."

Craig walked over and gave his dad a hug. "I'm sorry to hear that Dad. I was here a week back and you weren't yourself. It was hard to see. You ran me out." Craig gave him a smile. "We'll handle it together the best we can."

Mike turned and walked back to his chair. "I suppose we will, not anything I can do about it, but I think that is pretty frustrating."

Craig sat on the sofa as Mike made himself comfortable. "I suppose I could help you out." Craig smirked at Mike, hoping he would get the joke.

Mike looked at him a little confused for a moment, then his face fit up. "Oh! Goodness, that's a thought but I'm not sure I want to go down that road." Mike smiled and chuckled a little bit. "How is that coming along? Have you had any luck finding, what shall we call them? Any takers?"

Craig stared off at the TV for a moment and tried to formulate what to tell his father, but there was no good way to say it. He couldn't come up with anything that didn't sound as awful as it really was. "Yes. I have had, as you say, a couple of takers to the pyramid scheme."

Mike nodded, knowing that Craig didn't like what he was doing. Quietly Mike asked. "Do they know what they have signed up for?"

That got to Craig. He knew he was hurting people in the long run, cheating them, leading them down a dark path that they didn't sign up for intentionally. These people trusted that he had their best interests at heart when really, it was a completely self centered, self motivated, terrible thing he was doing. "No. They didn't read their contracts." Craig could feel a giant lump building in his throat so he could almost not speak. "They trusted me."

Mike could tell Craig was hurting from what he was doing. "They did, and you have done what you believe you have to do. It's self preservation. You have to let that go, those people had the chance to read the contracts and not sign. Right?" Craig nodded because he couldn't speak, and realized the incredible clarity that was coming from Mike. "Then it's on them."

Craig took a moment to think about it and let his guilt subside. "I know ultimately it's on them, but I am sending them to hell. We've talked about this before, I still don't feel comfortable with it, but at this point, I'm carrying through with my end of the contract."

Mike was sitting on the edge of his recliner with his elbows on his knees, his hands on his cane, leaning toward Craig. "Do you want to tell me about the souls you have recruited or would that make it worse?"

Craig pondered that for a moment and wasn't sure he wanted to think about it. "I'm not sure I want to go into great detail. I'll tell you that there are two of them so far, a young athlete and a young law student that wants to be a journalist." Craig hesitated, thinking about other people he had considered. "I have been looking into helping a husband and wife. My neighbors, actually. She has become ill and they are having troubles finding the medical help they need. I think I can get them into the university hospital, but I think I want to tell them up front what they're signing up for. I don't want to leave them to chance reading it in the contract." Craig looked up at his father waiting for a response.

Mike seemed to be thinking about it. "Do you think that would help you feel better about doing what you need to do?" Craig nodded and Mike thought for a moment. "Do you think that they will still accept your help?"

Craig leaned back in the sofa. "I have no idea. they might be desperate enough that they are willing."

Mike moved to the back of his chair and leaned back setting his cane across his lap. "What are the dangers to you if they decline?"

Craig looked at Mike with a bit of a shocked expression. "Dangers? What do you mean? Do you think that could be dangerous?"

Mike shrugged his shoulders at the question. "It could be. They could tell other people what you said. That they think you're crazy. They could tell others that you believe in the Devil or that you're a Devil worshiper, and that seems to me like it could be bad for your career, which, at this point, is all you have and the only way you have contact with enough people to recruit for the Reaper."

Craig's face went ash white, his jaw dropping open. "Oh dad. I hadn't thought of any of that. If it were to get out that I am recruiting for the Devil, people would think I'm nuts. They wouldn't believe that I actually have spoken to the Grim Reaper, they would just think I'm part of some Devil worshiping cult or something. That would be really, really bad."

Mike sat silently, nodding his head, letting the gravity of

Craig's discovery sink in. "So while your trying to decide if you should tell anyone about what you are dealing with, I think you should consider the negative 'what ifs'."

Craig's color had come back some to his face. "I know you're right, I'm glad you brought that up before I made a potentially huge mistake. I will have to tread very lightly before telling them anything."

They both sat in silence for a while, not looking at each other or moving at all. Craig's face showed his sleepless nights and the anguish he was feeling. Mike saw it when Craig first walked in the room.

"You haven't been sleeping well, I can see it on your face."

Craig shook his head. "No, not really. I've had some pretty terrible dreams, they make me not want to go to sleep."

Mike was watching his expression. "What kind of dreams?"

Craig took a deep breath. "They are a little bit dark, the falling kind of dreams, the kind where you're lost and can't find your way, or the ones where you're being attacked by bugs and birds and can't defend yourself. You know the good kind of dreams." Craig cracked a weak smile.

Mike smiled back. "It's pretty understandable to have those dreams in your situation. Is everything else okay?"

Craig immediately thought of his trip out to the mountains with a gun in his hand. "Yeah, everything is fine."

Mike knew he wasn't telling the whole truth but didn't push the issue. "You know you can tell me. I wont think you're crazy." They both laughed, but it was weak and tinged with disgust.

"Have you seen Glen?"

Mike smiled at the question. "I have, but I haven't spoken to him. I would prefer not to open that door if you know what I mean."

Craig did know what he meant. "I don't blame you at all for that. I spoke to him for a moment as I was leaving here once. He wasn't very forthcoming with any information that I could use."

Mike adjusted his seating position and leaned his cane to the side of his chair. "What did you hope to get out of him?"

Craig shrugged. "I'm not sure, I was just looking for answers, I guess, about how this whole scheme works. I think I have the gist of it, but I was trying to make a decision at that point of what I was supposed to do. Now here I am."

Mike was getting tired. "I think I need to rest. It has been very good seeing you."

Craig nodded. "Okay, I will leave you be. I'll keep you up to date in a couple days." Craig let himself out and heard the TV turn on as he closed the door behind himself.

Craig had all the thoughts of the conversation running through his head as he walked outside. The air was muggy from the rain the day before, the heat of the day was almost intolerable. When he got home he stood in the front yard looking at the porch and the swing, remembering the dreams from the day before as if they really happened. Not like most dreams, that fade away quickly and are hard to remember. He looked at the floor for signs of spiders and the yard for debris that was blown in the wind. He couldn't find anything that would suggest a tornado had touched down in his front yard. *'But that was such a vivid dream!'* He went inside and found his satchel next to the front door where he had left it from the night before. He wanted to look through the paperwork for the medical center application. Craig sat at the kitchen table to start looking through the papers. He noticed immediately that the paperwork had all been filled out. He started flipping through the pages, reading a few lines, then moving to the next page, every bland question, no matter how mundane, was filled in with Tom and Sue's information. As he got to the back section he found the pages for the doctors recommendations were complete as well, the reason for the applications, the personal information, everything. *Some of this is going to be hard to explain, how could I know all of this.* Craig started tapping nervously on the table with his index finger, staring blankly at the forms laying in front of him. *Maybe I don't have to let Tom and Sue know that it was all filled out, I can just turn it in and find out if the application is accepted. But when do I tell them that this deal comes with a price.?* Craig leaned hard against the back of the chair, letting the pages slip from his hand. An emptiness in his stomach made him feel sick. He pressed his hands onto his gut to try and relieve the feeling. *I'll just turn in the paperwork first and see how it goes.*

Craig stood and put the papers back in his satchel, then went about making some dinner to alleviate the pit in his stomach. As he mixed his rice bowl together, the satchel caught his eye sitting on the table, calling to him. *I've missed something.* He went over and pulled the packet out again, flipping through the pages to discover, just before the doctor recommendation section, there were two blank lines with Tom and Sue's names before them. 'Signature,' written in fine print below each line. *Damn! I have to get them to sign before turning them in.* Craig sighed, dropped the pages closed again, and returned to his meal to fill the empty pit.

14

The Skinny Kid

Craig sat in his Mercedes in the staff lot Monday morning, not ready to face the day. The sun was already beaming down with intense power, especially for a fall day. Craig put his head back against the headrest, feeling the heat come in the open window, trying to muster the will to get out of the car, sort of like trying to fight the urge to hit the snooze button, procrastinating going to his office and preparing for the day's classes. As he relaxed further into his seat, he could feel sleep starting to wash over him. His thoughts fighting between whether to give in, or to snap out of it and get out of the car. Something else entered his mind as he drifted farther towards a nap, a screeching sound with rhythmic under tones. High pitched, then low, up and down, getting louder. *'What is that?'* Craig forced one eye open, then the other. He glanced in his mirrors, then from side to side. *'Where is that sound coming from?'* Craig popped the door open and put one foot out on the ground, the sound was getting louder still, more rhythmic now. *'Music?'* He thought it could be but there was another sound with it that didn't mix. Moments later, the sound whizzed past him. Across the parking lot zoomed a little shit box car with the belts squealing and a thumping sound coming from the exhaust as it drug behind the car, slamming over speed bumps as if they were there for sport. Music blaring from inside, something loud and screaming with no discernible words. Craig stood up quickly to watch it roar past to the other end of the lot near the auditorium. The car came to an abrupt stop, nearly jumping up the curb. The noise stopped, both from the car moving and the music from inside.

Moments later, as Craig stood gathering his satchel, dumbfounded at the ruckus across the lot, the occupant of the shit box opened the door with a loud screech and a pop of hinges as the door fought to remain closed. The occupant emerged, tall and skinny, long dark hair, wearing black pants and a tattered black t-shirt with some imprinting Craig could't read from his distance. *'What in the world?'* Craig was intrigued and started to walk towards the skinny kid. He was struggling to pull something from the back seat, the trunk of the car tied down, too full of gear to close and latch. He noticed Craig walking his way.

"Good morning, sir."

Craig was a little surprised at the politeness of the young man. "Good morning. Quite the load of gear you have there."

The skinny kid freed some equipment from its tangle in the back seat and set it on the ground. "Yeah, its kind of tough moving all this stuff in my car, but I do it when I have to." The kid half climbed into the back seat again to retrieve something else as Craig stood several feet away, watching the circus unfold.

"Yes, I can see that. You aren't supposed to park back here

unless you're faculty."

The kid looked under his arm, sideways out the side of the car. "Huh? Oh yeah, parking. I'm not going to park here, I'm just unloading into the auditorium, this is the closest I can get."

Craig nodded his approval as the kid drug another large box of equipment and cords out of the back of the car. He slammed the door with as much gusto as he could. The door creaked and popped more than when he opened it but appeared to close all the way.

Craig flinched as he watched it happen. "What's your name?"

The kid moved to the back of the car and pulled the bungee loose on the trunk, the lid popped up without hesitation. "I'm Jake."

Craig stepped forward and offered his hand. "Hello, Jake, I'm Craig Newman. What program are you enrolled in?"

Jake stepped back from the trunk of the car and shook Craig's hand. "I'm in music production, that's what all this stuff is for."

Craig surveyed the pile of boxes and crates in the trunk, it didn't look like much to him. "Music production? Wow, that seems interesting. How long have you been in the program?"

Jake started picking at the pile of goods in the trunk, setting items on the ground next to the other boxes. "This is my second year, I have to take it kind of slow. I work full time too, so I can pay for the classes."

Craig's face lit up. "Yes, that is a common dilemma. Do you play instruments as well?"

Jake reached into the trunk and pulled out his guitar case and held it up. "Yeah, I'm a guitar player. I figured it would be a good idea to have a baseline of production as well as being a musician. Trying to be more well rounded."

Craig smiled at him as he looked him up and down again, from his grungy high tops to his short sleeve, rock band t-shirt. Craig took another look at all the equipment Jake was unloading. "What are you doing with all this equipment today?"

Jake set a box overflowing with cords and gadgets on top of an amplifier. "We're recording a demo today, then we're playing a show this evening at the arena."

Craig's brows raised. "Really? You have a show tonight?"

Jake pulled yet another guitar from the floor of the trunk and leaned it carefully against the side of the car. "Yeah, I'm pretty excited about it. We're opening for Egregious. We got the call last week. I guess their usual opener had all their gear stolen and haven't been able to get the insurance to cover the replacements yet."

Craig was listening intently, noticing how excited Jake was to talk about his opportunity. "That's a bummer for them, but a stroke of luck for you. What is the name of your group?"

Jake's face flushed red. "We have gone through so many names. We just can't settle on a good one, nothing seems to feel right. Right now we are going by 'Adaptive' because we seem to adapt to every situation we get put in. I don't know if it will stick."

Craig ran the name through his head a few times. "It's not bad. I could see that working out."

Jake smiled. "Thanks, it would be good to finally stick with a name so we could start building a following."

Craig looked again at all the gear spread out in the parking lot. "Do you need a hand moving this stuff inside?" He glanced at his watch to make sure he still had time.

Jake closed the trunk with a hefty slam. "That would be great! Could you wait here for a minute while I run in and grab a cart? I should have gotten that first."

Craig nodded. "Yes I can, you go ahead."

Jake grabbed one of his guitars and walked quickly around the corner of the auditorium, out of Craig's sight. Craig stood guard over the pile of equipment, waiting patiently. *This could be a wonderful opportunity to recruit another soul. I think he would jump at the chance to make it big, and what rock star hasn't sold his soul to the Devil.'* Craig could hear the rumbling of a cart with wobbly wheels echoing off the buildings, getting louder as it got closer.

As Jake neared, he looked Craig's direction. "Mr. Newman I really appreciate the help. This usually takes such a long time that I end up not getting much recording done."

Craig waved it off like it was nothing. "I'm happy to help."

They carefully loaded and stacked all the gear they could on the cart. When no more would fit, Craig grabbed the last couple of loose items and followed Jake into the building. It was a maze of hallways that Craig had never been in before. "I've never had a reason to come into this building. I had no idea this was here. How long did it take you to learn your way around this building?"

Jake led the way, left, right, through a set of double doors, down the hall, left again to a door marked 'Studio 6'.

"It took some time for sure, I've gone into the wrong room on more than one occasion." Jake laughed at himself as he entered the studio and held the door for Craig. "Just set that stuff over there," he Pointed to the left of a drum kit on a small stage riser.

Craig did as requested and stopped to take a look around. "How often do you get to come in here?"

Jake shrugged. "Since I'm in the program I get priority access, so my band gets in here once a week if we have material that's ready to go. Other wise it's about $400 an hour to have an amateur producer set up and record your band. Considerably more if you want a professional producer."

Craig gave a little whistle and raised a brow. "Wow, and I didn't even know it existed. How many studios are there?"

Jake waved Craig over to the glass in between the studio and the recording equipment. "This board in here is where we adjust the sound that is being recorded. There are four studios with this same set up, two studios with an even bigger board and more data capabilities and four of the older studios with older technologies and eight and sixteen track tape recorders."

Jake was really excited to share his knowledge about the studios with Craig. Craig had read something about newer recording technology and that the new tech wasn't as pure of a sound according to some people in the industry, it was apparently too sterile. "Which is your favorite?"

Jake's face lit up. "I really like to use a combination, the effects you can get from new tech are really amazing, but the warmth you get from recording on tape is hard to beat. The problem I have with it is the cost, tape is very expensive to use so you have to be sure it's something you want to record or it may be a waste."

Craig was finding it very interesting and lost track of the time, only realizing it when he glanced at his watch. "Oh, Jake! I really have to be going, I have a class starting in 15 minutes. When is your show?"

Jake smiled. He spun around, looking at all the boxes they

brought into the studio. Spotting the one he wanted, Jake rummaged through it, pulling out a colorfully printed piece of paper. "Here's a flier for the show. Will you come? We go on about seven."

Craig smiled back. "I would love to. You have very much caught my attention with this tour of the studio. Thank you for showing me around." Craig stepped forward and reached out to shake hands with Jake. Jake did the same and as they clasped hands, Craig felt a frozen hand in his. He paused for a moment, holding Jake's hand. "It was very nice to meet you Jake, I'll see you tonight."

Jake smiled, but this time it seemed to be a bit more of a wicked grin than a friendly smile. "I hope so, we could use the support, I'll introduce you to the band."

Craig slowly released his grip and took a step back. *What am I witnessing right now?*' "I'll try to find my way out."

Jake pointed toward the door. "Just follow the exit signs, they will take you right outside."

Craig waved a shallow, unsure wave as he left the studio, looking up and down the hall for exit signs. He was soon back outside, passing his car in the lot, feeling a tad uneasy now about Jake. He still felt like there might be an opportunity, he wasn't sure if the cold interaction was from himself or from Jake. *'Could he already be involved with a Reaper? Seems a bit young to have already run past a contract term.'* Craig quickly let it go when he reached his class and was in front of everyone speaking about Roman history.

15

The Big Show

Craig was overall, quite happy with his conversation with Jake. As he walked to his office he considered Jake's offer to visit him at his performance or even at a practice session. He wasn't sure whether he would like the music but it was more about getting to know Jake and finding what his passion was about, and ultimately offering him something he couldn't refuse.

Craig was just passing the fountain when a strong feeling of guilt struck him. He stopped in front of the splashing water, his face blank but behind his eyes he was envisioning the hell he was offering each of the clients that he was recruiting. It made him feel sick to his stomach as he stood in the courtyard in front of the fountain, water crashing, sending mist into the air, creating beautiful colors in the sun, a stark contrast to the darkness he envisioned if he didn't succeed in his recruiting duties. Craig hung his head and took a deep breath, letting it out slowly before moving on toward the Great Hall. Once in his office, Craig set out to get the student papers reviewed before his 10 o'clock class. He was reading but not understanding what he was seeing, his mind couldn't concentrate, every few sentences his thoughts came back to Brandon Wells. He was so excited to have a spot on the football team, it's all he wanted in life. Craig tried to convince himself that there was no chance he could have done that without his contract. He leaned back in his chair, trying to calm his mind. So much had happened in the last few weeks, it had all been a bit over whelming, life, and possible death, had flashed in front of him. He went from seeing himself as a decent, upstanding person. Albeit with some skeletons in the closet. To someone as low as a worm in the dirt, or in Craig's mind, as low as the devil himself. When he thought about what he had to do in order to survive, he hoped that he would become numb to it over time, and the sooner the better. '*I would like to not feel these emotions doing what I have to do to these unsuspecting people. They trust me, they like me, they think I am helping them just to be nice.*'

He took another ragged breath to calm himself and set his mind on something else. Craig decided to take Jake up on his offer to attend his concert at the city arena. It was a fairly large venue, he discovered when he looked it up to purchase a ticket. The arena has seating for 8,000 people for a concert, with nearly 3,000 just on the floor for general admission. Craig purchased a general admission ticket, thinking it would be the easiest to get in and out if he wanted to leave early. He smiled to himself after buying the ticket, he really liked Jake for some reason, even though he had just met him. There was some kind of feeling he got when he talked to Jake. He had a personality that drew a person in. It made Craig want to know more about him. It made Craig want to be friends with him, it must be that he was so easy to talk to. He showed

141

genuine interest in what you had to say. *'Smart young man. Qualities you don't find every day.'*

* * *

That evening, Craig found himself walking into the arena a little early. The seats were starting to fill and the lines at the merchandise counters were long. It seemed people of every age were attending, from early 20's men and women wearing jeans and tees, to 50 something rockers wearing leather and studs on their jackets. There were even 40 somethings men accompanying their pre teen daughters, all dressed in black. *'Interesting crowd,'* Craig thought as he scanned the faces at the merchandise counter and those standing in line. He walked into the auditorium at the general admission level to get a feel for the arrangement. Up on stage he could see the opening bands equipment crammed to the front of the stage as they had made due with whatever room was left over from the main act setting up their gear. Craig thought he recognized one of the amplifiers Jake had pulled out of his car sitting off to the right hand side of the stage. *'Ah-opening act. Now it all makes sense.'* Craig had begun to wonder how much help Jake could really need if he was already playing an arena show. Craig walked nearly to the front of the floor where he could get a good look at the stage set up. It was for sure the same amp out of Jake's car, the sticker that read 'eff the man' emblazoned down the side was unmistakable. It had been the name of Jake's band at one point in the past. Not so original, but bands tended to go through many names before one really stuck.

Craig turned around when he had seen enough to know for

sure it was Jake's equipment, but by that time the arena was getting full. He checked his watch, ten minutes to show time. *'I may as well stay here. At least if Jake spots me he will know I came to support him.'* Ten minutes turned into thirty and the crowed seemed to be getting impatient. Craig hadn't been to a rock concert, ever. The closest to it was seeing the aging Beach Boys at a state fairgrounds show that he happened upon by accident. He had enjoyed it, but was feeling that this might not be the same experience.

About the time that thought passed through his head, the lights dimmed in the arena. The crowd roared with excitement and anticipation. Craig turned away from the stage and looked at the sea of people, the floor was filled, the seats were packed to the roof of the building. Craig was overwhelmed, he had never been among this many people before. He turned back toward the stage in time to see the band come out and pick up their instruments, the speakers popping to life.

Someone made an announcement. "Please welcome to the stage our first act of the evening, Adaptive!"

There was a polite amount of applause with a few ruckus yells and screams. It gave the impression those people were either close friends or family of the band members. They didn't wait for any applause to pick up or die down, they jumped right into their set. It was loud for Craig, a little too loud, but after the initial shock he started to enjoy it. He could pick out some of the guitar parts Jake was playing, he was trying to follow along.

Craig turned to the crowd, who seemed to be getting into the music more than the initial response would have let on. Fans all over the arena were really getting into it, screaming and head banging was happening everywhere. Craig was in awe of the sea of people crammed shoulder to shoulder, pumping their fists in the air, screaming the words of each song.

Craig couldn't make out the words, he could barely make out a melody or tune, it was starting to make his head hurt, his eyes were getting blurry. Craig lifted his glasses for a moment to try and alleviate some of the pressure he was feeling in his head. Just then, he was shoved abruptly to his left. The sea of people was unstoppable, his glasses flew from his hand, tumbling over the shoulder of someone three bodies away. He looked frantically that direction but knew there would be no hope of getting them back. As Craig looked up to the stage, spotting Jake who was working over his guitar in a spectacular riff, another sudden jolt pushed through the crowd smashing Craig to the right this time as if he were hit by a battering ram. The next wave of shoving came from behind, smashing Craig into the people in front of him, as if it were water smashing into rocks, the wave came back the other way, the people in front slamming back into Craig. He got the back of someones head into his chin, forcing his jaw up and back, mashing his teeth together, just about making him loose consciousness. The surges kept coming, forward and back, his head was pounding with every beat of the drums. He had made a mistake, he didn't belong here. Craig tried to look over the crowd, *'Where are the exists? I need to get out of here.'* The surges kept coming, pushing harder and harder. His feet were being mashed by what felt like everyone in the arena all at once as they bounced up and down to the throbbing beat of the bass and drums. The screeching guitars ripped at his ear drums. *'Where are the exits?'* Craig tried to squeeze between the people he was being smashed against, but he couldn't break through. It was like they were holding him there on purpose, they were an impenetrable human wall. The pressure on his chest as the surges continued made it hard to breath, he felt he might pass out any minute. Again he pushed, trying to move in between shoulders that seemed stuck together. He managed to break through one set, then another, his feet were being crushed, he took an elbow to the ribs as he tried to push though a third row of people. He winced at the pain but kept pushing against the surge of the crowd. Craig tried again to look over the sea of bobbing heads, up and down, jumping, pushing, pumping their fists into the air. They all seemed to love it, but for Craig it was excruciating. Then, finally a glimps of a red exit sign.

Far to the back of the arena, thousands of people in his way. He kept pushing, not feeling like he was making any progress. A piercing pain shot into his head, the guitar wailed out a high pitched scream, Jake's fingers flew across the fret board, bending notes that seemed to dig directly into Craig's ear drums. Craig reached for his ear, he thought for certain that he felt blood running down his neck from his ear. Another slamming blow from behind as the crowd surged, Craig lost his balance and tumbled to the floor, banging his knees into the concrete, his hands slapping down as everyone around him jumped with the music. He wasn't sure how he was able to fall, there are so many people shoulder to shoulder that he didn't believe he would be able to get knocked down. Craig's fingers were crushed, he was kicked in the stomach and head, more people stepping on him, holding him down. Craig crawled through the forest of legs, a maze of moving tree stumps, knees and ankles slamming into his body as he tried to navigate through these obstacles.

Craig moved about 20 feet when he felt a large pair of hands grab him by the shoulders and pull him up. Craig was grateful and yelled a thank you, but was shoved toward the back of the arena through several more rows of bouncing, fist pounding, concert goers. He tried again to look over the crowd for the exit signs at the back of the general admission area but he couldn't see it. *'I swear it was just there.'* He jumped with the crowd, looking for the red exit signs, but then he was in sync with them. He had to try to jump opposite of the crowd so he could see over them. It was more difficult than he had thought, it took several attempts to get the timing right. He was facing opposite the rest of the jumping fans, who gave him dirty looks and shouted at him as he bounced on the off beats. He was grabbed by several of the fans that he was facing and pushed again toward the back of the arena.

Just before getting pushed again, he spotted it. *'There! The red sign.'* It seemed farther away than it had before he'd hit the floor. He turned to his right, still facing away from the stage, another exit sign glowing red, pointing the way to freedom. This one seemed within reach. Craig made another push between surging shoulders and flying elbows, each hitting him in the head. His feet continued being trampled, he was sure he had broken toes. He was getting closer to the sign, just a couple more people to push through, he lowered his shoulder and pushed in between the last couple rows of bouncing, rowdy fans.

Finally he was at the door to freedom, he leaned into the crash bar and gave a shove. The door didn't budge, he tried again, still it wouldn't release him to freedom from the insane circus of noise and pain. Craig turned around, looking back at the stage. Everything had gone black, the stage was dark. There was still a sound but it didn't seem like music any more. To be fair, it didn't seem much like music before either, but now the rhythm was gone, or at least it wasn't the same. The tone had changed too, there was something different about the crowd. Their surging and cheering to the band had become more of a chant, low and mono toned as their bodies swayed back and forth like waves in the ocean.

Craig could make out the dark shadows of the crowd still bouncing, but slower, still surging, forward and back, side to side. He pushed on the door again with his back against it, nothing. He could hear the crash bar clank when he leaned on it, but the door wouldn't release. The glow from the stage was getting even dimmer. Craig couldn't make out the shapes of the heads in front of him any longer, he could feel the crowd push back and forth and a low rumble was building from deep within the arena. He couldn't tell if the sound was coming from the stage or deeper within the building. The sound was almost mechanical, churning like a giant machine running its motor at a low RPM, building up momentum.

Craig's eyes had started to adjust to the darkness, he was starting to make out the shapes of heads in the crowd once again, but they looked different now for some reason. There were just as many as before but at first they were all somewhat even in height, now they were all different sizes. He could see that some of the figures were much taller than before. *'Are they holding people up on their shoulders?'* Craig thought about concerts he had seen on TV where people surfed the tops of the crowd, being passed over the heads from one person to another. *'No, that's not it.'* It was still hard to see, the light was very gray, almost as if there was none. He focused harder,

147

squinting a little, the figures became more defined. *'They're wearing hoods!'* Craig was stunned. *'How? They weren't like this when I came in.'* Craig wracked his brain to remember anything like this when he'd arrived at the arena. *'I don't remember getting here.'*

Craig started to panic, he pushed on the door at his back again, hammered at the crash bar, then turned around and kicked at it. The door wouldn't open. He was making a great amount of noise, the arena echoed with the sound of him kicking at the door over the mechanical hum. Craig spun around again to face the stage. Rows and rows of people were turned toward Craig, only they weren't people. Craig was staring into the deep dark hoods of thousands of Reapers! Eyes glowed red under the hoods. The rumbling mechanical sound built in the distance, coming from somewhere toward the center of the arena. Craig was frozen in place, somehow not completely surprised at what he was witnessing, but his soul filled with dread. His chest was tight, he clenched his fists by his sides and stood completely still, staring back at the red glowing eyes of the Reapers looking back at him. Slowly, they began to turn away from Craig, back toward the stage.

Craig felt his chest ease and he released his clenched fists. He was aware of the pain in his jaw and then moved it back and forth, trying to loosen the tension. Craig held out his hands in front of him, opened and closed his fists. He was able to see everything now, even though there were no lights on in the arena. He turned his hands over, palm up to palm down, several times, inspecting them for damage after being stepped on repeatedly while he had been on the floor. He could feel the pain of what he was sure was a broken finger, beginning to fade, the scrapes from shoes on the tops of his hands didn't hurt, and the pain in this jaw was gone completely. Then came the biggest revelation, Craig was wearing an all black robe. He noticed his sleeves first, then looked down at his torso. He patted himself down, trying to make sense of where the robe came from, wondering what happened to his other clothes. He reached for his pockets, his sport coat, his wallet and phone. He couldn't find them. In fact, it felt like he didn't have his other clothes on at all. *The robe is so comfortable!'* Craig was shocked at how comfortable it was, the fabric was the softest thing he had ever felt on his skin. *'There isn't anything I can compare it to.'* Craig suddenly reached for his head. He felt nothing but his thinning hair, he grappled at his shoulders and the back of his neck. *'No hood, I don't have a hood.'* Craig looked across the arena and saw thousands of beings, all with hoods. *'What am I doing here? Am I dead? Did I die trying to get out of the arena? I've heard of that happening. People get crushed at concerts all the time.'*

Craig noticed the sound of thousands of Reapers start to get louder. *'Are they chanting? Almost sounds like a hum.'* The droning hum sound was getting louder as well, it started taking on a rhythm, a slow churning, clanking sound.

Craig wasn't sure what to do, he glanced to his sides, one way, then the other. He couldn't see a quick way out. The doors behind him wouldn't budge and the other exit signs weren't lit up any more. He looked at his hands. *'I can see my hands but not the exit?'* He looked around the building and couldn't make out any structure around him. He looked for doors again but wasn't sure the doors would open even if he could find them. Just as he was looking to his right, trying to peer over the tops of several hundred hooded beings, a wall of sound came screaming from the stage. Jake stood at

149

the center of the stage with a lone spotlight beaming down on him from the ceiling, his white guitar was slung over his shoulder with a white guitar strap, it stood out on his long black robe. Under Jake's hood, red eyes burned bright and his left hand gripped the neck of the guitar as his right hand flailed on the strings. The amplifiers screamed out in agony as the sound erupted across the arena. The hands of the thousands raised to the roof in what appeared more like worship than the excitement of a rock concert. Craig stood in awe of what he was witnessing. *'This is shocking, scary and incredible all at the same time.'*

Craig noticed, as he stood gazing at the display, that his hands were freezing, his ears and face were numb. He brought his hands to his face and blew warm air into his cupped hands. It wasn't effective, but he noticed that his body wasn't cold at all, only the parts that were exposed outside the robe. Craig tucked his hands inside the robe where they warmed instantly. *'The robe protects me from the cold. Amazing!'* His face, nose and ears were still freezing but he was so intent on watching what was taking place that he hardly noticed.

The scream of Jake's guitar continued to fill the arena, he was joined by other members of the band and it started to feel like the concert was continuing where it had left off. The crowd, still full of black-robed Reapers, didn't have the same surge to it, they weren't pushing and jumping like before, no head banging or fist pumping either. They stood calmly, facing the stage, swaying slightly with the music.

Craig watched intently, more the crowd than the stage. He was scanning the crowd, looking for anyone without a hood like himself. *'What am I doing here? Maybe I am dead and this is some sort of induction ceremony.'* At that thought, the already freezing arena got much colder. Craig stiffened as the cold blast hit him. *'What was that?'* A heavy fog developed over the sea of heads, it enveloped the stage. Jake moved backward, still playing the melody of the song that the band was in the middle of. The music began to swell, louder and louder still, as a dark figure came into view, dropping down from above the stage. Craig was enthralled with the theatrics of it all. *'Was this rehearsed? How is this happening?'* The figure lowered onto the stage without the help from wires or a stage crew that Craig could see. He thought this could be entirely possible from what he had seen of Grimm during his short acquaintance with him. Craig was standing at the very back of the arena where he had tried to escape but he could see everything now as if he were front and center. His eyes had zoomed in on the dark figure as he lowered from above. Every being in the arena was quiet and focused on the dark cloaked, other worldly figure, he (or it) commanded attention without saying a single word.

The music had died down to a tolerable, low background rumble, just as the figure reached the stage. It hovered there for several moments before stretching out its arms, as a preacher would to his congregation, welcoming them into the house of worship. The audience erupted into a deafening roar, cheering louder than any of the rock music had been up to this point. Craig was astounded, he pulled his hands from his cloak to cover his ears. It hurt to put his warm hands over his nearly frozen ears, but the pain from the sound seemed much worse. The cheering continued for an uncomfortably long time as the being floated from one side of the stage to the other, coaxing more cheering from the congregation at each turn, his arms continually outstretched. Finally, he lowered

151

his arms and the cheering calmed to a dull roar until it raised its arms above its head to calm the crowd. The sea of cloaked onlookers fell silent and waited to be addressed by what Craig thought must be their supreme leader. The theatrics he had never witnessed before, the command and adoration it had over all of these people, it surely must not be of this world. But what was it? Who was it?

After moving across the stage and back again, looking into the souls of thousands of beings in front of him, lining the arena, wall to wall, standing room only, he spoke. "My faithful followers, my disciples that have done the work of the One Most Evil for eons, since the beginning of darkness. You have made him the most powerful, the most feared, the most redoubtable, imminent, and frightening being of all time!"

He raised his arms and the crowd erupted with a deafening roar of adoration. He lowered his arms and the arena went silent once more, awaiting the next words from the all mighty showman.

Craig was intrigued and bewildered at the same time. He didn't feel any type of draw to the being, he wasn't sure yet who it was. *'Is it the Devil? Is he a Reaper? What am I witnessing?'*

The being was in no hurry, he floated from one side of the stage to the other, then back to center. "I sense betrayal," he said with menace in his voice. "There is one amongst you that has not done as promised. The contract has been breached!" His voice boomed and echoed off the walls of the arena. "I know who you are. You believed that I wouldn't find out, you thought you could out smart me!" Again his voice boomed and echoed. "My disciples that have been faithful will know who you are, they will see you pay for your transgression. They will watch as you are sentenced to be tortured in hell for all of eternity!"

The throngs of cloaked beings started to murmur and shuffle uncomfortably, looking around, turning to one another, wondering if they could pick out the being that had crossed the Devil. Many of the beings turned their gaze toward Craig. Their glowing eyes drilling holes into his skull with no hood on his cloak to hide under.

The being on stage brought attention to Craig. "It is not him! I feel your attention to the newest Recruit at the back. He has not failed yet."

Craig realized he was the one the being was talking about. Craig desperately wanted to crash through the doors behind him as thousands of red eyes were now on him. His face burned, which he didn't think was possible as cold as it was in the arena.

"Look away from him!" The being yelled, booming so loud the walls shook. Immediately all the red eyes turned away. "This is the one who transgressed!" His speech held the S a little longer with a hard D for emphasis.

He reached out with his right arm, his bony palm facing upward. Slowly he raised his hand toward the ceiling and with it, from the middle of thousands of others, a single cloaked being rose into the air. His arms at his sides as if they were restrained, his legs flinching, his body squirming, seeming to struggle under immense pressure. His groans were muffled, he tried to scream in anguish but was cut short by the thundering voice from his captor.

"This is the one that failed to keep his word. He didn't believe that the All Mighty Evil Lord would make him pay his debt. He was wrong!"

Craig stood frozen, both from fear and the temperature, his

mouth hung open, his tongue dried out and frozen, lips about to crack from the cold. Again, the being's words boomed and echoed, shaking the foundation Craig stood on. Thousands of beings erupted in adorant cheers. The leader raised his skeletal hand farther into the air, as he did, the captive went higher toward the ceiling, squirming as he went. The crowd, as if knowing what was coming, cleared a space on the floor of the arena below the captive, as he was being lifted.

"Let this serve as a warning to you all! The Most Evil will not be betrayed!" With a flash he struck his raised hand toward the ground and the captive soul plunged into the earth as fire erupted like an after burner from where he had been thrown into hell. The heat from the hole in the earth was so intense that everyone near it had to retreat, lest they be melted into a puddle. The rafters of the arena were charred in mere moments. Though the flames died away in ten to fifteen seconds, it felt much longer. To Craig, it seemed to happen in slow motion. He watched in horror, knowing if he were not able to keep up his end of the contract, that would be him, thrown into the fiery depths of hell.

The being on stage went back to moving from one side of the stage to the other, contemplating what had just happened. "What you have just witnessed can and will happen to you, if you choose not to adhere to your contracts. Every one of you got what you asked for in return for your souls. You all agreed to abide by this arrangement. I assure you, I enjoy sending you to be tortured for eternity and the Ruler of Darkness and Hatred is overjoyed to have you to torture. So please, by all means, do as you wish, just know the next gathering could be for you."

Craig had still not closed his mouth, his eyes were wide and unblinking when there was a great flash of lightning from the stage, followed by an immense crack of thunder. Everyone recoiled from the light and sound, shielding their eyes. Craig fell back against the door that he had tried to open to escape from before the supreme being landed on stage. The door flew open when he hit it and Craig tumbled out of the arena into darkness, falling into nothing. He couldn't see anything, he just kept falling, flailing his arms and legs, tumbling head over heels into silence and warmth. It was getting warmer wherever he was falling, it was warmer than where he had been. *I'm falling into hell, its getting so hot. It's never the fall that kills you, its the sudden stop.'*

BOOM!

Craig's fall stopped, the air rushed out of his lungs, his feet up over his head, the back of his head hitting something incredibly hard. He winced in terrible pain, his arms raised over his face , eyes closed. He felt his tweed sport coat on his face, the rough jacket scratching his forehead, pushing his glasses onto the bridge of his nose. *'My glasses!'* Craig opened his eyes, pulling his arms away from his face to see he was staring up at the ceiling of his office. He had fallen over backward in his office chair. *'Oh my lord!'* He cringed at the words, remembering what he had just been through in his dream. *'It felt so real.'* Craig rolled on his side, struggling to get out of his office chair. He managed to get on his hands and knees and recoiled from the pain he felt. *'Huh, that's odd.'* He remembered falling in the crowd and trying to crawl to the door. *'What has happened? Was that real?'* He saw the backs of his hands, scratched and bruised. He sat down on the floor and rubbed his hands together, noticing that one of his fingers was in a lot of pain. *'It might be broken but maybe just really bruised.'* Craig checked the knees of his pants looking for wear or dirt, they were scuffed and discolored at the same location he could feel the bruises. He brushed them off and got to his feet. He stood there for a moment taking bodily inventory. His feet hurt, especially when he bent them. The tops of his feet felt bruised. He remembered his feet being trampled by the crowd. The tops of his shoes were terribly scuffed as well. *'The show hasn't even happened yet. How can I have been there to get this beat up? I was just sleeping in my office chair.'*

Craig looked at his watch. *'I could still make it to Jake's show, that seems like pushing my luck at this point. Though now I am very curious what will happen at the show tonight. Is Jake a Reaper already?'* He stood the chair back up and straightened up his office before leaving for the day. As Craig walked to his car, he had a sudden urge to go see his father. *'It's still early, only 3:30, I'll go have a visit and fill him in on these dreams. If nothing else, it will feel good to talk it out with someone.'*

16

Mike the Dream Doctor

Craig drove slowly out to the Winding Tree care home, he was trying to review the dream he had about Jake's concert-turned devil sacrifice. *'I am certain that it was real but how did I end up back in the office? How are my knees bruised? Was Jake really there? Is Jake already involved with The One Most Evil?'* Craig realized he just called him The One Most Evil and cringed. *'That's what Grimm calls him, he's in my head. Before you know it I'll be acting like him. I really need to figure out if Jake is already a client of a Reaper.'* Craig's mind raced with everything that had been taking place lately. He jumped from one thought to the next, never getting resolution, to any of them. It was causing his anxiety to overwhelm his thoughts so much that he couldn't focus clearly on any task.

Craig walked into Winding Tree tentatively. His last visit hadn't gone very well. Plus, Glen the Reaper could very well be roaming the halls. It was between meals, there weren't very many residents out in the gathering areas. Craig looked into the cafeteria just to check for Mike, but there wasn't anyone inside. He sauntered down the hall, taking note of the moderate temperature, it hadn't fluctuated from the time he'd entered the lobby to arriving at Mike's room. Craig listened at the door before knocking, he could hear the drone of the television, then tapped on the door.

"It's open," came Mike's response from the other side.

Craig opened the door slowly and stepped inside. "Hello Dad."

Mike was just getting up. "Oh, Craig! Good to see you."

Craig was relieved at the recognition. "Good to see you too, feels like it's been a while."

Mike met him half way across the room and gave him a hug. "It hasn't been too awful long. Glad you're here. It means you haven't messed up your deal with that Reaper yet." Mike gave him a half sideways smile to show his sarcasm.

Craig laughed a bit. "No, I haven't completely failed yet. I actually feel like I'm doing pretty good. I'm about to get two more contracts signed. Three people actually but I think that two of them will count as the same contract. I haven't checked with Grimm on that one."

Mike shuffled his way back to his chair. "Well, that sounds good for you, bad for them I suppose."

That brought Craig back to reality. "Mostly true, the couple I am dealing with knows what the stakes are. At least the husband knows, she isn't well and may have a hard time comprehending what he is telling her."

Mike was listening as he eased into his chair and set his cane to the side. "Let me put it together, see if I understand this correctly. She is sick, he wants to save her, but they both have to commit to make it work?"

Craig nodded. "Yes, mostly, she could do it on her own but she isn't well enough to sign the contract."

Mike glared at Craig. "Does the Reaper care if she knows what she is signing?"

Craig stared blankly back at him for several seconds. "I don't know. I suppose, it's possible not, however, I don't think I can take that chance."

Mike looked across the room, contemplating the situation. "I see where you're coming from, it would be a hard pill to swallow if you were counting her and then the Reaper disagrees."

Craig felt a twinge of remorse about the Tom and Sue predicament and needed to move off the topic. "The other guy is in a rock band."

Mike started to laugh before Craig could finish the sentence. "What rock band member hasn't sold his soul to the devil!" He laughed some more and leaned back in his chair with a big smile on his face. "You should specialize in rock bands. You would have plenty to go around."

Craig smiled, he was glad to see that Mike was enjoying the situation. "I agree, seems like there should be plenty of them. I think there might be a problem with this one though. I'm concerned he may already have a deal with a Reaper."

Mike's smile died away. "Ah, yes I could see that as a problem. Have you asked him?"

Craig looked at Mike dumbfounded. "No. I didn't really consider it. I had such a hard time telling Tom that I work for a Reaper that I didn't think about asking Jake."

Mike shrugged. "Maybe you should. What's the worst that can happen? He thinks you're crazy and doesn't sign the contract?"

Craig nodded emphatically. "Yes, that's exactly what could happen. I need him to sign it. He will only be number 4 if

Tom and Sue count as one and I only have a month left to finish for this year. Gotta meet the quota."

Mike let out a sigh. "What makes you think this kid, Jake, has a contract already?"

Craig sat down on the sofa and laid his head back. "That's what I came to talk to you about. Not Jake specifically, but the dreams I've been having. Crazy stuff. Not all of them have been related to specific people. But Jake was in the most recent one. I actually think it may not have been a dream."

Mike had leaned in, with his elbows resting on his knees. "Dreams can come from a lot of different places. Stress is probably the biggest one, followed by major life events. I would say this whole ordeal ticks both of those boxes pretty soundly. What makes you think the dreams aren't really dreams?"

Craig had his eyes closed now. "Jake was in the last dream, on stage with his band. I had agreed to go see his show. I had fell asleep in my office chair at work right after I purchased the ticket. Next thing I know, I'm at the show, its loud and crowded, and I realize I've made a huge mistake, it's just too much for me. So I start trying to move to the exit but it's so crowded that I can't make very good progress. I tripped on something or someone, and fell. I hit my knees really hard and while I was trying to crawl to the exit people were stepping on my hands." Craig held his hands out so Mike could inspect them.

"Wow! Those bruises are from your dream?"

Craig pulled his hands back and pointed at his pants. "They seem to be, and my knees are bruised! How does that happen?"

Mike's eyes were wide and he had a concerned look on his face. "I can't even imagine how that happens. You're tied up in some other worldly matters though. So suppose you were pulled or forced into a dream, then somehow you got bumped and scratched like you have shown me, then dumped back into reality. Why do you suppose you would be put through that? And by whom?"

Craig leaned his head back again, exhausted. "I think it was to show me what will happen if I don't succeed."

Mike's face turned stern. "Was it bad? Really bad?"

Craig nodded without lifting his head. "Worse than I thought or imagined when Grimm told me about being tortured in hell for all eternity."

Mike cringed and paused for a minute. "Did you say Jake was in your dream?"

Craig nodded again without lifting his head. "He was there, he was playing his show to start with, then he was on stage when the lead Reaper was punishing the soul that didn't follow through with his contract. He didn't have any interaction with the Reaper though, so I'm not sure if he was just a conjured image because I know who he is or how that works."

Mike was silent for a while staring at the TV, not watching it, but looking that direction as he thought about Craig's dream. "Here's my take on it. It was definitely a message from the Reaper. He wants you to know what's coming. He's sending a message that you need to take it seriously. But I don't think this Jake kid was really there. I would say you need to find a way to ask Jake if he is already under contract with the devil or a Reaper or whomever takes their souls as payment."

Craig rolled his head back and forth. "Okay, I'll figure out how to approach that subject with him. Do you think all the dreams are sending a message?"

Mike gave him a questioning look. "What do you mean?

There are other dreams?"

Craig lifted his head and looked at Mike. "Yeah there have been a few. This is the first one that I knew someone in the dream. Also the first one that I had injuries from. The others were dark and sort of terrifying in different ways, you know, things like spiders, attacking birds, dark caves, things like that."

Mike was listening intently. "No reference to the Reaper or the devil?"

Craig shook his head. "No, not that I can recall."

Mike leaned back in his chair and seemed to relax a little. "I doubt any of the other dreams were relevant to your Reaper friend. Probably just brought on by the stress of the situation. It's pretty likely that he has planted some deep, dark, scary things in your head just to mess with you, but that's what you get for being in this situation to begin with. Or, maybe, you just have some dark shit in your head that is now coming out."

Craig looked at Mike and rolled his eyes. "I know you're right Mr. Dream Doctor but you don't have to jab at me."

Mike smiled. "I couldn't help it."

Craig stood up and started pacing the small apartment. "Have you seen Glen the Reaper? The one that hangs around here?"

Mike nodded while squinting his eyes. "I have, he goes up and down the halls here every day. The mortality rate in this place is rather staggering. I don't know if it has anything to do with him or if that's just the way it is here. He keeps busy though."

Craig paused his pacing for a moment, deep in thought. "Have you had any interactions with him since he tried to recruit you?"

Mike shook his head. "No, so far he doesn't even acknowledge me when I see him in the halls. Did you see him in your dream?"

Craig paused and made eye contact with Mike. "No, I'm not sure he was there, he could have been. There were thousands of them. Dad, you would not believe how many Reapers were there. The arena was packed, at least 8,000 of them. I have no idea if they are all from this area or where they all came from."

Mike smiled and chuckled to himself. "You mean you didn't have a meet and great session and find out where everyone came from? A little go around the room and do introductions at the Reaper convention?"

Craig looked at Mike and smirked. "I'm glad you're enjoying this today and that you haven't lost your sarcasm."

Mike chuckled again. "It's not all funny but if you can't laugh at something serious once in a while you'll end up in the loony bin."

Craig hung his head but smiled anyway. "I guess that's true. I might end up there anyway." Craig checked his watch, he had been there an hour and a half. "I'm going to head home now. You'll probably be going for dinner soon anyway."

Mike looked at the time as well. "Sure enough. I'll head down there in a little bit, you sure you don't want to stay for dinner? It's meatloaf night."

Craig smiled at him. "Thanks, I'll pass on that, don't have much appetite lately anyway."

Mike got up and gave Craig a hug. "Take care of yourself, and stop by more often, I want to hear about your next dream."

Craig laughed. "You know there will be another one. I'll keep you posted."

17

Tom and Sue

Craig hadn't turned the paperwork into the university hospital yet. He had sat at his kitchen table staring at it a week ago but every time he thought about talking to Tom the emptiness in his stomach came back, he would push the feeling down and stop thinking about what he had to do. When he noticed the paperwork was magically filled in, and realized that he would have to tell Tom about it to get his signature before submitting the mountain of paper to be reviewed, he lost his nerve. He didn't have a good reason not to talk to Tom sooner, just procrastination and the pit in his stomach that he didn't like. It was a conversation he wasn't excited to have. *'How do I go about telling someone that I am a representative of the Devil.'* Put on a smiley face. *'Here's your contract to become a Reaper or be tortured in hell for all eternity. Just sign here.'*

Craig stood in his office, staring out the window but not seeing anything specific. A familiar cold blast of air hit Craig from behind, snapping him out of his window trance. He turned around slowly, knowing who he was going to see but hoping it wasn't true. Grimm hovered a few inches off the floor, his glamorous dark robe soaking in all the light from the window, his presence using all the heat in the room. Craig breathed out, exasperated at the sight of Grimm.

"Hello, Craig."

Craig waited a moment before responding in a monotone voice. "Hello, Grimm, I would ask how you're doing but that seems trivial."

Grimm scoffed at the retort and got straight to the point. "So it is. Why have you been waiting to turn in the paperwork?"

Craig looked at Grimm's hooded head with a questioning expression. "The paperwork?"

Grimm moved to the chair in front of Craig's desk and sat with his bone hands on the arms of the chair. "Please, don't be a fool. You know what paperwork I speak of. Sit down Craig, lets discuss this."

Craig's posture relaxed as he sat in his leather desk chair. Feeling small, as if he were sitting in front of the school principal for shooting spitballs at the teacher across the room. "Yes, I know what paperwork you are talking about. I have been getting a painful feeling whenever I consider that paperwork."

Grimm clasped his fingers together in his lap. "Craig, do not make me remind you, there is a contract in place. This is your obligation. You must not fail to meet your quota."

The temperature in the room seemed to drop another ten degrees.

"Of course, I am aware of the contract. I will move forward with the paperwork."

Grimm nodded slightly, his hood slowly moving up and down. "See that you do, there is no reason for hesitation. The

165

paperwork you have is correct, there will be no problems moving forward."

Craig nodded in return. "I want to tell Tom and Sue what they are getting into, I am afraid they might not believe me or think that I am crazy."

Grimm held up his right hand to stop Craig, the robe sliding down his arm slightly, revealing his radius and ulna bones. Cracks in each one healed with thick lines of scar tissue, much lighter in color than the gray ash of the rest of the bone. Craig couldn't take his eyes off of them.

"You must not doubt yourself, it rarely matters if you tell a prospective client that they are making a deal with the Evil One. I have told you this before, they may not believe you and often think it is a joke. Others may be hesitant and not entirely sure if they believe you, thinking there may be a possibility that you are telling the truth. Either way, no matter what they think, many people sign anyway because the opportunity is too good to pass up. I know you think you owe it to these people to be up front with them that is up to you. You don't need to do that in order to sleep good at night, it wont help."

Craig's eyes darted from Grimm's arm to his hood. *'He knows about the dreams!'* Grimm lowered his arm and stood before Craig could say anything about the dreams. "Don't waste any more time, present the paperwork and turn it in. You will be that much closer to your quota." Grimm hovered backward, not bothering to go around the chair, his robe floating out slightly as he passed through it. "I will check back with you soon enough." Grimm disintegrated as he got to the door and the temperature started to come back to normal.

Craig sat, stunned at the thought of Grimm knowing about his bad dreams. *'Is he causing the dreams? Is he messing with me? Is this some form of torture that he gets a kick out of?'* Craig shook his head in disgust. *'What have I gotten into?'*

The rest of the day was a challenge for Craig to focus, his classes were a blur and now that he was driving home, he wasn't sure what he talked about in class or if he gave out an assignment. *'That's embarrassing, I'll have to admit to the class that I don't remember and ask if I gave out homework.'* Craig's mind wandered again while he was driving, thinking about presenting the paperwork to Tom and telling him about the contract with the Evil One. *'How do I present that? Hi, Tom, nice to see you. I work for the Grim Reaper who, in turn, works for the Devil. Here's your contract, still want to sign it? Sure that would work, don't want to sugar coat the issue.'* Craig smirked at himself, letting his sarcasm take over. *'Look at it this way, you can get Sue the treatment she needs and you both can become employees of the Dark Lord working for eternity. The benefits are amazing, you might really like it.'* Craig cringed at the thought as he sat at a stoplight. He glanced at the car next to him, the lady looking back at him had a strange look on her face, having seen Craig outwardly cringe for no reason. Without making another face he turned and looked forward, waiting for the light to change.

He drove home without too much more thought on the matter, until he pulled into his driveway. Tom's car was sitting next to his house. *'He's home, I should just get this over with.'* Craig sat in the car with the AC blowing for a few moments before taking a deep breath and getting out. *'Here goes.'*

He grabbed his satchel and stepped out into the heat. On the way into the house he detoured to the swing on the front porch, he hadn't spent much time there since the spider dream but decided to give it another go after going inside to get a cold beer. He sat pushing back and forth on the swing, sipping his beer, watching the neighborhood go by, people in the park walking dogs, playing with young kids on the play sets. Craig had hoped Tom would just happen to come outside so he didn't have to make that awkward phone call asking him if they could talk. He finished one beer and started a second one, sitting on the swing for over an hour. His wish finally came true, Tom came outside, headed to his car.

"Tom!" Craig shouted across the yard. "Do you have a few minutes?"

Tom waved and started walking toward Craig. "I do, I was just headed to the store for a few things but it can wait a little bit."

Craig held up his beer. "Can I get you something to drink?"

Tom thought about it for a second. "No, I'm okay for now, thank you." Tom came up on the porch and leaned against the rail. "What's on your mind?"

Craig could feel the pit in his stomach growing. "I have some news about the university applications."

Tom's face lit up. "Is it good news?"

Craig nodded and shook his head simultaneously. "It is, but, it comes with a catch."

Tom's excitement faded quickly. "It usually does, that's what we have been up against since this whole thing started."

Craig nodded. "I completely understand how you're feeling. There is positive news though. It has a bit of a story to go with it if you have time."

Tom nodded slowly. "Maybe I should have that beer."

Craig got to his feet. "I could use another one myself, I'll be right back."

Tom took the opportunity to sit on the swing while Craig

went for refreshments. Craig was relived that Tom had sat down, he wouldn't feel like he needed to look directly at him while he laid out his story of Evil.

"Here you are. Thanks for taking a few minutes to hear me out." Craig didn't stop for a reply. "I spent some time at the university hospital gathering the needed paperwork and trying to figure out where to turn it in. I discovered that there is quite the process to getting accepted into any of the programs including having a doctor referral. It didn't look very good for a while but there is a way." Craig stopped for a moment and glanced at Tom who was staring intently at Craig from the side. After a drink of beer he continued. "It involves something that can be life altering and most people wouldn't believe was possible. Most would consider it to be myth or a wives tale, in the end it may not be for you but I am going to lay it out for you to decide." Craig was pleased with how this was coming out, he hadn't planned anything that he was going to say, it was just coming to him. "I have contacts that are able to get Sue into the program and most likely will be able to cure her from whatever the issues are. It comes at a price. A very large price." Craig glanced at Tom again, his expression was tentative and anxious. "I myself made a deal with these contacts quite some time ago and it worked out very well for me, so I can vouch for the legitimacy of the parties. Are you with me so far?"

Tom cleared his throat. "Yes, I think so. Are we talking about the mob?"

Craig turned his head quickly at Tom. "What? No! No, I'm not involved with the mob." Craig was startled at the response but then realized it might be better if it were the mob. "Actually, these contacts are a bit more serious than the mob."

Tom was surprised at that. "More serious? Dang! Who are these people? Russians?"

Craig cocked his head, looking at Tom. "Russians? Like Russian Mob?"

Tom shrugged. "Yeah, I guess. I hear there are better health care opportunities in other countries, so yeah, maybe something like that."

Craig shook his head. "No, not Russian Mob. I guess I just have to come out with it." Craig paused, took a drink, then looked at Tom. "No judgment."

Tom nodded. "Okay."

Craig looked away. "I work for the Grim Reaper." Craig winced a little as it came out, wondering if there would be a reaction.

Tom squinted at Craig. "What?"

Craig let his breath out, realizing that he was holding it. "I'll tell you the story." Pausing to formulate his words and where to start, Craig waited a beat. "I signed a contract a long time ago, agreeing to do something that was not all the way above board, if you catch my drift." Craig looked over to see if Tom was following. The slow nod signaled he was still on the same page. "I completed my side of the contract and never thought about it again." Craig was having a hard time coming up with the next part, he wanted to land it softly so it didn't sound totally crazy. "Until, it was time to pay the piper, so to speak."

Tom was shifting in his seat a little. "So, you were asked to do something a little shady. Then you thought you were done with it once you did whatever it was. Come to find out a little later that there was more to it.?"

Craig nodded. "Yes, basically. The two things weren't really connected except there was some language in the contract that tied me to something else. I didn't read the contract so I was stuck with it. These individuals will not budge on a contract."

Tom blinked hard and looked at Craig with a stern face. "You said 'Grim Reaper.' What does that mean?"

Craig took a deep, uneasy breath. "That was the part of the contract that I didn't read. I signed my life away to the Devil. The Grim Reaper is the executor of the contract. He oversees my work as a contractor for the Evil One. I sold my soul to the Devil."

'There, I said it.' Craig looked at Tom again waiting for his reply.

Tom was processing, staring at Craig through squinted eyes. He paused for a very long time before breaking a weak smile. "You're joking. You're just saying you sold your soul to the Devil like anyone says when they make a bad decision and get involved with something that they really didn't think through."

Craig cocked his head sideways. "You could look at it that way. But, no, I really do work for the Devil, through the Grim Reaper. Right now I am offering you an opportunity to get Sue the help she needs, but it comes at a price. A really huge price. Yours and Sue's soul will be the required payment. I wanted to tell you instead of tricking you into this. I wanted you to know what you are getting into."

Tom sat back with a glazed look, staring out across the lawn, past the park, over the trees, far away into the clouds. "You're serious?" he said slowly, softly.

Craig, in turn, was staring at the floor after a quick glance at Tom. "Yes, I am." He paused to let Tom process. "Now, your service wouldn't start right away, It could be paused for many years or may even wait until you pass away, but I recommend not waiting until then."

Tom was still in deep thought, gazing out into the sky. He was silent for several minutes before lowering his head and closing his eyes. "What do you mean, my service wouldn't start right away?"

Craig cleared his throat slightly. "The agreement would be something like, Sue gets cured and you two can lead your normal lives for 'X' number of years, at which point the Reaper will come calling for you to start your term of service, where you will have the option to recruit others like I am doing now. If you decide to wait until you pass on naturally, then there are other, less appealing, duties you would have to do, basically for eternity, which, to me, sounds less appealing."

Tom shook his head slowly at first, then snapped it back and forth like a dog, trying to un-hear what Craig was saying. "You're not serious!"

Craig flinched a little. "I'm sorry, Tom. I am serious. This appears to be the only way I can help. I just wanted you to know that this comes with a catch."

They both sat silently on the swing, watching the neighborhood pass by for several minutes. Tom finally drew in a deep breath and spoke softly. "This seems very surreal to me, I don't really believe what you are telling me. However, in case you are telling me the truth. How long would we have before we are required to serve the Devil, or the Reaper?"

Craig slowly nodded his understanding of where Tom was coming from. "It could be as long as 15 years, that would be a good long time for you and Sue to enjoy retirement, do some traveling and watch the grandchildren grow up. And it's not like you die right away or anything. You have the opportunity to recruit other people and live your otherwise normal life while you do that."

Tom smirked at Craig's description of *'just living a normal life while recruiting people to work for the devil.'* "Just like that? Easy?"

Craig knew he was over simplifying the contract with the Reaper but he also didn't want to go into more detail, he had to get them recruited after all, as part of his own contract. "Pretty much, just like that."

Tom stood up and handed Craig the mostly empty bottle. "I will have to speak with Sue about this. It doesn't seem to be something that should be taken lightly. How long do I have to decide?"

Craig gave a little shrug. "You should definitely speak with Sue and it would be good to make a decision inside of a week. I don't think Sue is getting any better by the day. Time is of the essence."

Tom nodded as he walked away. "That it is." He paused in the yard, looking at Craig still sitting on the swing. "I'll let you know."

18

Runnin' With the Devil

Craig was still spooked by his dream about the concert with Jake and his band, Adaptive, but he still wanted to talk with Jake and find out if there was any chance he needed help with his music career. Craig had been watching the parking lot for the rattle-trap car Jake drove so he could try to visit him in the studio. It took nearly a week before he spotted the heap of a car in the same spot that he helped him unload equipment from previously. *'I knew he wouldn't move his car after unloading.'*

He walked down the halls, trying to remember the sequence of turns and doors they had gone through. He made several wrong turns and had to back track, but eventually found studio six. It was empty. Craig stood in the hallway outside the studio doors, looking up and down the hall, wondering which way to go, he had passed three other studios on his way to find this one. Everything seemed to be empty. He looked down the hall that he hadn't been down yet, deciding that was his best bet. He had walked 50 or so yards, wondering why all this time in this huge building he had never seen another person. Just then, up ahead someone emerged from a set of doors letting out an enormous blast of sound. That had to be the studio he was looking for.

Craig quickened his step as the young man that had emerged stood in the hall outside the doors, talking on his phone. Craig discerned it was a dispute with the young man's girlfriend or wife, from the tone and the few words that he caught before his voice was hushed. Craig grabbed one of the doors and let himself into the studio without asking permission. Craig was hit in the face with a frigid blast of cold air and a wall of sound that made him stop in his tracks. *'He's here!'* He looked around the room and noted that the bystanders, friends and or girlfriends of the band were wearing jackets. Not usual dress code for New Mexico, even in the winter. He continued into the room and was happy to see it was the right place.

Jake was standing up front playing his guitar, unaccompanied, presumably as loud as it would go. *'Turned to 11 I'm sure.'* Jake finished his riff and looked at his band mates, giving them some instruction of what would come next in the song. One of them nodded toward Craig, causing Jake to turn his way.

"Mr. Newman!" Jake raised his arm and waved, having the biggest smile on his face that Craig had ever seen. "Come on in! It's awesome to see you. Let me introduce you to everyone."

As Craig walked toward the center of the room, Jake's hand waved him in enthusiastically. Jake went through all the names of everyone in the room, including the students that were there just to take a break between classes and watch the band practice. Craig knew he wouldn't remember any of them in just a matter of moments.

"What brings you here, Mr. Newman?"

Craig didn't expect an audience when he'd thought about having this discussion with Jake, he wasn't ready to answer that question. "Uh, well. Can we talk outside? I don't want to stop your session though, so if this is a bad time we can meet up later."

Jake took his guitar off. "This is fine, we are about wrapped for the day." Jake led him out of the studio.

Craig shook off the cold when they got out in the hall. "Did you notice how cold it is in there?"

Jake smiled and let out a laugh. "Oh yeah, I do that on purpose. We get super hot when we play, so we crank the AC in there so we don't get so sweaty. Everyone else hates it, but it works for the band so they have to wear jackets. It's kind of funny to me."

Craig was relieved to hear that, but quickly realized it could be a cover up. "Oh, that is interesting, good idea."

Jake seemed fidgety and couldn't stand still. Craig had gathered that Jake was an excitable person just from the one meeting they had, but this seemed a little extra.

"Are you okay? You seem wound up."

Jake looked at Craig a little sideways. "Yeah! I'm good man! I get wound up when we play. It takes some time to calm down afterward. Hey! Did you make it to our show?"

Craig didn't know how to answer. "Yeah, I did, it was great." He couldn't believe he just said that. "You didn't see me? I was up front for a while."

Jake raised his hand to Craig, wanting a high five. Craig obliged and slapped his hand. "That means a lot, so glad you made it, bummer I didn't see you but still, that's awesome. What did you think?"

Craig was on the spot now, all he could think about were

the black hoods and the glowing eyes staring at him. "I was mesmerized, I truly couldn't take my eyes off the show. It was a little loud for me but I managed."

Jake nodded. "I should have warned you about that. Next time bring some ear plugs."

Craig held back a smirk. *'Not likely going to be a next time.'* "Yes, that would be a good idea. Your guitar playing is really amazing, you really have a lot of talent."

Jake blushed a little with another big smile. "Thank you, I really appreciate you saying that. I've put years of practice into it."

Craig reached over and patted Jake on the shoulder, then immediately felt weird about it. "It shows. There is a lot of dedication involved in what you are pursuing."

Jake stopped fidgeting for a moment and looked at the floor, embarrassed. "Thank you, I hope I can make it pay off, I would really like to make a career out of music."

Craig noticed Jake had calmed down almost instantly. "Jake, I think I might be able to help you on your path if you're interested."

Jake looked up at Craig with an astonished expression. "Really? How's that?"

Craig moved his satchel to his other shoulder. "Yes, really. I Have some friends around town that might be able to help you get your music career fast tracked."

Jake hadn't looked away, he was staring straight into Craig's eyes, making Craig second guess what he was about to do. *'What happens if I offer a contract to someone that already has one?'* "I would be interested, but why would you want to do that? We just met."

Craig returned Jake's stare, trying to break him first. "True, we just met, but I like you, you have good energy and enthusiasm for what you're doing. I like to help students get what they need to succeed, and, in this case, I think I know the right people." Craig was watching Jake's eyes, looking for signs of the Evil One. "But I need to know something first, it's very important that you're 100 percent honest with me."

Jake never looked away, more calm than Craig had ever seen him. "Of course, what is it?"

Craig matched his calm tone. "Have you signed any contracts? For any reason? And I do mean *any* reason?"

Jake shrugged, finally lifting his gaze from Craig's eyes and smiled as he looked at the ground, his eyes shifting left and right. "Hmm, no, no I haven't."

Craig was watching his face and expressions change. "Are you positive? If you have, I need to know."

Jake looked back at Craig and smiled again. "I'm sure, I haven't signed anything."

Craig stood silent, looking at Jake for a few moments. "Okay, make sure you don't until I come see you again. I'll reach out to my contact and arrange something for you. It will be worth it. Remember, don't sign anything."

Jake was still smiling. "Got it. Can I tell the band?"

Craig pondered the ramifications. "No, you should keep it to yourself for now. I'm not sure if the deal will be for the whole group or just for you."

Jake looked disappointed at first, but then grinned. "Okay, cool. Can't wait."

Craig pulled out his wallet. "Here is my card. Call me if you need anything. My cell number is on there."

Jake took the card and shoved it in his pocket without looking at it. "Thank you, I will."

Craig reached out, shook hands with him and turned to walk away, then stopped suddenly and turned back to Jake. "Do you have a demo CD I can take with me? I'll need to be able to show off your skill."

Jake's face lit up. "I do! Hold on, I'll get one." Jake spun around and ran into the studio. He emerged moments later holding out a CD. "Here you go. That's the latest one we've been working on. It's got our newest songs on it."

Craig took it from him and dropped it into his satchel. "That's great, thank you." Craig looked down the hall, and not seeing an exit sign in front of him, turned around, spotted a sign and walked away. "We'll talk soon, Jake."

Jake waved as Craig walked away. "I appreciate the help," then he disappeared back into the studio.

19

Tom's Struggle

Tom thought about Craig's offer for days. Mostly returning to the same conclusion. Craig was crazy. Tom was in total disbelief, what Craig was offering couldn't possibly be real. Each day, he tried to make sense of Craig working for the Grim Reaper and offering him and Sue the same opportunity. Sue was getting steadily worse, she was nearly at a point that he wouldn't be able to talk with her at all. She was getting far too weak, she slept 18 hours a day, and when she was awake it was only to have a coughing fit. Tom was only able to share a few words with her each day. He tried to comfort her and get her to eat but even that was getting harder. He knew he would have to make a decision within the next day or two, otherwise it might be too late.

Tom sat next to Sue while she was propped up against the headboard in bed. He was trying to help her eat, she needed nourishment. "Sue, we have to make a decision." He looked at her eyes, hoping she was listening, her eyes followed him. " We have an opportunity to get into the a medical program at the university." Sue's arm stiffened, pushing against Tom, so he grabbed her hand. "Yes, it's a real opportunity, I think. Our neighbor Craig has some contacts at the U that he believes will get us in." He was watching her closely to make sure she was following what he was telling her. Her eyes were brighter than he had seen them in months. "It comes with a catch." Tom could feel her slump. "Yes, I know, every avenue we have gone down has come with a roadblock. This one seems too strange to be real." Tom paused to formulate his words. "If we agree, we will have to do things later in life to pay back the debt."

He gazed into Sue's eyes, looking for understanding. She seemed to understand from the grief in his tone that the debt would be hard to repay and that it might be something they wouldn't want to do. She made an attempt at a nod to say, *'Carry on'*. Tom got it.

"We might not like what we have to do, or who we have to do it for. As I see it, right now, we don't have many, or really any, other options. Craig said it's literally making a deal with the Devil."

Tom never stopped looking into her eyes and he could tell that she wasn't hearing him any longer, her eyes had all but closed and she was slumping down. Tom set the bowl of soup aside and helped slide her down into the bed, covering her so she could sleep again. *'I think she heard some of it, but I don't think she gets the depth of what it will entail.'*

Tom left the room, closing the door most of the way as he walked out. He checked his watch, 4 pm. *'Craig will be getting home soon. I have more questions about this.'* Tom paced back and forth across his living room, feeling completely lost and unable to make this decision. It felt impossible. *'How can I make a decision for her that she will have to deal with? Is this*

181

even real? Would we really have to work for the Devil? Would Sue take that offer if she were deciding for me? Would she accept the offer for herself? Am I willing to take this offer?' He stopped at the thought and broke down into tears, falling to his knees, covering his face with his hands, sobbing uncontrollably. *'Yes! Yes! I will, I will take the offer to save my love, the love of my life is worth my life in return!'*

Tom stayed on the floor sobbing off and on for 30 minutes until he heard something that snapped him out of it. He started to gather himself together, drying his eyes, trying to breath normally. He slowly got off the floor and looked outside. Craig had gotten home while he was falling apart. *'I have to go talk to him.'*

Tom peeked into the bedroom to see if Sue was still sleeping, she hadn't moved. He checked the mirror, his face was all puffy and his eyes were very red. *'It doesn't matter, I'm sure he would understand.'* Tom went out the front door, slowly walking into his yard, stopping to admire the surroundings, feeling different about everything, realizing he had been taking the whole world for granted now that he was faced with turning himself over to evil. He looked across the street to the park, up at the trees, into the sky. *'Does it change? Does it look different after?'* He stood still, pondering the life he had, wondering if this is the right choice. *'People die all the time, we have to accept that as part of life, should I just let it be?'* Tom could feel tears welling up again at the thought of letting go, when he knew that there was something he could do about it. *'Is it worth selling my soul? How many people are faced with this decision?'* He started to cry again at the thought of not saving Sue in order to preserve his own life. He doubled over in pain at the thought.

Craig had looked out the front window about the time Tom had walked into the front yard. He watched as Tom stared off into the distance and knew what he was struggling with as he saw him break down in tears. Craig grabbed a box of tissue, and stepped out onto his porch. He sat quietly on the swing, waiting for Tom's tears of desperation to subside.

Tom's pain was acute, but the tears had slowed. He stood upright again, looking out to the park, then up and down the street, taking note if anyone had seen him falling apart. He turned toward Craig's house and started walking that way with his head hung down. He eventually looked at Craig's porch and saw Craig sitting on the swing. He hesitated, embarrassed for falling apart, but then saw the look of empathy on Craig's face.

"You have turned my world upside down in just a couple of days." Tom's tone was rough and slightly accusatory.

Craig didn't take offense from it. "I understand, my friend. I didn't mean for it to be hurtful, I only offered as a means to an end, to try to preserve your relationship. By no means are you obligated to accept the offer."

Tom continued onto the porch. "I didn't mean to come off harsh or sound mad. It's just such an impossible decision to make. Sue isn't well enough to understand what I am telling her and what the consequences are, that is, if what you are telling me is real."

Craig sat in silence for a few minutes, looking at Tom. "It is real, I assure you. I wish it weren't. I understand what a terrible decision it is to have to make, but like I told you before, I wanted you to know what was happening and to have the choice about your future."

Tom was still standing at the top of the steps with his head hung, staring at the floor. "I want to take this on for Sure. Let me make the sacrifice for her, so that she can live her normal life."

Craig got an uneasy feeling when he heard Tom say that. He hadn't considered that Tom would want to take the proverbial bullet for Sue. "Tom." He said with a sad, exasperated feeling. "I don't think it works that way. This is something you both want, you both would have to sign the contract. At a minimum, Sue would be able to sign for herself to preserve her life, but you couldn't do it for her. I guess, I figured that you would want to do it together, so you could be together longer and be in the same circumstance. Does that make sense?" Craig wasn't sure where this knowledge came from, he just opened his mouth and the words came out. *I'm going to have to speak with Grimm about this.'*

Tom stood still, only shrugging in response. "So Sue could take this on her own? I wouldn't have to commit to the Devil?"

Craig watched the pain on Tom's face. "Technically, yes, but I wonder about her ability to sign the contract, you might have to sign it as well as a witness to her signature, which, as I see it, binds you to the same contract."

Tom shrugged a little more and tears started to stream again. Craig held out the tissues and Tom came to sit on the swing. "I really don't know if Sue could agree to such a thing, even to save her own life. She isn't spiritual but a deal with the Devil might be a step too far."

Craig sat in silence, looking out into space, his mind starting to wander in the silence. He started to wonder if this feeling he was having, as he sat there daydreaming about nothing, was what his students felt when he saw those blank stares on their faces in the middle of his lectures. He smiled to himself, then snapped out of it, hoping that he didn't smile and Tom saw it. *'That would be awful. This is not the time to smile.'*

Tom finally broke the silence. "I am going to try one more time to talk to her, I'll have to make it fast when she's awake, before she fades off again. It's going to have to be soon too, she's slipping away quickly."

Tom stood and pulled his shoulders back, only to hunch down again in defeat.

Craig stood up and put his hand on Tom's shoulder. "Tom, I feel terrible for what's happening. I won't judge you, no matter what you choose."

Tom turned and gave Craig a hug. "Thanks for your understanding, it means a lot, even though what you've presented to me is incredibly evil. It feels weird to appreciate what you've done for me, but, thank you."

Craig didn't respond, he just gave Tom a knowing look. Tom left without saying another word and went back to his house to check on Sue.

20

Air Guitar

Craig sat in his office thinking about the transformation of Brandon and Haley, considering his next steps. *'I need to get Jake a contract. I can only imagine what his transformation would look like.'* He fumbled with his satchel for a moment, pulled the three pages out that he had stapled together and looked over the front page. Jake Ramsey's name, Music Production Program, full scholarship. *'This should help, at least he wont have to pay for school.'* Craig pulled out his laptop and searched local recording studios. He found three not too far away. He saved the addresses, then searched reviews. In Motion Sound had the best reviews by artists. *'I'll pay them a visit. I guess I'm blowing off my responsibilities today.'*

In Motion Sound was about a 30 minute drive in silence, no radio, windows up, only the AC blowing on low to keep him cool in the afternoon sun. He was becoming reluctant to use the AC, it reminded him of Grimm when it got too cold.

As Craig pulled into the lot next to In Motion, he evaluated the business based on the condition of the building alone. It was a little run down and didn't look all that professional.

'Not sure I would want to use this place, based on the looks of the building alone.' Craig parked in the middle of the lot, only four other cars were there besides his. None of them screamed *'music executive.'* Just your basic sedans, each a few years old. *'Doesn't seem like they are raking in the cash either. Maybe that's a good thing. Maybe they will be more eager to strike a deal.'*

Craig stepped out of his car into the midday sun. He felt the hot pavement radiate up into his shoes. He took another look around the lot and up and down the side of the building before walking toward the front doors. At the front of the building, Craig saw several band posters, advertising coming albums and concerts. He didn't recognize any of the band names or album covers. He shrugged it off, knowing he didn't keep up with current music, those bands could be multi million album sellers and he wouldn't know.

The doors to the studio looked more like doors to an old drug store than a high end recording studio. Craig pushed through and was met with an assaulting, musty, smoke smell that seemed like it was 30 years old. The carpet in the lobby was from the 70's, probably the source of the smell. Craig took four steps into the lobby and considered turning around. His eyes were adjusting from the sun to the darkness of the lobby, as they did, he could see a newer reception desk with a lovely woman sitting behind it, looking at Craig expectantly, waiting for him to approach. Beyond her desk, Craig looked through a large window into a sound room, with large speakers arranged throughout the room and two plush looking leather sofas. The sound room was more what Craig expected a professional studio to look like.

Craig put a smile on his face and approached the desk. "Good afternoon, how are you today?"

She smiled back at Craig. "I'm well, thank you. What can I do for you?"

Craig introduced himself and discovered her name was Sarah. "I'm here to speak to someone about a recording client of mine."

Sarah's smile said, *'Yes, you and everyone else that walks in off the street.'* "Do you have an appointment?"

Craig felt his face burn red. "Oh, I should have thought of that. This isn't my usual job, I'm actually trying to help a student of mine at the university, I was hoping that someone would be available."

Sara picked up the phone. "You're in luck today, James is here, I'll find out if he has time to see you." She hit a couple of buttons and waited. "James, there is a Craig Newman here to see you."

Craig couldn't hear the other side of the conversation but it was obvious.

"He has a client he wants to pitch if you have a moment." Sarah hung up the line. "You can go into the listening room. He's in a good mood, you got lucky." She smiled and pointed to the heavy glass doors to the right of the room.

Craig let himself in and looked around at the equipment. *'This is more what I was expecting from a recording studio.'* A few moments passed before a scrawny man wearing jeans and a button down shirt came rushing into the room. He had a heavy five o'clock shadow and the start of a mullet hanging just over his collar.

"Hello, I'm James Miles." He walked straight to Craig, reaching out to shake hands.

Craig shook his hand. "Hello, Mr. Miles, nice to meet you, thank you for seeing me. I didn't even think to make an appointment."

James smiled and waved it off. "Not a problem, usually I'm too busy for drop ins but we got a light day today. What would you like to talk about? Let me guess, you have the next big rock star and you need me to promote him?"

Craig was a little embarrassed as James smiled at him with a very sarcastic look on his face. "I must admit, I didn't really consider that these kinds of things probably happen to you all the time."

James nodded agreement. "They really do. Often people believe they are, or have, the next music star. Some people do have some talent but it is rarely the type of talent it takes to make it big." James paused to read Craig's face. "It looks like you don't really know what you have, just from the look on your face."

Craig made a face that gave him away. "You're right. I'm a little out of my element. This type of music isn't my thing, I don't know if it's any good or if it's just noise. I hope that you will give it a chance."

James held out his hand. "Let's have it. Now I'm curious what you've brought me."

Craig handed over the disc and watched as James put it into the enormous sound system. The volume started out fairly low. James leaned against the back of one of the sofas, his eyes closed, his head tilted back as if he was soaking in the sound. Craig watched James closely, trying to read his body language. James hit the remote and the sound level increased. The bass was thumping in Craig's chest, the guitars were crunchy and sometimes pierced at his eardrums. Craig, still watching James, winced with the loud notes hitting his ears. James didn't flinch, he stood there with his eyes closed

189

absorbing the music. Suddenly, the song changed. James was skipping tracks, he would listen to a few seconds, then fast forward into the middle of the song, listen a little longer, then on to the next track. Each time he paused on a song, it played for an even shorter time then the one before. There were a couple of times Craig thought he saw James tapping his hand to the beat.

The music abruptly stopped. James went to the player and pulled out the disc. He walked over to Craig and handed it to him. "Thanks for coming in, I don't feel that this is a band I want to pursue."

Craig automatically took the disc from his hand but was disappointed in James's reaction. "Are you sure? You didn't listen very long."

James went back to leaning on the sofa. "Yeah, I've got a good ear for this kind of thing. It's not that they aren't good. Musically, they are tight, but it's just not a salable product."

Craig was surprised at the response. Granted he didn't know anything about the music business, but it seemed like James wasn't giving these boys a fair chance. "I really think you should give it another listen, you clearly know what you're talking about, but there is more here than what you are giving them credit for."

Craig held out the disc. James just looked at it but didn't reach out for it. Craig shook it a little, urging James to take the disc. James didn't take it. He stood up off the edge of the sofa and took a couple steps away from Craig.

"I don't need to listen again, I heard all that I need to. I've been doing this a while now and know what I heard."

Craig could feel the opportunity slipping. "You really should give it another listen." At that moment, the room began to get cold. Craig stepped forward, holding the disc out again. Craig's eyes were focused on James's eyes, staring into his soul. James took a step back. Craig took a step forward. "Take the disc."

James saw Craig's eyes dilate, there was no color to be seen. The room was getting colder and now James noticed. He rubbed his hands up and down his arms for warmth.

Craig took another step forward and thrust the disc at James. "Take the disc and listen to it again." This time, Craig's voice boomed louder than the speakers in the listening room. It shook the glass wall and Sarah stood up from her office chair, thinking there was an earthquake.

James reached out and took the disc. He slid it back into the player and turned the volume up. The music played for several minutes before James finally changed his focus from Craig to the sound filling the room. James got lost in the music, he didn't seem to notice the cold in the air anymore. He was tapping to the beat and swaying to the groove.

Craig watched him soaking it in, but still couldn't find a groove to the music himself. *'I personally don't hear it.'* Craig reached over for the remote and turned the volume down. Keeping his voice low and somewhat menacing, just not as loud. "Now, what do you think?"

James broke out with a smile "This is great! I think you have something here. What is the name of the band?"

Craig relaxed slightly, his voice softened but the room remained cold. "They're called, 'Adaptive.'"

James smiled. "I love it, I think this is something we can work with."

Craig stopped the music and James looked at him, wondering why. "I am their agent. I want to see what your normal contract looks like."

James was still under the influence of Craig's power. "Sure, I have some templates, let me grab one from my office." This is not something James would normally do, but he was in an agreeable trance. James went through a door at the end of the listening room to his office, Craig followed. James dug into a file in the corner of his office and produced a document. "This is one of our agreements, we use it as a template for each artist we sign."

Craig was standing in front of a large mahogany desk centered in James's office, there were several records on the walls, band photos inlaid between silver albums. Craig didn't know any of the bands or how many records sold was represented by each of the framed albums. James turned around with the contract template, looked at it for a moment then slid it across the desk to Craig. It was shorter than Craig had anticipated.

"There really isn't much here, are you basically having the artist give everything to you?"

James smirked and nodded. "Yes, that's very standard for a new artist. We take everything except about ten percent, but they have to pay for studio time out of their own pocket and they are required to use this studio so the money stays here. The other option we give them is eight percent plus we keep the rights to all the music they create on the next five records, but they can record wherever they want."

Craig let the contract sit on the desk as James explained the terrible terms within. When James was done Craig stared at James, locking their eyes, James couldn't look away. He was trying but he physically he could not turn away. Craig's eyes darkened again as his pupils dilated until there was no color left.

Craig spoke calmly but very stern. "I will make some needed changes to the language and terms of this agreement. Jake will sign it and I will bring it back to you. You will then sign and honor the agreement. You will not be disappointed in your decision."

Craig held his cold gaze for an uncomfortably long time, James finally was able to nod agreement and Craig let him look away. At that moment, Craig felt amazingly powerful, it was gratifying, he had never felt that before. There had been something similar when he'd spoken with Gavin Scott, the athletic director, but he hadn't been able to put a finger on what it was. Now he felt like he understood what true power was. *'I could get used to that feeling.'* Craig felt like a puffed up, overly confident version of himself, like nothing could stop him. He had never been ten feet tall and bullet proof, but he imagined this is what that felt like.

The room was still cold, Craig had James under his control, he would do anything Craig wanted at this point. "Remember me, when I come back with this contract, you will be excited for it and ready to get to work with Adaptive. You're going to do all you can to make them famous."

James was locked into Craig's words, his eyes didn't leave Craig's. "I am very excited to work with them."

Craig relaxed and picked the contract off the desk, then moved back into the listening room. He hit play on the remote and paused by the large glass door. Craig looked at James before he opened it, just to make sure he was still paying attention. James was reaching for the remote while watching Craig at the door, waiting to see if Craig was going to say anything else. Craig waited a moment, then opened the door and left the listening room. The temperature started to come back to normal right away.

Craig heard the volume increase as James cranked up the sound system in the listening room. James yelled, "This is the best new rock band I have ever heard!" He was stoked that he just made a discovery that would be a hit.

Craig looked back through the glass into the listening room as he reached the door to leave the lobby, James was throwing his head back, playing air guitar to the demo like he was a teenager jamming to his favorite album.

Craig smiled, Sarah looked over her shoulder at James. "He must really like what you brought in."

Craig nodded. "He came around to it. By the way, you should consider getting rid of that smelly carpet."

Sarah laughed. "Yes, I keep suggesting that but it was part of the original studio that was started in the late 60's. James is a little nostalgic for it."

Craig made a face. "It smells awful." Then he turned and left the building.

21

I'm Stuck!

It felt like forever had passed since Craig had been to visit Mike, when in reality, it had only been a week. Craig didn't have too much new to talk about, but wanted to stop in and say hello anyway. As he walked down the hallway of Winding Tree toward Mike's room, he felt a chill pass through him. He hesitated slightly, looking around, knowing it was likely a Reaper. *'What's his name? Glen? Yes, that's it, Glen the Crotchety Old Reaper.'* Craig toyed with that in his mind a little, trying to make fun of the situation, making it feel not so dreadful.

He tapped on Mikes door and turned the handle before getting a reply. "Yes, come in."

Craig stepped inside to find Mike still in his sleeping clothes. "What's going on? Are you okay?"

Mike was slightly propped up on pillows laying on the couch, watching the television. "Oh, I'm okay. I was feeling a little under the weather today and didn't get dressed. I'm a bit better now."

Craig went to Mike's usual seat and made himself comfortable. "That's good, have you had anything to eat today?"

Mike pointed at the tray left on the side table. "Yes. Nancy brought me a plate this morning. I called to the front desk and told them I wasn't feeling well and wanted to eat in my room."

Craig squinted at Mike like he was a three year old. "If you say so. I felt your local Reaper when I was coming in. Don't let him get a hold of you."

Mike rolled his eyes, playing along. "Oh, I have no intentions of letting that Reaper anywhere near me. I'm doing fine. Probably going to outlast you." Mike chuckled.

Craig didn't think this was so funny. "You could be right, but I'm going to do my best to stick around as long as possible."

Mike pushed himself up on the sofa, allowing him to have a better conversation face to face. "How is that coming? Any progress with those two needing medical help?"

Craig nodded. "Yes, a little progress. Poor Tom really has a difficult decision to make. His wife, Sue, doesn't have the capacity to make a decision herself so he has to take it all on. I probably shouldn't have made them an offer, or just not told them what the consequences were. I'm afraid he will regret his decision no matter which way he chooses."

Mike was shaking his head. "I don't know that not telling him would have been the right choice. I think you did the right thing, unless you weren't going to help them at all. And by 'help' them you know what I mean." Mike put air quotes around 'help.' "I understand what you mean though, it's a choice he will have to live with forever."

Craig pressed his lips together, thinking about Tom and Sue making a choice that they would have to live with forever. "Quite literally for eternity." Craig shifted uncomfortably in his seat, crossing his legs and leaning back, with his head on the back rest. "I'll find out what they want to do in a day or so I believe. What I wanted to ask you about though was another client that I am working with."

Mike used air quotes again around 'client'. "Is that what you're calling them? 'Clients?'"

Craig gave him a sideways look. "Yeah, I don't know what else to call them. What's with the air quotes?"

Mike laughed. "I don't know, I just thought it was funny. Who is your other client?"

Craig shook his head and let it go. "He's the musician kid I told you about last week. You laughed about all rock stars having made a deal with the Devil."

Mike chuckled again now. "That's right, I do love the stereotype of the rock star musician making a deal to hit it big. It's so fitting."

Craig nodded. "Glad you enjoy it so much. I went to speak to a record studio guy and he is going to take a contract and promote this kid and his band, everything is set up, I just want to edit his contract a little bit so that he has a good deal at least for the amount of time that he gets to be a star."

Mike got a more serious look on his face. "Okay, maybe I can help talk through that with you. What kind of deal would they normally get? From what I have seen they aren't usually very good."

Craig dug into his sport coat pocket and pulled out the contract. "Here you go. This is what James, the studio guy, gave me. I told him I was going to make changes and bring it back."

Mike took a few minutes to look through the pages. "It doesn't leave much for the artist once they sign it. May as well be a deal with the Devil." Mike smirked at Craig.

"Go ahead, keep jabbing. I see what you did there." Craig paused for a minute to gather his thoughts. "What I would like to change is the percent the artist receives as a base. I think the ten percent isn't good enough."

Mike nodded. "I agree, I don't have any idea what a good number is, but it seems like anything over 20 percent would be good. Understanding that the record company will have things they need to pay for when promoting an artist."

Craig listened and was processing the information. "Sure, I'm sure there are plenty of costs associated. Along those lines, I want to add that the band doesn't have to pay for recording time, that should be included, as well as touring. If the band goes on tour that should all be covered by the record label."

Mike nodded again. "That's got to be plenty expensive. Do you think this James guy you talked with will go for all of that? If this is the contract he normally gives out, then what you've come up with will be a big stretch."

Craig got a big smile across his face. "Yes, I am quite sure James will take anything I bring him. I don't really want to break his bank but I want it to work out for the band better than the average." Mike readjusted himself on the sofa. "Well, then put in 25 percent for the band off of all sales and the couple of things you mentioned there and get it done."

Craig laughed. "Get it done, just like that. There might be a couple other things I'll add in as well. Thanks for your help. I wasn't sure how far off base I was thinking."

Mike slid down the sofa a little bit and rested his head back. "You're welcome. If there isn't anything else I can do for you, I'm going to take a nap."

Craig smiled. "No, you've helped enough for today. It was good to see you." Mike waved a little. "Don't mind me if I don't get up to see you out."

Craig got up and went to the door. "No worries Dad, see you later."

Craig left Winding Tree in the very hot afternoon sun. When he got in his car he didn't start it right away, his mind wandered to where he might be able to recruit his fifth soul. *'Athletes are good, they always want to do better.'* Craig's imagination took over, envisioning the different sports available at the university; football, track, baseball. *'Who wouldn't want an opportunity to be the best?'* Craig heard something behind his car, he checked the mirrors and didn't see anything. He craned his head around to look out the back window and caught a glimpse of something black moving quickly behind his car. Craig checked the mirror again but didn't see anything. He twisted around in his seat even farther to take another look. Then he saw it, a being in a black cloak. *'Oh Grimm what now?'* Craig opened the door and stepped out of the car, quickly turning to the back. He was feeling overwhelmed and tired of dealing with Grimm.

"What do you want?!"

Craig suddenly realized it was not Grimm. It was the Winding Tree resident Reaper, Glen. Glen was stopped just behind the Mercedes, his black robe fluttering at the ends, devouring all of the suns rays and not casting a shadow.

"Never return. Never return here, this is my territory. I know you work for Grimm, you cannot come in here and take my Recruits."

Craig raised his hands in defense. "I'm not here to take any of your Recruits. My father lives here."

Glen hovered two feet off the pavement. "Yes, Mike Newman. I've watched you enter and leave that room several times."

Craig got an uncomfortable feeling about that. "Why were you watching me?"

Glen remained silent for a few moments. "It is my duty to know what is happening in my territory, who is coming and going." Glen paused. "It does not matter why! You should never return here!"

Glen was getting angry and started to move toward Craig. Craig instinctively backed away as Glen rushed at him. Craig turned to run the other direction, out into the street. He looked over his shoulder, trying to spot Glen and gauge if he was going to get away. *'He's a Reaper you fool, he can catch you in an instant.'*

Just at that moment, Craig felt like he couldn't run very fast, he was trying but he couldn't seem to get anywhere. His steps felt slow, he was trying to move his legs faster but they wouldn't cooperate. He felt like he was tethered to his car with a bungee. Craig looked at his feet and saw the pavement was hot and sticky, he could barely lift his shoes. The tar was stuck to the bottoms, making it hard to take a step. Craig managed three more steps then looked at his feet again. *'They're so hot!'* His feet were covered in tar now. With each step the tar got deeper and deeper until it was over the tops of his shoes, spilling into them at his ankles. He looked back over his shoulder again, Glen was gone. He looked all around just to make sure, Craig couldn't see him anywhere. He was, however, a bit stuck in the middle of the street. Craig could barely lift his feet now, his left shoe came off and caught him off balance, down to his knees he went, squishing into the hot tar in the middle of the road. Craig looked toward the sidewalk, hoping that someone would be nearby that could help. The tar was burning his skin, his hands were covered from the fall.

Craig looked up and saw Tom Downy on the sidewalk. "Tom, can you help me?!" Craig reached out to him with his tar covered hand. Tom just stood there with a blank look on his face, like he didn't understand what Craig said. Again Craig yelled out. "Tom! I'm stuck, I really need your help."

Tom's expression changed, he had an angry look on his face. "Like you helped me? You want me to help you after you helped me by offering me a deal with the Devil? Why, Craig? Why would I do that?"

Craig pulled with all his strength to get his left leg loose, when it came free he lost his balance and plunged his hands back into the goo. "That's not fair, Tom. I wanted you to know what you were getting into. That's why I told you, I didn't want you to be blindsided by it."

Craig pulled his right hand out and some of the tar flung onto his face. He winced from the heat of it but couldn't do anything about it. Craig looked back up for Tom, but he was gone. Farther down the street he saw Brandon Wells.

"Brandon! Brandon, can you help me?"

Brandon walked slowly to the very spot that Tom had been standing moments before. He just stood there looking at Craig, not offering so much as a word of encouragement. Craig was motionless, trying not to make his predicament worse by moving unnecessarily.

"Brandon, can you please help me get out of this mess?"

Brandon shifted slightly from one foot to the other. "Why would I do that? Didn't you sentence me to a life of hell just like you're living now? I think it seems fitting that you're stuck in the hot tar. Imagine how hot the tar is, burning and being tortured for all eternity in hell."

Craig shifted his weight back some to get a better look at Brandon. "How do you know that? We didn't discuss any of that."

Just at that moment, Craig sank deeper into the tar, his calves were submerged and the tar was well up his thighs. Craig managed to pull both hands free and his torso upright. He had hot tar to his elbows and didn't know what to do with his hands.

"Brandon, did you read the contract?" Craig looked back to the sidewalk but Brandon was no longer there, instead it was Haley Turner. "Oh! Haley! Can you help me?"

Haley furrowed her brow. "And I thought you were helping out of the goodness in your heart. It wasn't that at all. You were just trying to save yourself at the cost of others."

Craig, feeling deflated, sat back on his heels, plopping his butt into the tar and sinking even farther into the muck. "Haley, you're right, I've done an awful thing to others just to save myself. Can you please help me get out of this mess?"

Craig could feel the hot tar burning through his clothes, the chemicals eating away at his skin, melting it from his body. Craig heard a noise behind him and twisted his torso to try and see what it was. As he twisted he felt a pop in his back, the pain was searing like needles in his spine. He fell to his side into the hot tar, struggling to keep his head above the goo. He managed to get a glimpse of what was behind him. "Jake! Jake, please help me!" Craig was floundering in the tar, struggling to move, it was so thick and heavy, the weight of it pulled him in farther and farther by the second.

"Mr. Newman, you used me. You offered me something you knew I wanted in order to trap me into your Devil scheme. I guess the positive is I probably would have made a deal with the Devil at some point anyway. So I'm not too upset with you."

Craig tried to reach a hand out to Jake but was too off balance and fell face forward into the tar. Everything went black and silent. Thoughts were spinning in Craig's mind like images in a kaleidoscope, all crashing into one another. Everything from childhood memories to more recent memories of recruiting innocent souls. *'What have I done? Is this the end?'* Craig could feel himself slowly sinking deeper and deeper into the goo. *'How did I get here? Where did this tar come from anyway? How did they all know I used them? Why are they all in front of Winding Tree?'*

Craig jolted, gasping for air and slapping the horn in his car where he had fallen asleep in the hot sun. He was sweating and stuck to the seat but very much alive. He sat still for a moment, taking a few beats to catch his breath and look around. There were no signs that anyone had been nearby as he had yet another dream. He looked out at the street, he could see heat radiating from the pavement, but it was solid, he wasn't going to sink through it as he drove away. Craig started the car and turned the AC as low as it would go. He sat there just long enough to start feeling the cold air come out of the vents, then left the lot and headed home.

22

The Servant

As Craig walked across campus he mumbled to himself, *'Grimm, I need to talk to you.'* He was walking with a purpose today, not looking around, not noticing students passing, not looking at the fountain as he passed it. *'Grimm, please meet me in my office, we need to have a discussion.'* Craig grumbled under his breath. *'I don't really want to have a discussion, but there are things I need cleared up.'* Craig bounded up the stairs of the Great Hall, his shoes echoing off the stone tile, clacking each time he took a step. Craig stopped at his office door for a split second before inserting his key and letting himself in. He didn't feel the icy presence of Grimm, and went into his office. He made his way behind his desk, took his blazer off and hung it over the back of his chair. *'Grimm, when you have a few spare moments I could really use to speak with you. I Promise, it wont take long.'* A cold blast of air hit Craig in the face when he went to sit at his desk. He gasped a bit as it took his breath away.

"What is it?!" Grimm appeared to come out of the floor rising into the room on a blast of cold, dusty wind from below.

"I've heard you all morning grumbling about needing to speak with me. I am not at your beck and call!" Grimm started moving back and forth across the room almost immediately. "Now that I am here, What do you want?!"

Grimm seemed agitated. Craig had never seen him hover back and forth across the room before, he had always been very stoic, never seeming ruffled by anything. Craig knew this was his best opportunity to ask Grimm about Tom's dilemma. "I need to ask a question about a potential Recruit."

Grimm stopped pacing and turned to face Craig. "I believe I know what you're going to ask but go ahead, I want to hear it from you."

Craig swallowed hard and dabbed at his nose with a tissue from the desk. "I have a potential client, or two, that are in a tough situation."

Grimm went back to pacing. "Yes, yes, Tom and Sue Downy. I am aware of them."

Craig nodded agreement. "Right, then you know that Sue isn't well, and may not fully understand what the document is that she is agreeing to. With that in mind, will the contract be valid? Secondly, will it count toward my quota?"

Grimm stopped again, not facing Craig. The room seemed to get even colder. He clearly had something else he was concerned with. Grimm pondered Craig's question as a thin fog started to form just above the floor. Craig's hands and face were turning bright red in the cold room. He thought for a moment he saw ice crystals floating in the air, visible as the sun beams from the window reflected off of them.

Grimm spoke suddenly. "If Sue is cognizant when she signs the contract, I'll allow it. But if Tom has her sign not understanding what it is, it will not count toward your quota.

I will however honor her wishes set forth in the contract and she will be bound to it just as Tom will be. Understood?"

Craig had a sinking feeling in his chest, he had known it would go this way but also knew that it was not likely that Sue would understand and sign on her own accord. "I understand, I will relay the message to Tom as well."

Grimm nodded his head slightly in agreement, then started rubbing his fingers together. Click, click, click. Craig tried to block it out but was unsuccessful and he cringed as the sound sent chills up his spine. Grimm went back to pacing back and forth across the small office. "What else do you wish to discuss?"

Craig was drawing a blank, his disappointment about Sue leaving him flustered. He watched Grimm move silently back and forth. When Grimm turned, Craig caught a glimpse of Grimm's glowing red eyes. He flashed back to Jake's concert at the arena. *'Oh, that was it!'*

Craig took a deep breath and held it for a moment, he was tentative with Grimm seeming agitated. "I do have something else I want to ask about."

Grimm turned to face Craig. "Very well, out with it."

Craig flinched a little at Grimm's tone. "I would like to know if the dream that I had the other day was more than a dream. Was it real?"

Grimm stood still, waiting for Craig to give more details. "Did you want me to reach into your mind and have a look around?" Grimm's tone was dripping with sarcasm. "I assure you, I won't stop at just your dreams, it might get a little uncomfortable."

Craig shifted at his desk, rubbing his hands together, trying to warm them. "I seemed to fall asleep right here in my office and while I was out dreamt that I was at a concert, that morphed into what appeared to be a convention of Reapers. At one point, one of the Reapers was-."

Grimm raised his hand and cut Craig off. "He was sent to serve his time with the Center of Evil himself."

Craig sat astonished, nodding his head. "Yes, that's exactly what happened."

Grimm paced out and back once. "That was real. You were there. All those thousands of Reapers and dedicated souls were there. Did you understand the point of you being there?"

Craig brought his hands to his mouth and blew into them, trying to get some warmth. "I most definitely did get the message. It was very clear to me what will happen if I don't follow through."

Grimm held his hands behind his back, rubbing his fingers together a couple of times. "That's correct, it was not just for your benefit, each of those Reapers is a Servant and has a quota to meet. Just as I am a Servant to his Darkness. It's important to make sure that all of you, the Recruiters, know what is at stake."

Craig nodded with a look of amazement on his face. *That is an incredible amount of Reapers.* "So Jake is already spoken for?"

Grimm was still motionless. Click, click, click. "No, Jake is yours for the taking. He was there as part of your manifestation. While you saw Jake on stage, other Recruiters saw someone that they know or are working with. It's the power of suggestion. Proceed with your plans for Jake. Be swift, get the contract completed."

Craig relaxed slightly. "Thank you for clearing these things up for me." Grimm turned to face Craig but before he could speak Craig jumped in. "You said Servants a minute ago when you were talking about the gathering of, whatever it was. What is a Servant?"

Grimm's red eyes glowed darker than Craig had ever seen before. "I will explain in a moment, but first, I need you to know that you are now required to collect six souls before your deadline. You have approximately three weeks."

Craig's mouth dropped open, he was shocked. "What do you mean!? What did I do wrong? Why am I being punished?"

Grimm went back to pacing, the fog forming at the floor swished back and forth as he crossed the room. "You asked about the Servant?"

Craig nodded. "Yes, was that wrong?"

Grimm paused a moment before he turned around. "No, it's not wrong, I told you, I will explain." Grimm was frustrated with these questions. He didn't have time to waste on Craig's trivial issues or explaining the entire organization to him. Grimm was having a hard time meeting the terms of his own contract. That's the issue with pyramid schemes, there is always someone above, expecting you to perform. Grimm had been recruiting souls for millennia, he had always been a top performer. The Evil One had relied on him to continually turn in new souls. The loss of another Recruiter at the gathering in the arena was a way for Grimm to get his point across that he expects everyone to step up, he needed numbers now and couldn't afford to have anyone do any less than what was agreed upon. Grimm was already serving at the right hand of the Devil, if he didn't meet the requirements of his contract it would be much worse for him. The One Most Evil would take Grimm and torture him for eternity without forgiveness, even though he is the top Reaper in the organization. Grimm knew it would be 100 times worse than the existence he knew now.

Grimm came up through the ranks of Recruiters just like all the other Reapers, he had never faltered, always bringing in new souls that perform well without defaulting on their contracts, he had built a successful pyramid. Grimm had done so well over the last thousand years that he had the longest tenure in the history of Reapers. No other Reaper had lasted as long as he has. At some point, every other Reaper had failed to complete the terms of their agreement and was sent into the bowels of fire and darkness.

Grimm continued to pace and spoke in a monotone, low voice. "The pyramid looks like this: The Devil is supreme, he is at the top of the pyramid and commands all that is required of the others below. The Servants, also known as Reapers, report to the Evil One, they are his captains, Reapers bring in all the others to do the dirty work for the Center of Hatred. The Soul Collectors, also known as Recruiters, you, work for the Reapers, or Servants, recruiting Mortals who will eventually move into the Recruiter position after their grace period, or their contract expires. Devil, Reaper, Recruiter, Mortal. Each Recruiter is responsible for collecting contracts for five mortals per year. As I have 200 Recruiters under me, this equals 1000 new Recruits each year from each Reaper. Each of those mortal contracts comes due at different times, there are so many Reapers working that there is never a shortage of Recruiters to call on." Grimm paused his pacing, the fog settled to a standstill, the room dropped another 20 degrees. Craig shivered as the chill went through his body. Grimm stared out the window as he continued. "However, the only one that can call up a mortal to be a Recruiter is the

One Most Evil himself, that's where it gets difficult for the Reapers to maintain their quota of 200, the Center of Evil will only refill the Recruiters annually. If a Reaper has any of his Recruiters fail to meet their quota, or suffer a breach of contract, then that Reaper needs to make sure he or she has the rest of the Recruiters make up the difference." Craig watched Grimm closely as he sat at his desk. Grimm still didn't move, deep in thought. "You are an exception. There have been very few exceptions during my time as a Servant."

Craig didn't take his eyes off of Grimm. "What do you mean exception?"

Grimm returned to pacing. "You were granted to me mid year. That is a rare occurrence. In the past there was usually a catch to being granted a new Recruiter mid year. It doesn't usually end well for the Servant."

Craig swallowed hard, feeling an icy lump in his throat. "What do you mean it doesn't end well?"

Grimm stopped and waved his arm through the fog, animating a slit throat. "The Servant usually pays with his soul tortured in Hell. I am trying to keep that from happening, that is why I need you to make sure you do not fail collecting the required six souls. If you fail, I fail, and that is not good for either of us."

Craig felt another cold blast of air, he was sure his nose would have frostbite as he sat with his hands between his legs, trying to keep his fingers warm. "How did I end up drawing the short straw to make up the difference?"

Grimm turned and started pacing again. Click, click, click. "You have opportunity."

Craig squinted his eyes at Grimm, trying to think of what he might be referring to. "What opportunity is that?"

210

Grimm stopped and stared at Craig, his eyes got bright as if he were drilling lasers through Craig's skull. "The Recruit you are going to have sign a contract has friends that would nearly beg you to sign a deal with them as well. How can you not see that?"

Craig looked away embarrassed. "You're speaking of Jake's friends?"

Grimm was still staring at Craig but didn't respond. Craig heard Grimm's voice in his head, dark and menacing, meaner than he had felt Grimm ever before. *'You fool, it was in front of you the entire time. You could have had the contract complete already. Go to them and get it done, do not delay, do not miss this opportunity.'*

Craig cowered back in his chair trying to escape the intrusion into his mind. "I will, I will do it right away."

Grimm was done with the conversation, he didn't waste any time with pleasantries. He vanished into a particle cloud that spun in a vortex and descended through the floor, a great swirling wind pulled the fog down with him and out of the room. Craig sat stunned at his desk, feeling the warmth return to the room, trying to soak in the sun through the window. He felt numb and foolish that Grimm had to tell him to hurry up and get it done. *'He's right, I could have had this done already, then I would have had more time to get another contract done. Only three weeks left!? How am I going to make it?'* Craig gathered his things, stuffing them into his satchel. He checked the contracts for Jake, as well as his blanks, *'I'll need to use these for the rest of the band.'*

23

Meet the Band

Craig had been feeling like things were getting out of control. He was jumping from one thing to another, trying to get contracts wrapped up without forgetting any important details. He had everything he needed now in order to get Jake's contracts completed. Craig walked the halls of the music production building, looking into each studio as he passed it, listening for the sounds of Adaptive practicing. He had been wandering for ten minutes without finding anyone related to the band. There were two other bands playing in different studios that Craig looked into. *'I'm sure I saw Jake's car in the lot this morning. There can't be too many unfortunate people driving the same type of beat up car.'*

Craig turned down a hallway he was sure he had never been down before, walking slowly down the hall, looking into each room as he passed by. At the third door from the end, Craig pulled the door open just enough to look in. Jake was sitting with the band at a couple of tables in the middle of a standard classroom. They had food spread out on one of the tables and a pile of notebooks on the other.

Jake heard the door open and looked over as Craig was looking in. He waved with an excited smile on his face. "Mr. Newman! Come in." Jake jumped up from his chair and went to greet Craig. "Good to see you, how are you?"

Craig reached out to shake hands. "I'm well, how are you?"

Jake shook his hand enthusiastically. "Great! We're just having some lunch and doing some writing, while looking over some of our older music, hoping to come up with some fresh ideas. Do you want some lunch?"

Craig smiled at the offer. "No, thank you. I came to get your signature."

Jake smiled so big he lit up the room. He jumped up, turning around in mid air, then ran circles around the room with his hands in the air like he had just won a sporting event. "Oh my gosh! This is the best day ever!"

Craig pulled both contracts out of his satchel. "I have your contracts right here." He stopped short, remembering that he asked Jake not to tell his band mates. They were all looking at Craig and Jake with questioning expressions.

Craig looked at them staring back at him. "I'm sorry everyone, I don't recall your names. The last time we met it was such a hurried introduction."

Jake took the initiative and started introducing everyone. "Craig, let me fix that." Jake went to each person in the room. "This is Edward, he is our bass player, also vocals, backup and some lead. This here is Christopher, he shares guitar duties, also sings back up vocals." Jake ran to the other side of the table, always full of energy. "This is Richard, he is our lead vocalist, he and I are in the production program together. Next up, last but not least, our drummer Jeff, no vocal duties for him, he is too busy flailing his arms and legs keeping us in time to worry about singing." Everyone laughed at Jake's description of Jeff.

Richard got up to shake hands with Craig. "Nice to meet you. What exactly did you bring?"

Craig held up the paperwork. "Yes, this. Well, I have been working on something for Jake and I finally have the final documents for him to sign. Jake, if you don't mind, I can fill them in on what it is."

Jake was so excited he could barely stand still. "Oh, Yes! Please do!"

Craig moved to the end of the lunch table and made a little room so that Jake could sign the documents. "These documents are contracts that I have been working on for Jake, that will also be very beneficial to all of the members of this band."

Everyone stirred a little, wondering what exactly Craig was talking about. Jake couldn't contain himself and ran another lap around the room yelling. "We got a record deal!" Jake ran yet another lap around the room with his hands in the air.

Richard's jaw dropped open. "What are you talking about? When did that happen?"

Jake ran over to Jeff and gave him a high five, then did the same for Richard. "We started talking about things a few weeks ago and Mr. Newman offered to help. We've talked a couple times since then. He even came to our last show."

Richard had a concerned look on his face. "Why didn't you tell us something was in the works?"

Craig could sense Richard was feeling a little left out. "Richard, it was at my suggestion not to tell everyone, I wasn't sure I would be able to come through with a suitable contract and didn't want anyone to get their hopes up."

Richard seemed satisfied and his concern changed to excitement. "This is surprising and amazing news."

Christopher raised his hand and spoke without waiting. "I think it would have been a good idea to bring us all into the loop so we could have a say in what the contract terms are."

Craig stiffened a little. He didn't expect to get resistance to getting a recording deal, then also remembered that Christopher was in the business program. "That is a good point. However, each of you are not tied to this contract, this deal was made for Jake. I'm sorry that I was not able to have each of you as an individual on the contract deal. You, as a member of this band will have to work out your terms of agreement with Jake."

Jake was still smiling and as happy as ever, not thinking that this would be a problem since the group had always gotten along and it never occurred to any of them how a record deal would get done. "Guys! We're good! This opportunity presented itself to me and I accepted it. It does put us in a position that we will all have to come to agreements, but I think we can work it out."

Craig looked around the room, taking note of everyone's expressions. They were a mixed group, but overall, accepting.

"Jake, let me show you the terms." Craig pulled the deal with In Motion Sound from the paperwork and laid it on the table. "A normal record label contract will only get the band ten percent of the proceeds to split amongst the members, while still requiring you as a band to pay for recording time and touring fees." Craig glanced around to see if everyone was following. Satisfied that everyone was engaged he moved on. "I was able to negotiate 25 percent proceeds, plus your studio time and touring costs are covered." That news was met with some happy chatter in the group. "The band can make any internal contracts as you see fit, the only catch is that Jake is the holder of the contract with In Motion Sound Studios, so as long as he is part of the band, you will have a recording contract."

Richard had a pleased look on his face. "Excuse me, Mr. Newman, who owns the music? I have heard that often the studio gets to keep the music."

Craig nodded. "I'm glad you brought that up. You, as a band own the music, so, as a band, you all should decide how to split that up, or who takes ownership if something were to happen with any one member of the group."

Jake had been standing off to the side of the lunch table the entire time Craig was going through the contract details. "This is amazing! Guys, I hope you're all happy with what we have here. I know we can come to an agreement on all the shares and how to split up any proceeds. This is good, really good." Jake looked around the room at each of his band mates. "Do you all agree?" Each of them gave some sort of affirmation. "Great! Craig, where do I sign?"

Craig turned to the last page of the contract and set a pen next to the line. "Right here."

Jake came to the table and scribbled his name without hesitation, dropped the pen on the table like he was dropping a mic. "And it's done!" Jake started a victory dance.

Richard noticed the second set of papers in front of Craig. "What are those?" Pointing at them.

Craig put a hand on top of the other papers. "These are for Jake, he is getting help with tuition for the production program."

Jake stopped his victory dance and came back to the table.

"I forgot about that. Can I sign that now?"

Craig slid the second contract in front of Jake, along with the pen. "Please do."

Jake scribbled his name a second time, this time setting the pen down without as much fanfare.

Craig gathered both contracts and his pen, putting everything into his satchel. "Thank you, Jake. I will get these filed with their respective agencies. You should be hearing from the school before next semester and I will set up a meeting for all of you at In Motion Sound to meet your producer, James."

"Jake was still giddy with the exciting news. Jeff, Edward and Christopher had turned their attention to each other as they discussed the new record deal and what that might mean financially for them. Jake seemed to be in his own celebratory world, dancing around the room like no one was watching.

Richard moved in closer to Craig to have a word. "Are there any more spots available for tuition assistance? I could really use the help. Both Jake and myself feel that it's very important to get educated about producing our own music. I think it will pay off down the road."

Craig looked Richard in the eyes and thought about Grimm telling him to get the rest of the band to sign a contract. *'Don't delay.'* Coming into the meeting, Craig blocked it out of his mind, he was already having guilt about Jake. *'He's too nice, I hate doing this to him.'* Craig withdrew into his thoughts, seeing Grimm hovering back and forth in the office, reaching into his mind, telling him this was what he needed to do. Craig snapped out of it. "You don't need a scholarship now. You've got a record deal."

Richard smiled. "I'm sure at some point the record deal will be much more financially lucrative than scholarship money, but I don't know when that is going to happen. If I thought the cash were going to start rolling in tomorrow, or shoot, even by the end of the semester, when I have to pay for the next block of classes, then I wouldn't be too concerned about it. But there are no guarantees that we will make any money. No one has heard of us. We still have to record a good record, then probably go on tour in order to get our names out there. That's a really long process before we'll start to see any return on our work. What happens if we stop getting along and I get booted from the band, then there's nothing. I mean, I trust Jake like a brother, but at the same time, I don't trust my brother."

Craig was astonished that Richard had all those thoughts about the record deal ready to go. *'He's thought this through.'* Craig's gut reaction was to pull back. Now he was really having reservations about getting another band member to sign a recruitment contract. "Well it would really only be tuition assistance, you would still have to pay."

Richard shook his head. "No, I think what Jake signed was more than assistance. I think it was a full scholarship."

Craig looked Richard in the eyes. *'How does he know that? I wonder if Jake said something to him about his deal.'* "Richard, really, this might not be the best thing for you to do."

Richard shook his head again. "I think it is the best route for me. I think this is exactly what I need. please look into it for me. I would be *eternally* grateful."

Craig looked at Richard's eyes. *'Why did he say it like that? What does he mean eternally?'* Craig couldn't do anything except agree. "I have another scholarship contract with me, but I can't say for sure that I will be able to push it through. I know that scholarship funds are running low, so I can have you sign it now and I will do what I can to make it happen." Craig pulled one of the three page stapled contracts from his satchel and looked at it before putting it on the table in front of Richard and spoke in a hushed voice. "Sign this on the last page, like I said I will do what I can."

Richard leaned over the paperwork and started to read it. Craig's palms started to sweat. *'If he sees the language buried on the last page he might tell Jake what he saw.'*

"Don't take too long, I don't want the others to see that I gave you this."

Richard glanced up at Craig with a stern expression, then went back to reading, flipping to the second page. As he turned to the last page, Jake made a lap of the room. Craig stepped in front of Richard in order to block the view of the paperwork.

"Richard, what are you doing?"

Richard looked over at Jake. "Just reading your contract to see what's in it."

Jake continued his lap of the room, stopping at Edward to chat about recording.

Craig stepped closer to Richard. "If you're going to sign it, do it now."

Richard grabbed the pen and neatly signed his name on the line with the date next to it. He flipped the papers over and slid them toward Craig. "Done. Will you let me know if this goes through?"

Craig grabbed the papers and put them in his satchel with the others. "Yes, either I will let you know or someone from admissions will contact you when registration opens up."

Richard turned and walked away to join the others. Craig stood at the end of the table, waiting to catch Jake's attention.

"I'm going to leave you all to your celebration. I'll get these turned in and let you all know when our meeting with In Motion will be."

Jake came over to Craig and gave him a big hug. "Thank you Mr. Newman. I really appreciate all you have done for us."

Craig let the hug happen. "You're welcome. I'll be in touch. See you soon."

Craig walked out before any of the others could corner him, feeling dirty that he just sentenced two boys to an eternity working for the Evil Master.

24

Signature

Tom tried to get Sue to understand what they were faced with multiple times. Finally, on the third attempt, she seemed lucid.

"Sue, I have to make this quick before you fade out again. If we accept this contract to get the medical help that can heal you, we will be making a deal with the Devil. I'm not just saying that as a figure of speech. We will have to work for the Devil in the future. Do you understand?" Tom waited and watched Sue's face. She had a look of tired concern, mixed with confusion. Tom jumped in again. "Just nod that you understand the words I said."

Sue blinked hard. Tom thought he saw her head nod just slightly.

"Just know, I'm not joking, it's real. Would you sign it to stay alive?"

Tom watched her intently. It took longer, but she blinked hard again with the slight head flinch. Tom squeezed her hand, his heart sank a little bit. He hadn't taken the time to consider how he would feel if she said yes. He just realized what that would mean. He was feeling deeply sad. He would be working for the Devil. *'Is that really what we want?'*

Tom saw Sue close her eyes, she was slipping away again. "Okay, I'll have Craig come over with the paperwork." He leaned down and gave her a kiss, then pulled the covers up, and left the room.

Tom went to the front of the house to see if Craig was home. It was dark outside, he was sure it was light out when he'd gone in to talk with Sue. He saw that the lights were on at Craig's house. *'Now's as good a time as any.'* Tom slipped out the front door quietly to be sure Sue wouldn't hear him. He walked to Craig's house quickly and knocked on the door with no hesitation, he had to get this done before he lost his nerve.

When Craig opened the door, Tom jumped right into it. "I was able to speak with Sue. She understood what I was telling her." Tom paused and took a breath. "She agreed, she wants to sign."

Craig waited for a moment, thinking Tom might have more to say. "Hello, Tom. Does that mean that is what you want to do?" Craig knew he was baiting Tom, giving him a chance to back out.

Tom didn't answer. He backed away from the door, his face had gone blank and pale.

Craig came out and guided Tom to the swing. "Here, sit down. You haven't really thought about it, have you?"

Tom sat and looked at Craig blankly, shaking his head. "No, not in any context other than saving Sue's life. I didn't consider what that meant down the road. You know, after. What happens then?"

Craig sat down next to Tom. "It's a heavy burden. I can't talk about it too much. The thing is Tom, once you're in this position, there's no getting out. You either do well, or your situation gets worse." Craig sat back for a moment, staring across the street into darkness. "I hadn't ever admitted to myself how terrible this situation is, how absolutely never ending this is."

They both sat in complete, dumbfounded silence for minutes on end. Both staring out into darkness, a perfect representation of the situation they found themselves in.

Tom finally broke the silence. "Please bring me the contract."

They glanced each other's direction. Craig gave him a head nod, then got up to get the paperwork. Craig returned moments later with the medical enrollment contract. He stood in front of Tom but didn't hand it to him right away.

"Tom, you don't have to do this. I know it's difficult to hear, but people die all the time. You'll die someday too, then you'll be together again, if you believe that kind of stuff."

Tom held his hand out for the contract. "I know you're right about people dying all the time. But how many of their spouses would save them if they had an opportunity? Please give me the contract."

Craig handed him the paperwork and a pen. "There's a line for each of you on the last two pages, I'll need to see you sign it, then you can have Sue sign it."

Tom thumbed through the pages until he got to second to last page. He opened it up and signed the top line without conviction, then flipped to the last page and did it again. Craig watched Tom look up at him as he finished.

"Now you can have Sue sign it, I will need it today so both dates are the same. Please use the same pen."

Tom got up from the swing and started to walk toward the

stairs. "Why don't you need to see Sue sign it?"

Craig looked Tom in the eyes and spoke in a low tone. "You belong to the Devil now, he sees everything. He will know who signed the other line."

Tom got a terrified look on his face. "What if she can't sign on her own?"

Craig pointed at the pen. "Put that pen in her hand, hold her hand if you have to help her sign it. As long as she is holding that pen, it will be valid."

Tom held the pen up and looked at it. "Craig, I can't do it alone. I don't think I can handle it emotionally. I may not go through with it."

Craig stiffened, he knew he had Tom's signature and that Sue's signature would count if she understood what the contract was. "Okay, I'll help you, we need to do it tonight, if you want to be together on this, you'll need the same date next to the signatures."

Tom shook his head, "She went to sleep a while ago. If we wake her up she may not be all there and understand what she is signing. Can't we wait till tomorrow and put today's date on it?"

Craig got an astonished look on his face, like he couldn't believe Tom could suggest such a thing. "Tom, you work for the Devil now. The One Most Evil, the Master of Darkness. Do you think it's a good idea to try and deceive him?"

Tom was sobered by the rant but certainly got the point. "No, I see what you mean. We should go wake her up and get her signature." Tom led the way over to his house. "Would you mind waiting here? I'll go see if she's awake."

Craig shook his head. "I don't think that's a good idea. If she wakes up lucid you may only have a few seconds to get her to sign."

Tom nodded. "You're right, come to the doorway and let me wake her." Tom went to the bedroom door and motioned for Craig to wait. Tom went in and turned on a soft light. "Sue, my love. Sue, wake up." It didn't take too long before she opened her eyes and focused in on Tom. "Sue, I have the paperwork to sign." Tom laid the paperwork in front of her, then put the pen in her hand. He helped prop her up against the headboard. "Can you sign this? It's the paperwork we talked about earlier."

Craig could see from the doorway that Sue looked very confused, and was starting to drift off as soon as Tom propped her up. Tom reached up and stopped her head from falling to the side.

"Sue, please wake up. We need to take care of this paperwork right now. We talked about this earlier today, you agreed that this is what you wanted."

Sue's eyes were open but she was squinting at Tom, she looked unsure again at what was going on. Tom reached over to her hand with the pen and pulled it over to the contract, drawing her attention to it. Tom helped her scribble her name on the second line, with the date.

"She was awake the whole time. She signed the papers, does that count?"

Craig looked at Tom expressionless. "It does count, you're as good as enrolled in the program , I'm sure you will be getting a call any day to get her admitted." Craig took the contract from Tom. "I'll get this submitted tomorrow."

Craig was feeling quite low. He knew that Tom didn't really want to sign the contract, but he was sure that Sue agreed to it, so he thought that's what she wanted. Craig didn't think she knew what was happening anyway, but he was selfishly disappointed that he wouldn't get to count her soul toward his quota.

25

The Investment

Craig was unaware there had been a career fair happening over the next two days, in the lower level of the Great Hall. As he entered the building, he noticed tables set up across the building where it was usually open space, used for general gathering and activities. These functions were not unusual, Craig had seen them pop up from time to time over the years.

As he ascended the stairs to his office, it occurred to him that this might be an opportunity to meet people with big dreams. He stopped half way up the stairs and looked over the edge at the booths being set up for a welding shop, mechanical HVAC, and IT groups. A sign pointed to a small lecture hall for real estate, medical sales, nursing, a plumbers union, electrical, automotive repair. As Craig glanced through the area nothing really made him feel like people would be overly anxious to get into these fields, but each of them should be considered. *'Maybe somebodies dream is to become a plumber and for some reason they just cant make it on their own. Poor sap.'*

Craig continued up the stairs slowly, still looking down at the meeting space. Just as he reached the top, he saw a woman walk out to adjust the sign pointing to the real estate seminar. He paused for a moment and decided to go back down the stairs. She didn't stay in the area long enough for Craig to catch up to her, so he followed the sign to the lecture hall to try and find her. He wasn't sure what he wanted to say, he just thought that there might be something that a young real estate professional could use to get ahead.

Craig found himself standing at the top of a set of riser seats, all empty, looking down on a podium and projector screen that read, "Welcome to Real Estate." He had lost her, he was sure she had walked into this room but she was clearly no longer there. Craig went back out into the hall and saw that the first presentation started in 45 minutes. *'I'll go drop my things at my office and come back.'*

As Craig returned from his office he was thinking about why he felt drawn to return to the lecture hall. *'She was very attractive, but I could really use another Recruit.'* He hadn't been attracted to someone in a very long time. Craig spotted her again as he walked toward the lecture hall.

She smiled at him as they approached each other and she reached out to shake his hand. "Hello, I'm Becky Tran. You don't look like you attend classes here."

Craig smiled back at her. "You're right. I'm actually a history professor here."

Becky was looking Craig in the eyes. "Are you interested in real estate?"

Craig had to think quick on his feet. "Oh, well, in a round about way. I have investor ties that work in real estate." He was blowing smoke now, just so he could stand there and talk to Becky, realizing that she was more attractive than he had noticed from a distance.

A smile spread across her face. "Are you going to attend the seminar?"

Craig shuffled his feet nervously. "I hadn't planned on it, I just noticed your signage and was curious what you had to offer. I am assuming this is more for those that want to pursue a career."

Becky nodded, but the look on her face was more than just business. "It is really just that, but if you have other investment questions I would be happy to answer them. Please, stay for the seminar, we should talk afterward."

Craig blushed. "I would like that."

He wasn't sure if she wanted to talk business or if she actually felt a connection and wanted to get to know him.

Becky Tran had been working in real estate for only five years. She had worked hard making contacts, trying to break into the commercial market. She knew that's where the real money was. She'd had small wins, here and there, brokered some decent lease options with downtown property management companies, made great contacts and trustworthy business partners along the way. Becky had her eye on a vacant building on the edge of the high-rent office district. The building needed renovation before any tenants would be interested in leasing the space. Renovation required capital, a building with eight floors that took up half a city block would require more capital than she could get with her short time in the industry

Becky motioned to the empty lecture hall behind her. "You're welcome to sit anywhere." She laughed, then checked her watch. "I hope I get at least a dozen people, it can be pretty hit or miss doing these things. I'll get going in about 30 minutes."

Craig checked his watch as well, not that he had a time concern, he was only thinking about what to do to fill some time before it started. "I would like that, I'll come back in a little bit and find a good seat."

Becky turned toward the stage and pointed at the front row. "I suggest that one down there, right in front of the podium. Would you like me to reserve it for you?"

Craig laughed. "Yes please. I expect front row treatment."

Becky laughed as well. "Very well, I'll see you in a little while."

Becky waited at the doorway, greeting students and passing out seminar fliers as they came in. Craig went back out into the main hall and wandered from booth to booth, saying hello and making small talk with some of the visitors, finding out what each of their businesses were about. When Craig returned to the real estate lecture, Becky was walking to the front of the hall. There was indeed a decent turn out, Craig casually counted about 20 people scattered throughout the seats, no one sitting up front. Craig went to the front row as instructed, he thought it was the only polite thing to do. As he went to sit down about four seats from center, he looked at the seat in front of the podium, it had a flier propped against the back of the seat, he could see something written on it. *'Oh, did she really put my name on that seat?'* He glanced at Becky as she was crossing the stage, she was looking at him and smiling. Craig got the hint and moved to the marked seat. Craig was felling a bit anxious. Not by the real estate lecture, he was barely listening to that. He hadn't had a woman notice him in so long, that he wasn't sure what was happening. Craig thumbed through the flier that his name was on and noticed on the back page that she had written her name and phone number on it for him. Craig quickly folded the flier and put it in his blazer pocket. *'What do I do?'*

Craig sat still in his seat, watching Becky go through her presentation, admiring how she spoke to the audience. She was very clear and confident and worked hard to hold their attention. She seemed to be somewhat successful in engaging them, as there were several people asking questions, interested in pursuing real estate as a career.

Craig's mind started to wander. *'Why am I here? With all that I have going and the dark things that I have to deal with, this is not the time to be chasing a woman.'* Craig looked up at Becky and smiled at her. *'But she is very attractive. Could it hurt?'* Craig looked away and glanced around the room. A few people had left but the engaged were still listening intently. *'Is she really interested in me? Or is she just naturally flirtatious? Maybe she just wants to talk business.'*

Craig's thoughts were broken by a smattering of applause. He snapped back to reality and looked around the room, noticing that people were gathering their things and leaving the hall. Craig stood as well, not sure what to do next.

Becky stepped off the stage and approached. "Well, are you ready to start your career selling real estate?"

Craig laughed. "I'm convinced, where do I sign up?"

Becky pretended to rush to get him some paperwork to sign. "Tell you what, I'll be your private instructor."

Craig felt his heart jump. "Now I really can't refuse. Would you like to go talk for a little while?"

Becky checked the time. "Yes, I do want to, I have about 45 minutes before I get to do this again."

They made their way out of the Great Hall to the courtyard and found a bench in the shade. Craig started the conversation as they walked. "Do you get anything for signing someone up to sell real estate?"

Becky sighed a little and sounded frustrated. "No, actually it feels counter productive, it dilutes the field to have more people selling but it's a requirement for the group that I work for. We each have to take turns recruiting new sales agents. The group makes more money that way. As they see it, more people can sell more property, but to each agent that means fewer properties per selling agent."

Craig nodded. "Sure, I get the economics of it. I heard you say you've been doing this about five years?"

Becky nodded and smiled. "Yes, I have. In that time I have studied a lot. More than my peers. I really want to get into the commercial space. Not just selling. Selling is very lucrative, don't get me wrong. But I want to get into development and renovation. I feel like I'm ready. I don't want to put it on hold any more. I am super confident in my plan and my abilities, I just need the financial backing to make it happen. Even if I could get a giant loan, which I probably can't because I have no collateral or commercial loan history, I know I could make it work." Craig was captivated by her enthusiasm. *Just keep talking, I just want to listen to you talk.'* Becky watched Craig's expressions as she spoke to him, she could see he was very engaged in what she was telling him. "I've worked really hard making contacts all over the city with property management groups, as well as property owners. I've watched the leasing trends over the last five years and I feel like it's the right time to move on this project."

Craig was sold on the idea, as well as Becky, if he had the money he would have pulled out his bank info right then. The breeze shifted slightly as they sat in the courtyard. Becky's perfume hit Craig like a truck to his senses. *'What is that? Good grief, she smells amazing!'* Craig's mind was distracted as they sat on the bench. There was an awkward silence for several moments as Craig's mind wandered. *'How do I go from this to asking her out? I don't think I have ever been this attracted to a woman.'* Craig shifted and glanced around the courtyard taking note of the students and staff crossing from one building to the next. He snapped out of his daydreaming head space. He needed to get her talking again.

"What's your plan? Sell me on your idea."

Becky was ready for this question, she had rehearsed what she would say 100 times if she ever got the chance. "I've got my sights on a property right on the edge of the high rent district, I want to buy it! Renovate and update the outside. Make it look like the class A buildings just down the street. Gut the inside and clean it all out. Make it a blank canvas. As long as the outside shines that will attract tenants and buyers. The inside will be tenant improvement anyway, a build to spec office opens more doors to potential tenants then a space that has an existing layout that may not work for everyone. I believe my plan will work and the investment will pay off within five years." Becky spoke with enthusiasm using her hands when she spoke. She only stood five feet 6 inches, thin build, with sandy brown hair. Her green eyes were intense when she spoke, looking directly at Craig as if he were the only person that mattered. It made Craig feel engaged like he never had before. Craig had never had a serious love interest but Becky was making him feel different. *'Sure now that I'm heading down an evil path, I finally meet a woman that's interesting to me.'* Craig was listening to Becky but the daydream was pulling his attention away from what she was saying again.

"What makes you think the market can support another class A office? Isn't that a huge gamble?"

Becky smiled and stared into Craig's eyes. "It's a risk for sure, the market is good now and occupancy is way up, but you never know what can happen in three months time. As we transform the building it could all fall apart, but everything is stable at the moment so now is as good a time as any. I just need the capital to get it started."

Craig was listening, but not. He was captivated by her smile, her eyes, her demeanor. He desperately wanted to get to know her farther. "I am interested in your journey. I think you've done your research and know what your talking about." Craig dug into his pocket for a business card. "Here's my card. I'm going to reach out to a friend of mine in the commercial investment field and let him know about your plan. I'll try to set up a meeting."

Becky's smile faded. "That concerns me, I just gave you my plan. What's to stop you from diving in and taking that property out from under me?"

Craig almost laughed at the thought. "I don't have the talent or the backing for that."

Becky watched Craig's expressions. "Maybe you don't, but you're telling me you have friends that probably do have that ability."

Craig nodded. "Yes, true, they probably have the contacts and ability to get it done, but then what? They are the money backing, not the types to get the building renovated, let alone occupied."

Becky's smile came back. "That's what I wanted to hear. Do you really think you can make something happen?"

Craig smiled and blushed. "I will give it my best effort."

Becky stood up, looking at the time. "I need to go get ready for my next presentation. Before I go, can I ask what you get out of helping me?"

Craig stood as well. "I don't get anything really. Maybe a small finders fee, but mostly I just really like your energy and enthusiasm for what you're doing."

Becky smiled and extended her hand. "Thank you for hearing me out, I hope to hear from you soon."

Craig shook her hand. "Do you have a card?" Becky gave him a sideways look. "What did you do with the flier I left on your chair?"

Craig laughed at himself. "Of course, thank you, I have it right here." He patted his blazer pocket and smiled. "I'll reach out as soon as I have some information for you."

Becky walked away as Craig stood, watching her leave, enjoying the view. *'I've really put my foot in my mouth now. I'm not going to want to send her down the path to the Controller of All That is Evil, but that's the only way I would be able to help. And she's so good looking, I wonder if she is always that friendly, she can't possibly be interested in me.'* He pondered asking Becky on a date, then shook his head as he walked away. *'Nah, that's not going to happen.'*

26

Transformation

The days seemed to be running together. Craig had a hard time remembering what day it was, he had to look at his phone for a reminder several times a day. It was Tuesday morning, typically one of Craig's easier days. Grade papers, lesson plan, read historical articles trying to keep up on current findings. He had to lecture in one class but that always seemed to be the easy part of the job.

Craig walked from the staff parking lot toward the center fountain. It was a very typical sunny day, about 65 degrees at 8 AM. He had Tom and Sue on his mind a lot lately, he'd turned the paperwork in to the medical admissions office a few days ago but hadn't heard from Tom since he signed the forms. Craig was wondering if anything had happened yet, if the admission office had contacted Tom. *I hope everything was done correctly, I know Grimm said it was right but you never know about those medical files. Something could change last minute and they would never tell you beyond your application had been denied. Even that, you would have to call them to find out. There I go being cynical again. Maybe I should call over there and check to make sure everything went through without problems.'*

As Craig ran these thoughts through his mind walking towards the fountain court, he felt a familiar cold blast of air hit his face and blow through his jacket. He stopped in his tracks and stared down at the sidewalk, not wanting to look up. He didn't feel like he had the energy to deal with Grimm today. Craig started walking again, slowly, still looking down at the cement in front of his feet, watching the tips of his shoes come and go. His shoulders were tense, he could feel the muscles twinge up his neck. Craig noticed something was different as he walked, the temperature felt much lower than normal. He glanced up from the sidewalk and saw Haley Turner walking toward the center court on an intersecting path, she didn't look natural, her gate was stiff. She was still a fair distance from Craig but it looked like she had no expression on her face, blankly staring out in front of her. Craig was distracted by Haley but quickly looked to his left when he heard footsteps. Brandon Wells was passing him on the grass next to the sidewalk, Brandon was walking with a purpose, headed straight for the fountain, he also had no expression on his face. Then Craig realized the grass was crunching under Brandon's feet. Craig gasped a little *'It's frozen!'* He stopped where he was, turned around and looked back where Brandon had come from. The grass was frozen white from the point that Brandon had stepped onto it. Craig slowly traced Brandon's footsteps back to where he was now standing, next to Haley in front of the fountain. As Craig stood behind them he noticed the sound of the crashing water had changed, it was starting to crack and sounded like small pieces of glass hitting the concrete. *'The fountain is freezing too.'* Craig stepped closer to the fountain, but still ten feet behind

Brandon and Haley. He could see the water in the bottom of the pool had hardened and the spray was coming down in ice pellets. Craig looked around the courtyard, scanning for Grimm.

"Grimm! What are you doing?!"

He turned all the way around but didn't see him. *'Where is everyone else? There aren't any student or staff in the courtyard. There's always people in the courtyard in the mornings.'* Craig moved in front of Haley, looking at her face. Her cheeks were rosy with blue undertones, Brandon's nose was white, nearly frozen. He stood in front of them, waving a hand in front of their faces, trying to get them to snap out of the trance they were in.

"Brandon! Haley! What is happening? Can you hear me? Do you understand what I am saying to you?" Both of them stood still, not giving any response to Craig. Again, Craig looked around the courtyard. There still weren't any other people and no sight of Grimm.

"Grimm! What is happening?"

Grimm appeared behind Brandon and Haley, coming into view from a dusty cloud until he was fully visible, hovering several feet above the sidewalk. "Craig, why are you so frantic? They are merely going through the transformation."

Craig stood still, captivated at the sight of everything freezing around the two statuesque students. He glared at Grimm. "What do you mean, the transformation?"

Grimm spread his arms out wide in front of him as if to show Craig all that he had to offer. "They are drawing all of the energy from the area, much like I do. They are transforming their beings into dark souls."

Craig shook his head. "Why is this happening? Did they do

238

something wrong?"

Grimm had lowered his arms but remained hovering behind the students, his light consuming cloak hanging majestically from his skeletal frame. "They have done nothing to violate their contracts, if that is what you mean."

Craig stepped back slightly, holding his hands out to the two souls that appear to be freezing to death. "Then what is happening? Why are they going through this?"

Grimm laughed, a demonic chuckle that boomed in Craig's ears. "Everyone that signs a contract goes through this, you just happen to be able to see it."

Craig's jaw was open slightly, astounded at what he was hearing and witnessing. "Everyone? I didn't go through this."

Grimm stayed still and silent for a few seconds as the fountain behind Craig stopped throwing ice pellets and everything went silent. "But you did." Grimm replied calmly. "Everyone goes through the soul transformation. It is where you become one with The Most Evil himself, it is your first encounter with dread and evil. He is within you after the transformation occurs, he controls you at will. You may believe that you still have control over your life, and over your actions, and the Evil One may choose to let you make a decision now and then, but ultimately, he controls all that you do."

Craig had a confused expression on his face. "I don't recall going through anything like this."

Grimm's tone didn't change, he was calm yet menacing, he seemed almost gleeful that these souls were being trans-formed. "They wont remember going through this either. They will return to their lives and from this point forward be rewarded with their hopes and dreams that you gave them in those wonderful contracts and have no memory of this moment in time. Just like you. The others that you have given contracts to will go through a similar transformation. Not necessarily at this location, but it will be just as fantastic as this, I assure you."

Craig's shoulders slumped as he gave in to another of Grimm's explanations of something he knew he couldn't change or do anything about. He turned and started to walk away, slipping slightly on the icy ground around the fountain. When he reached the steps of the Great Hall he looked back at the fountain, Grimm was no longer there and Brandon and Haley had started to walk their separate ways, presumably back to class. The fountain had started to make noise again, ice pellets fell to the frozen pool below as the temperature started to rise in the courtyard, the grass started to thaw, returning to the lush green color it was before freezing white. Craig went inside, feeling deflated again, knowing he couldn't do anything about these strange rituals that he kept learning about. *'I need a manual for this so I know what to expect. 'Reapers for Dummies' might be nice.'*

27

Too Late

Tom paced back and forth in his living room most of the morning, holding a cup of coffee that had gone cold. His mind wandered and raced from the present to the future and back again. *'What will I be asked to do when this is all over? I can't believe I actually signed a contract with the Devil. What have I gotten myself into? When is the hospital going to call? Maybe I should just call them and check on the paperwork. It's going to be okay, as long as we can spend our lives together it will all be worth it.'* He put the cup to his lips to take a drink, then realized it was cold. Tom went to the kitchen and set the cup on the counter by the sink, then forgot what he was in the kitchen for. As he turned around to go back into the living room, his phone rang in his pocket. He fumbled it and nearly threw it across the room as he pulled it out, flipping it around to try and swipe to answer.

"Hello!" A nice but very businesslike woman's voice came from the speaker. "Hello, Mr. Downy. This is Erin from NMSU Medical, I have your program admittance paperwork here, everything is perfectly in order and it looks like we need to get your wife Sue admitted as soon as possible. Would you be able to bring her in this afternoon? We have a spot available right away."

Tom fumbled for the words to respond. "Uh. Maybe, she can't get out of bed, she's too weak to walk. I'll try and figure out how to get her there."

Erin had anticipated that this might be the case. "We can send an ambulance and EMTs to pick her up. Then you don't have to worry about having to move her. We don't want any injuries trying to get her here."

Tom was relieved. "When can I expect them?" Tom could hear Erin tapping on her keyboard.

"I'll dispatch them now if you're ready."

Tom thought just for a moment. "Yes, I don't see why not. The sooner the better. Is there anything I should do before they arrive?"

Again Erin tapped on the keyboard. "Please make sure there is a clear path from point of entry to the home to where Sue is located. If you have pets, please put them in another room. Is the address clearly marked on you residence?"

Tom thought for a moment. "Yes, the address is visible."

Erin was silent for a moment. "Okay, Mr. Downy, the EMTs are on their way. They will arrive in 10 to 15 minutes. Do you have any questions?"

Tom thought for a moment. "Should I do anything to get Sue ready? She's probably sleeping."

Erin took a few moments to respond. "If she is receptive, you can tell her what is going to happen so she won't be surprised. Other then that there isn't anything else we need. I do suggest you bring your own vehicle to the medical center when the EMTs leave."

Tom hadn't considered that, he wasn't thinking that far in advance. "Okay, yes, thank you. I'll do that."

Erin jumped in again, seeming rushed this time. "Thank you, Mr. Downy, the EMTs will be there soon, I've got to take another call."

Erin disconnected the call without waiting for a reply. Tom looked at his phone, then put it in his pocket. He glanced across the front room of his home, from the front door then toward the back of the house where Sue was in the bedroom. Tom went and pushed the chairs in the front room a little farther out of the way, making a wide path all the way to the bedroom. He glanced into the room, Sue was still laying flat where he had helped her slide down from the headboard. *'I'll wake her just before they come in.'*

Tom went to the front room again, looked out the window, then at his watch. He started pacing the small front room, feeling very anxious. Again, he looked at his watch, only two minutes had passed. *'This could be the longest 10 minutes ever.'* Back to the front window for a quick glance then back across the room. Tom's anxiety was building. He went to the front door and stepped out on the front porch, thinking he might hear sirens. *'Are they using sirens?'* He stood on the porch not moving for several minutes. His brain shut down, not knowing what to do in the moment. *'Just take a breath, don't forget to breath.'* Tom repeated it to himself several times. *'Don't forget to breath, it's going to be fine.'* He wasn't sure why he was anxious over this. *'Is it because we are finally going to get help or is it the way we are getting help?'* He shook his head and looked at the floor as he started to pace across the porch and back. He heard a vehicle coming down the street, he spun on his heels to look. It wasn't the EMTs, he checked his watch

243

and went back to pacing. What felt like several minutes went by when he looked down the street and saw the ambulance on it's way, driving slowly. Tom gave them a wave as they pulled to the curb in front of the house. He went inside after he knew they had seen him to try and let Sue know what was happening.

He entered the bedroom quietly, not wanting to startle her. Once at her side he put his hand on her shoulder, giving her a slight jostle. "Sue wake up." He waited a moment watching her eyes. "Sue. We're going to the medical center, wake up for a moment." He waited again, but she didn't respond. Tom was getting concerned, she usually stirred at least a little when he nudged her to wake up. "Sue. Sue, wake up for a minute." He shook her a little more this time and got a bit louder. "Come on, Sue!"

The EMTs entered the room as he was nudging her again. "Mr. Downy, I'm Eric, this is Kyle. Is she not responding?"

Tom looked at Eric, worried. "No, she's not waking up. Usually she wakes up at least a little bit."

Eric moved closer. "Can you please step back? I would like to check her vitals."

Tom moved away from the bed and let Eric step in. Eric pulled Sue's arm and checked for a pulse. He glanced at Kyle, who went directly to the other side of the bed while pulling a respirator from his bag.

"She's not breathing, no pulse."

Tom backed up against the wall in horror, he put his hands over his mouth to muffle his own gags. Eric and Kyle were working to revive Sue but even to Tom it didn't seem to be working.

Eric looked at Tom while working, "Mr. Downy, how long

has she been down? When was the last time you know she was awake?"

Tom was still against the wall, holding back his fear. He realized Eric was talking to him. "It was before talking to the lady at the medical center. Maybe 30 minutes ago, maybe more."

Eric and Kyle exchanged glances, then stopped what they were doing. Eric checked for a pulse and listened for shallow breathing. Tom stood silent, holding his breath. Without saying anything, they both went back to work. Kyle went to the front room and brought in the gurney. They both worked quickly without saying many words, they put Sue on the stretcher and moved her quickly through the house, out to the ambulance. Tom wasn't sure what was happening as he watched them work, stunned that all of this was going on.

"Is she going to be okay?"

Eric responded as they strapped the gurney into the back of the ambulance. "We're going to do all we can Mr. Downy. Right now we need to get her to the hospital. I suggest you follow us there and you can get more information once she gets admitted."

Tom was in shock, he stood in his front yard and watched as they closed the doors and drove away. Tom snapped out of his shocked state as the ambulance drove out of sight with the sirens blaring. He ran to his car, fumbling for the keys in his pocket, dropping them as he pulled them out. He fumbled more as he got in the car, he put the car in reverse and backed out of the drive like a madman, without looking for other traffic, bouncing over part of the lawn and off the curb. He jammed the car into drive, then sped away, chasing the ambulance toward the hospital.

* * *

Craig came home late after spending most of the morning with Becky, he had to make up for that lost time for grading papers and lesson planning. As he pulled into his drive he glanced at Tom's house, noticing the car wasn't in the driveway. He didn't think much of it until he noticed the front door was open. There didn't appear to be any lights on in the house and it had been dark for over an hour.

Craig stepped out of the car and went directly to Tom's front door. "Hello! Tom are you here?!" He hesitated, listening for a response, then tried again. "Tom, Sue! Anyone home?" Craig stepped into the house and turned on a light. "What happened here?"

He looked around the room, noticing the furniture didn't look natural where it was placed, things were strangely pushed aside. "Tom?"

Craig walked deeper into the house, slowly moving toward the bedroom. He stopped outside the room, the lights were on, the bed was a mess, but no one was in it. He stepped inside the room just to check next to the bed, making sure Sue hadn't fallen to the floor. *'I hope everything is okay.'* Craig pulled his phone from his pocket and called Tom. He stood there, waiting for a connection. When it finally went through, all he got was voice mail. Craig disconnected and walked out the front door, closing it behind him. He went to his car and retrieved his satchel, then went to the front porch and sat on the swing. *'This can't be good.'* He tried calling Tom again but got voice mail. He started pushing the swing slowly back and let it fall forward. *'I'm going to wait it out.'* Craig pulled a history book from the satchel and started reading in the dim porch light.

Craig could feel a strain in his neck as his head leaned forward, gravity pulling him to the ground. He became conscious enough to feel the pain but couldn't move through it. He didn't open his eyes right away, he could hear the wind blowing and something else, a scratchy sound, it was warm too. *'I fell asleep in the dark it wasn't this warm.'*

His eyes popped open and he was shocked at the sight. There was a drift of sand piled up at the front of his porch, sand had blown over the porch and against the front of the house, blocking the door. It was still dark, but very warm outside. Craig stood up quickly, stepping forward to the rail, gazing out at the front yard, now covered in wind blown sand. He could only see to the edge of the yard where he thought the sidewalk should be, there was the start of a mound where the curb used to be, about three feet tall now.

Craig looked over to Tom's house and was hit in the face with a gust of wind carrying sand into his eyes. He closed them quickly, but it was too late. He turned around and tried rubbing the sand out carefully, with the wind at his back. After a minute, Craig was able to open his eyes again. He turned slowly, looking at Tom's house, shielding himself from the wind and another airborne attack of sand. Tom still didn't appear to be home, at least his car wasn't visible. Craig walked off his porch, struggling to walk in the soft sand across his yard. As he got closer to Tom's house, he could see it didn't look right, the porch rail was broken, one of the gutters was hanging down, a side window of the house was broken out. It looked like the paint was peeling, though it was hard to see in the dark, still trying to shield his eyes from the sand in the air. Craig stood between the two houses, surveying the damage for a few minutes.

"Tom! Are you home?!" He waited for any sign that Tom might be there but nothing came back to confirm.

Craig turned toward the street and trudged through the soft blowing sand as if it were snow. He fought through the piles at the edge of the yard, walking into the street with shoes full of sand. He looked both ways but couldn't see very far and soon realized that only a few of the street lights lining the avenue were working. It was very dim, especially with the sand whipping everywhere. Craig turned back to his house and could barely see the dim light on the porch, he realized the house was half covered with the blowing grit.

Craig shielded his eyes from the attack and tried to walk back over the piles of sand that were even taller now. He sank into the one at the edge of the yard, burying him up to his waist. He leaned forward and tried to crawl out using his hands and legs to get on top of the loose piles. His arms sank in as he tried to swim through the sand on his chest, half crawling, half swimming his way to the front porch. The wind had blown sand up the steps and piled up to the handrail. Craig was sinking but trying to move forward. Suddenly, he felt something hit his head, then something else on his back. A sharp pain went down his calf, making him gasp. He turned over and saw a giant black bird pecking violently at his left leg. He kicked and tried to yell but his throat was dried out, his mouth full of grit from the blowing sand. The giant black raven flapped up into the air right above Craig's face, sand fell from it's wings, dropping into his eyes. Craig tried to cover his face but it was too late. His eyes stung as the sand dug into his eyelids. Craig rolled over, brushing at his sand filled eyes, hoping gravity would help clear the particles. He tried to wipe the sand away with his sleeve and successfully cleared his right eye, yet he could barely see, it was blurry and scratched.

The raven was still there as Craig turned around, standing just out of reach, eyeing Craig with his head to the side, waiting for the perfect moment to attack. Craig noticed black shadows against the tan sky, circling above in the darkness, hundreds of shadows swirling in the wind, dotting the sky while the airborne sand blew in every direction. The raven jumped at him and pecked at his legs again, ripping through his pants. Craig jumped back, crawling on his hands and feet, slipping in the deep sand. The raven followed, jumping forward at him with it's wings spread wide. Craig scrambled away, managing to pull himself up onto the porch. He went to the door but with sand piled in front of it he couldn't pull the screen door open.

Several birds flew into the porch, flapping past his head, pecking his shoulders. Craig crouched down and tried to move away, back toward the swing, stumbling over piles of sand. He fell to the floor but continued trying to get away. He pulled himself up onto the swing, still attempting to cover his head from the attacking ravens. Craig let out a sad excuse for a scream but his mouth was so dry and full of sand, the sound didn't deter the attack of the birds. One after another took turns dive bombing Craig, trying to peck at his head and back, driving their beaks into his shoulders. Craig winced in pain each time an attack landed on his flesh. He waved his arms frantically, hoping to fend off the airborne assailants.

* * *

Tom found himself sitting at a green light. A few polite people honked their horns at him, but he didn't move. He couldn't focus through the tears, the lights ahead were just a blur of color. Other cars passed by as he sat wracked with pain, unable to focus on moving forward.

Someone not so polite laid on their horn from where they sat behind him at the light, it snapped him out of his fog just long enough to start moving again. Tom drove home without knowing what he was doing. He pulled into his drive next to his house and sat motionless behind the wheel with the motor still running for a good ten minutes. When his emotions subsided momentarily, he shut the car off and stepped out. The evening was quiet, the air was still, there didn't seem to be anyone around. Tom felt dead inside as he looked across the street at the park, the darkness hiding it's contents, the silhouette of the trees and skyline in the distance was all he could see. He looked at Craig's house, the porch light was on and he could just make out Craig sitting on the swing. Tom hung his head, tears started streaming down his face again. Seeing Craig just reminded him of the situation he was now faced with, alone.

Tom took a few weak steps towards Craig, then stopped, unsure if he was ready to speak to him. For Tom, the unspeakable had just happened, exactly what he didn't want to come true had done just that. Tom took a couple more steps, then a few more. He wanted to stop taking those steps but eventually he was standing on the porch, looking at Craig as he slept, slumped over on the swing with his mouth hanging open. Tom stood there for a minute without saying anything, not wanting to say anything, for fear he wouldn't be able to hold back the tears.

Craig started to jolt side to side, his legs twitching, sometimes violently kicking the air. Tom forgot for a moment why he was standing there as he watched Craig twitch and squirm. *'What is wrong with him?'* Craig's movements became more pronounced until Tom thought he might fall off the swing.

"Craig! Hey, Craig! Wake up!" Craig's movements lessened. "Craig, wake up!"

Craig jumped one last time then opened his eyes and let out a rough yell. Tom waited for Craig to focus in for a moment.

"It's too late."

Craig closed his mouth and tried to swallow, but it was so dry. "What?" It came out very horse and rough.

Tom paused again, waiting for Craig to pull himself together. "It's too late Craig. She's gone."

Craig furrowed his brow, still trying to shake off the vision of ravens attacking, quickly looking around for piles of sand and circling, giant, black birds. "What's too late? Who's gone?"

Tom jerked in a breath, feeling his loss attack his emotions, knowing he was about to lose it again. "Sue's gone. She died before I could get her to the hospital."

Craig's face lost all color as he watched Tom's expression distort with grief that can only be caused by losing the love of his life. Tom fell to his knees and sobbed, burying his face in his hands. Craig didn't know what to do or say.

His mouth was still dry but he choked out a few words. "I'm sorry, Tom, that wasn't supposed to happen."

They sat there together in the dark silence. Craig tried to console Tom the best he could, while knowing the worst was yet to come.

28

In Motion

Craig had made plans to meet Jake at In Motion Sound on Thursday afternoon. He wanted to make the introductions to James himself. He felt a kind of obligation to Jake since he was the one that set the deal up. Craig was sitting in his C Class in the parking lot of In Motion, waiting for Jake to show up. Jake wasn't technically late yet, but it was only two minutes to the meeting time. Craig had the air conditioner on while he waited but suddenly felt a colder than normal blast of air. *'Oh no.'* He looked around the car but didn't see Grimm. Within a few seconds the temperature quickly returned to normal.

Craig heard Jake coming from at least half a block away and watched as he pulled into the lot and parked uncomfortably close to his car. They both got out at the same time. Craig flinched a bit as Jake's door slammed shut.

"Hopefully you'll be able to get a new car soon with one of the royalty checks."

Jake had his usual big smile. "That would be so cool. I am pretty attached to that old rattle trap though. I may have to keep it."

Craig started walking toward the front of the building as Jake followed. "Have you ever been here?"

Jake looked up at the In Motion Sound sign on the building. "This old place? Yeah, I've been here." He laughed. "Just for like ten minutes until I found out it was too expensive for me."

Craig chuckled at the comment. "Well, you don't have to worry about that anymore."

They reached the front of the building and Jake stopped to take another look. "I never noticed how run down and basic this place looks. Are you sure this is a good place?"

Craig pulled the door open. "It is. Just wait till you see the inside."

As they stepped into the lobby the musty smoke smell hit them both. Jake stopped in his tracks. "Smells like all the shitty dive bars we've played music in, all at the same time."

Craig laughed. "You should feel right at home then." Craig walked in looking for Sarah, but she wasn't at her desk. He looked through the glass into the listening studio but couldn't see anyone there either. James's office door was closed. "Hello! Anyone here?"

Jake was peeking into the listening room. "That looks pretty nice. I hope the studios are good." Jake turned to check out some of the records on the walls.

Craig went to the glass doors and started to go in. "Do you recognize any of these bands?"

Jake nodded as he went from one album to the next. "Yeah, most of them. That's pretty impressive."

At that moment, James opened his office door and was startled to see someone standing there. "Oh, shit! Wow, you scared me!"

Craig chuckled. "Sorry about that, there isn't anyone out

front, so I wasn't sure what to do."

James looked over Craig's shoulder at Jake. "Oh, yeah, Sarah ran out for something, I'm not sure what it was. Is this Jake Ramsey?"

Craig turned to see Jake still looking at the albums on the wall. "It is. Jake, can you come over here for a moment?"

Jake turned quickly and came over right away, extending his hand to greet James. "Hello, I'm Jake, very nice to meet you."

James shook his hand without hesitation. "Hello, Jake. James Miles. I was very impressed with the demo Craig brought me, I hope there's more just like that waiting to be brought to life."

Jake smiled his big happy smile. "Yes, there is! I'm very thankful for the opportunity, Mr. Miles. I can't wait to start recording."

James held his arms out. "Well this is where it's all going to happen. I am excited to have you signed up. Would you like a tour?"

Craig was enjoying the interaction, they seemed to be hitting it off nicely. Jake looked over at Craig, then back at James. "Yes, I would, I was hoping to get to see the studio today."

James took a couple of steps toward his office. "Great! Give me just a moment and I'll show you around. Why don't you hit play on that remote on the table and I'll be right back."

James walked into his office as Jake reached for the remote and pressed the play button. Sound started filling the room instantly. Jake's face lit up as he recognized the intro to one of his songs. The volume was building as the seconds passed. Jake seemed to be enjoying the sound quality as he closed his eyes, letting the music wash over him. Craig watched him for a moment as Jake stood facing the center of the room, motionless. He looked at the open doorway of James's office. James was standing in the doorway, facing the center of the room as well, with his eyes closed. *'Is this how you experience music the best?'* Craig glanced from James to Jake, then decided to join them. He closed his eyes. *'What am I missing? It seems like rhythmic noise to me.'*

A blast of cold air hit Craig without warning and he popped his eyes open. Jake and James were still in their same positions, listening to the music but it had changed, it was rumbling and cracking, not as rhythmic as before. The lights flickered and a louder rumble emanated from below the building. Craig could feel the floor vibrating under his feet. The room got noticeably colder after the floor shook. The lights flickered again, this time turning off. Craig saw a red-yellow glow coming from the opposite side of the room, behind one of the sofas. A heavier rumble followed by a boom and a crack that sounded like wood splintering. It sent a shiver through Craig.

Jake and James hadn't moved. The room got colder with yet another cracking sound. The wall across from Craig split from bottom to top, letting in a rush of steam and black smoke. The red glow got brighter with orange and yellow undertones. The smoke was thick, making the air heavy and hard to breath. An ominous weight pressed down on Craig, the feeling of evil surrounded him. The rumbling sound was growing from deep within the earth, vibrating the building with a low bass that Craig could feel in his chest.

Another explosive crack made Craig recoil, stepping backward. The center of the room filled with flames as the floor opened up, allowing the extreme heat from molten lava fill

the room. One of the sofas and a table burst into flames.
The red hot glow lit up the faces of James and Jake as they
stood motionless on each side of the crater in the center of
what used to be the listening room. Craig held his arms
in front of his face to shield him from the heat. He had
never experienced such extremes, going from sub freezing
temperatures to boiling lava in mere seconds.

The room was nearly split in two pieces. Craig could
see through the roof, the darkness outside was dotted with
circling crows and ravens, he could just hear them screaming
at each other over the rumbling earth below. The yellow and
orange glow showed their black bodies in the dark sky. Craig
could see through the split walls into the street behind the
building. Smoke obscured his sight as it rose from the growing
crack in the floor. The building shook again, this time harder
than before, causing sections of the walls and floor to fall into
the fiery depths below. The glass wall behind Craig shook,
warping the glass, Craig could hear it flex, bowing in and out,
making a distorted sound before straightening back to its
original position.

Craig nearly lost his balance as the shock waves traveled
through the floor, he had to step back again as the crack in the
floor grew into a crevasse. The flooring was splintering and
coming apart at his feet, pushing him nearly to the wall. The
burning sofa and table tumbled into the opening, along with
another large section of flooring. With all the debris falling
into the molten earth, the smoke and flames rose from below,
searing heat scorching Craig's face. He tried to move farther
away but there was no more room to retreat.

The once icy cold room became an oven as the lava started
to bubble and spew into the air, landing on what was left of

the floor, some of it making it out of the roof into the night sky. The building jolted again, Craig fell to his knees, the glass wall behind him shattered, sending millions of glass shards scattering across the room and into the fiery pit. More lava was spit from the chasm in the floor, through the roof, hitting parts of the ceiling. Roof structure blew off the building with tremendous force. Smoke and flames followed the eruption out the top of the building obscuring Craig's view of the sky and the circling birds above.

A giant figure of billowing smoke and half cooled lava began to rise from the deep. The earth was shaking, the broken walls crumbled even more.

Craig was trying to take cover from the heat but there was nowhere to hide. Jake was standing frozen near the doors, his feet uncomfortably close to the opening in the floor, while James was by his office. Their faces turned bright red as they burned from the extreme heat. Craig didn't know if Jake was aware of what was happening. The figure was growing larger and larger from below the building, Craig couldn't completely tell what it was. As the figure rose up to the height of the roof, Craig thought it looked like a feathered, fire breathing T-Rex demon.

Screaming sounds he couldn't describe came from within the giant being. Craig looked to his sides and through the broken glass to the lobby, he saw Grimm hovering nearby, watching the event unfold. Craig spun around and faced him. "Will they survive?!"

Grimm didn't speak out loud, Craig heard it in his mind. *'They will be fine. It's their transformation.'*

Craig spun back and looked at Jake, then at James by the office door. The beast was still rising from the gaping hole in the earth below the floor, its skin fluttered with tinder of burnt earth, shimmering like diamond covered feathers in the sun. *'Wait! What do you mean they?'* The beast roared, then screamed, billowing fire and smoke past its massive teeth. *'They are both going through transformation?'* Craig did a double take from Grimm to the beast and back. *'Who recruited James?'*

Another explosion rocked the remainder of the building, debris crumbled from the walls, some of the broken ceiling fell into the opening, causing flames to erupt around the great fire breathing beast. Grimm seemed to be unfazed by all of it, his robe fluttering from the blast but otherwise he hovered, unmoved. *'He signed the contract that you presented for Jake, did he not?'* +

Craig nodded *'He did. So, I get credit for James?'*

The beast let out a huge trail of fire from between his teeth, leaving the area thick with smoke. Grimm let out a thunderous laugh. *'No! Not at all! Had you made that your intention before he signed the contract you would get credit. Now it is too late, he is bound to the agreement and will by my soul to reap.'* Grimm needed the extra soul for his own quota, with now just one more left to fill the backlog.

Craig felt betrayed. He watched as the beast started to descend back into the earth. The transformation was almost complete. He wasn't sure how this building was going to look once this was finished, but he didn't want to be a part of this process any longer. He backed through the broken glass wall, keeping an eye on the beast as flame and lava shot from below the floor. Grimm didn't try to stop Craig from leaving so he continued out to the street, then on to the parking lot. He watched the building for a few more minutes as smoke and flame rose from the opening in the roof. The giant black birds still circled in the sky over the building. Craig looked around at the surrounding streets, not a single other person was nearby to witness the event. He had seen enough, he felt bad for James, he didn't know that was going to happen. Craig sat heavily into his Mercedes, realizing his exhaustion. He rubbed his face several times, feeling the tender, burnt skin as his hands went over it. He glanced in the mirror, looking for wounds, but couldn't see anything in the dim light.

Craig started the car and sat still for a little longer, gazing at the glow over the building, watching the smoke rise into the night sky. He checked again for any witnesses in the area as he drove away, glancing in the rear view mirror at the glowing flames as he drove toward home. Once the building was out of sight, Craig managed, with great difficulty, to keep his eyes open. Eventually he made it home, struggling to put the evenings events behind him, hoping his dreams wouldn't reflect what he just witnessed.

29

In The Dark

Craig hadn't stopped thinking about his time with Becky for more than a few minutes since they had sat in the courtyard talking. He was even more captivated by her now, after thinking about her for three days. He sat at his desk searching for the appropriate lending institution to recommend for her needs. He discovered it was going to be a little more difficult than he thought to procure the appropriate paperwork to secure a loan of such a large amount. *I'm for sure going to need the special Grimm paperwork on this.'*

After an hour of clicking through a hundred different financial web sites, Craig recognized a name on one of the pages. Rick Spencer, Commercial lending. The photo matched the Rick Spencer he remembered. Rick was the financial advisor at NMSU several years ago. Rick left the university to follow a different career path. *'This must be where he went.'*

Craig pulled out his phone and dialed the number next to Rick's name. He got a bit nervous as the phone rang in his ear.

"Rick Spencer, how can I help you?"

Craig stuttered a moment. "Hello, Rick, this is Craig Newman, we used to work at NMSU together. Do you happen to remember me?"

Rick did remember. Craig went on to tell him about his friend Becky and that he was hoping to get some help procuring financing for this big commercial project that she wanted to take on. Rick was very helpful and laid out all the steps and pre qualifications Becky would have to go through. Craig was slightly overwhelmed by it all, but figured that with the Grimm paperwork he would be able to make it happen. Rick agreed to send over the paperwork for review and have Becky complete it all. Craig thanked him and let him know they would come in and see him once it was completed.

It was already mid day and Craig hadn't done any of his actual job. He sent Becky a quick email, letting her know he had some good news and that he should have some paperwork for her by tomorrow afternoon. After hitting send, Craig gathered his things, stuffing them into his satchel, then rushed across campus to his class, trying not to be late.

After an hour and a half spent lecturing his class on Roman idealism, losing all train of thought about Becky and Grimm to his love of history, Craig found himself craving a nice sit on the porch with a cold beer to help wash the stress of his week away. He gathered everything from his class that he would need, stuffing it into his bag, and proceeded out the door toward the staff parking lot. Suddenly, he was doubled over at the waist, it was too painful to stand upright. Craig threw his satchel and sport coat into the back seat and sat in the drivers seat with the engine running, waiting for the oven to cool off from sitting in the blazing sun. Craig found himself feeling anxious, his heart racing and his chest tight. A piercing pain shot through his left shoulder into the center of his body. *'Am I having a heart attack?'* Craig reached for the door handle of the Mercedes, thinking he should try to get out of the car and seek help. He felt the hot metal handle in his hand and pulled. Nothing happened, it didn't pop open. He pulled again to no avail. Confusion raced in his mind as another piercing lightning bolt went across his chest. He gasped at the pain. *'What do I do?'* Craig pulled the hot handle again and leaned his shoulder into the door, trying to put as much effort into it as he could. It didn't open. A third piercing pain shot through him again, this time from his chest to his spine. Craig stiffened up, pushing his feet into the floor. His right foot mashed the accelerator, the cars engine spun out of control. Everything went black and he felt a blast of cold air on his entire body. His pain turned into fear as he anticipated Grimm being behind his sudden piercing pains. *'He's coming for me! He wants to take me now!'*

Craig grabbed at the door handle once more, giving everything he had to pushing the door open. To his surprise, the door opened easily this time and he fell from the seat, onto the scorching hot pavement. Craig scrambled to his feet, pain still in his chest, he grasped at it with his right hand, trying anything to relieve the tension. He felt another blast of icy cold air hit him from behind. Craig was scared and started to move away from the car, still grasping his chest. Craig's pace quickened as the chilly air followed him. *'I have to get away from here, I can't let Grimm take me now!'* He was almost at a jog moving across the parking lot. Craig ran toward a building near the athletic center but he didn't recognize it. *'Where am I? What building is this?'*

Craig looked behind him quickly, trying to see if Grimm

was chasing him. He didn't see Grimm but the cold blast continued to pound his skin, blowing through his clothes. Craig found a door at the side of the building and pulled it open, running inside. He took four quick steps into the dark room before the door slammed shut behind him. The room was void of light, the echo of the door slamming still ringing throughout the area. Craig stepped backward a few steps, thinking the door would be right behind him and he could retreat back into the sunlight. One more step with his arm stretched out behind, he touched what should have been the door and stopped. Craig turned around and felt for the panic bar of the door so he could escape. There wasn't one, there wasn't even a door.

"Where did it go?" He said out loud in a panicked tone, his voice echoing in the darkness.

Craig slid to the side, still with his hands on the wall, thinking he must have just moved to the side slightly and missed the door. *It's so dark, where is it?'* Craig was panicking, his breath was rushed and short, the pain in his chest was still there and growing more acute. After a few steps to the left he reversed and went to the right, Nothing! Not even a seam where the door should be.

Craig froze. It was bitter cold in this dark room. He turned around and leaned his back against the wall, staring out into blackness, hoping his eyes would adjust and he would be able to make out any shapes or dim light that he could move toward. His breathing was short and ragged, it was painful to try and take a deep breath. Craig started to slide his back against the wall with his hand leading the way, feeling for a light switch or an opening, a door handle, anything. There were no sounds in the room other than the echos of his feet shuffling across

263

the floor. His ears were ringing and cold, his nose started to run from breathing in the cold air and adrenaline from trying to find a way out.

Craig followed the wall for a very long time, anticipating a corner or doorway to be there somewhere. He stopped and stared into the void again, trying to focus into the blackness. Craig held his breath and listened intently for any movement. He couldn't hear anything, not even air moving from a ventilation system. He let out a gasp when he started breathing again but he had managed to stop hyper ventilating in his attempt to regain calmness. The pain in his chest reduced to a mild stabbing feeling right over his heart.

Craig stepped forward, leaving the comfort of having the wall at his back. He reached his hands out in front of himself so he wouldn't run into anything he couldn't see. After several steps forward, the echoes of his footsteps were drowned out by a rumble Craig could feel in his feet. He turned around and took several quick steps back to where he thought the wall should be. His arms still stretched out in front of himself, reaching for the wall. It wasn't there. He took a few more steps, still nothing. The rumble got louder, Craig tried again to find the end of the room, reaching for the wall. He couldn't find it and again the panic rose in his chest, causing even more pain.

Craig tried to run but stumbled when the room shook. A massive rumble followed when he hit the floor. "Oof! What is happening?"

Craig blinked hard, trying again to get his eyes to adjust to the black. As he started to get up, he felt something crawl across his hand. He scrambled to his feet right away, shaking his hand violently and brushing at it with his other hand to make sure whatever it was he felt wasn't on him any longer. Craig took several steps backward, his heart racing in his chest, then stopped and listened again. Finally, a sound from far away, clicking, tapping, scurrying. *'What is that?'* It was getting louder, closer. Something was coming toward him.

"Who's there? What is that?" Craig didn't expect an answer but it made him feel better to say it out loud, so at least he knew he could hear his own voice.

The tapping sound was all around him now. As Craig moved again, trying to find a way out of the room, a crunching surfaced under his feet. Whatever it was crawling on his hand was now covering the floor. The critters crunching under his feet echoed across the room. He stopped a moment and tried to calm his elevated breathing once again, he could hear the clicking and crawling of the critters on the floor. They were crawling onto his shoes and up his pant legs.

Craig kicked his legs, trying to remove the creepy crawlies from his feet and legs. Each time his foot hit the floor it crunched as he smashed the hard shells of the bugs. Craig moved yet again, searching for a way out, holding his hands in front of himself, hoping not to run into anything yet wishing that he would at the same time. His arms brushed something scratchy. Startled, he jerked his arm away. Then, curious, he reached out to find what he had touched. He moved his arm side to side, sure that he was in the right spot. He couldn't feel anything where he thought it should be.

Craig started moving in tight circles, crunching critters with every step. Suddenly, the scratchy object was there again, brushing against his face. He reacted violently, pulling away and grasping at whatever it was. Finally, Craig got hold of the object. A rope, heavy and rough. At least an inch thick, suspended from above. Craig could feel the course fibers protruding from its hemp core. He ran his hand down toward the floor but the rope stopped before it touched. Craig kicked his feet again, removing critters that had climbed onto his shoes. He ran his hands up the rope toward the ceiling as high as he could reach. There was nothing there that he could touch. He reached up above his head with both hands and gave a healthy yank on the rope. It gave a little but didn't come down. He gave it another tug, not as hard this time. Something clicked from above, the rope gave way a few inches.

Craig could hear a whirring sound from high above, then he felt a rush of fresh air. The creatures on the floor started to rattle as they scurried away from Craig's feet. He pulled the rope a couple of quick tugs with one hand, curious what was happening. More noise came from above, it sounded like gears turning.

Craig looked up into the darkness, as the floor below his feet gave way. He felt nothing beneath his feet for a split second as he instinctively grasped for the rope but came up empty handed. He felt a searing pain on the back of his head when it hit the floor as he fell through the trap door he had been standing on. The weightless feeling struck him before the realization that he was falling. He started grasping and flailing his arms and legs. His heart rushed, he could feel his stomach in his throat as he tumbled over backward. Panic filled his brain. *'What do I do?'*

As he flipped over, wind hitting his face, whistling past his ears, his eyes wide open searching for light before his free fall came to an abrupt stop.

The quote, "It's not the fall that kills you, it's the sudden stop," passed through his consciousness. *'When will it end? I'm going to die.'*

Moments went by, turning into minutes, then hours, still he fell in this cold dark space. He never touched anything during his decent. Craig became calm and relaxed during the fall.

Then nothing. Silence. Craig's consciousness came back to him slightly. His eyes were closed, breathing normal. He could see light on the other side of his eyelids. Gradually, the sound of birds crept into his ears. He moved his arms, they were very heavy, but he felt the soft sheets of his bed under his hands. His body was exhausted, as though he had used every ounce of energy available the day before and he hadn't yet recharged his batteries.

Craig struggled to open his right eye, peaking out a tiny slit, careful not to let in too much light. He was in his room, it seemed to be morning, the room was dimly lit from the sun streaming in from behind the shades over the windows. The covers felt good over his tired body. He didn't want to move. Craig struggled to recall what day of the week it was. He felt hung over, foggy in his brain. *'Have I been out drinking? I haven't done that in years.'*

Craig strained to get his legs over the side of the bed and sit up. *'What day is it?'* He looked at his phone on the bed side table. *'Friday, 9AM Six messages from Becky Tran!'* His thoughts went to his conversation with Rick on Wednesday. *'I wonder if those papers have arrived. Wait! It's Friday?! The last thing I remember was wrapping up class on Wednesday. Have I been out an entire day?'*

Craig opened the messages from Becky. The first message was received Thursday, 10AM. "Just checking in. Wanted to know when we can meet and look over the paperwork. Excited to get moving on the project." The next message at

1PM. "Did you get my message? It's not like you to not reply." Three more text messages wondering where he was, followed by "Please call me." at 10PM.

Craig texted her right away. "Sorry I didn't get your messages. I seem to have lost an entire day. I'll check on the documents and let you know."

Craig proceeded to fumble around, trying to get moving and shake off the heavy body feeling. He tried and tried to recall what happened to Thursday but nothing would come to him. *'Where did that time go? I feel like I was drugged.'* He shook his head and got in the shower, trying to wash off the strange feeling. After showering and making coffee Craig went to get his satchel so he could check his email, hoping to have something from Rick Spencer about the financing.

Craig stopped at the front door where he usually set his satchel and keys. He stared blankly at the spot on the floor where it should be. He turned and looked around the room. Nothing. A slight panic rose in his chest as he went to the bedroom and checked for his bag. Not finding it there, the panic grew. *'Not only did I lose a day, I've lost my bag!'* He went back to the front door and stepped out on the porch, intending to go check his car. As he pushed through the screen door he saw his bag sitting on the swing, tipped over, the contents half spilled out onto the seat. Craig stepped quickly to it, then glanced around the area to check if anyone was around. Tom's house appeared to be empty, no one on the sidewalk or in the park nearby. Something wasn't right. He looked around again but couldn't put his finger on what was missing.

He turned his attention back to his bag. As he started sliding things back into the pockets he took inventory of the items. His laptop, textbooks, student papers, a few blank contracts.

Everything seemed to be there, plus a yellow envelope. Craig picked it up, carefully inspecting it. He couldn't remember this package. His name was hand printed on the outside.

Holding the envelope, Craig looked around the neighborhood again to see if anyone was watching. Then it hit him. His car was missing!

"Damn!"

Craig dropped the envelope on the swing and ran down the steps and across the yard, hoping he had just pulled the car unusually deep into the driveway. No such luck. Craig stood barefoot in the drive, dumbfounded that his car wasn't there.

He couldn't remember the previous day, or why his bag had been sitting on the porch swing, looking like it had been gone through but with nothing missing. *'I can't explain any of this.'* He hung his head for a few moments, then slowly went back to the porch.

Craig sat on the swing, rubbing his face with his hands, hoping to regain some memory of what happened. After several moments and realizing it wasn't coming to him , he picked up the yellow envelope and pulled open the metal tab. He peeked in as if something scary might be inside. Just papers, bound together with an industrial sized clip. Craig pulled the packet out. It was heavy, he guessed 60 pages or so. He flipped it over so he could read the front page. *'Commercial financial loan documents.'*

"Oh!" Craig exclaimed. "How?" He was baffled, happy to see the documents, but having no idea how they got there was concerning, plus his car was missing. *'How am I going to find that?'*

30

Where Did the Time Go

Craig was stumped by the loss of time but decided to continue getting ready and hoped some clues would show up so he could piece together the missing day.

He pulled his phone out and called Becky. "Craig! Where have you been? I was concerned about you. Well, I was mad at first because you didn't text me back, but then I was concerned."

Craig laughed a little at her reaction. "I honestly don't know what happened to yesterday. I woke up this morning feeling like I was drugged. I had some really weird dream and my car is missing."

Becky gasped. "What? Your car is missing? Or was your car missing in your dream?"

Craig laughed again. "My car is really missing. I have no idea where it might be."

Becky was shocked. "Oh my, Craig! What can I do to help?"

Craig was getting the feeling that Becky might really be interested in him. "I was hoping you could pick me up? I have the papers for you to fill out for the financing."

Becky almost shrieked with excitement. "You do? You're a miracle worker! You bet, I can come get you! We can go get some coffee and talk about it. Send me your address and I'll head right over."

Craig was surprised by her excited reaction, holding the phone away from his ear because she was very loud at that moment. "Great, I really appreciate you taking the time. I'll text you the address. See you soon."

Craig didn't wait for a reply. Disconnecting the call, he immediately sent his address to her. Craig took his satchel inside the house and emptied it out on the kitchen table. He looked at everything that was there, trying to decide if anything was missing. Laptop, blank contracts, car keys, student papers, history book and the financial documents that weren't there before. *'Nothing missing. Actually more documents than what I had before. How did these get in there?'* Craig carefully put everything back in his bag and went about getting ready to go.

Within minutes, Becky arrived. Craig saw her pull up to the curb in front of the house, so he grabbed his satchel and went out to meet her. Becky had stepped out of the car by the time Craig got to it.

"Good morning, Craig. I hope you're feeling well. It seems like you've had a rough couple of days."

Craig didn't know how to great her, so he leaned in for a friendly, courtesy hug. Becky accepted it but didn't seem too satisfied by it. "I don't feel too bad, I just can't remember what happened over the last two days."

Becky wanted a better hug but shrugged it off as Craig was going around the car to the passenger side, completely clueless that Becky wanted more. "Do you know how you got home?"

271

Craig sat heavily into Becky's Lexus sedan. "I don't have any idea, I just woke up this morning feeling quite awful. I feel better now, just very confused about what happened."

Becky slid gently into the drivers seat, buckled in and looked over at Craig. "Where should we go first?"

Craig was struggling with the twisted seat belt, that wasn't twisted until he touched it. "I think we should go to the college first. That's the last place I remember being, so maybe my car is there."

Becky waited for the click of Craig's belt, then drove them to the staff parking lot. "Where do you usually park?"

Craig pointed to a row near the covered walkway by the music center. "It's always over there."

Becky drove through slowly, looking at each of the cars. "Do you see it?"

Craig shook his head. "No, it's not here. My other thought is that it might be at Winding Tree where my dad lives. Can we go there?"

Becky stepped on the accelerator. "Yes! Let's go! Just tell me which way."

Craig gave careful instructions, guiding Becky to the parking area in front of Winding Tree where he normally parked. "There it is!" Craig pointed out his Mercedes, baking in the mid morning sun.

Becky parked next to Craig's car. "That's wonderful, it looks like everything is okay with the car."

Craig popped the door open. "I should go inside and check on my dad, maybe he has an idea what happened. Will you wait here for a few minutes?"

Becky was a little disappointed. "Yes, I'll wait. Don't forget we were going to get coffee."

Craig stood up, noticing it was getting hot already. "Okay, I'll only be a few minutes, then we'll go. You might leave the AC running, it's hot already." Craig left Becky in the lot as he went inside to ask his father if he had seen anything unusual in the last two days.

Craig glanced at the dining hall as he walked past, not many residents at the tables this time of the morning. As he walked down the halls toward Mikes room he thought he should keep an eye open for Glen. *'I just don't trust that one.'*

Reaching Mike's door, Craig tapped on it lightly. "Dad? You home?"

Mike was making himself tea when Craig arrived. "I'm here, come on in." Craig entered the small apartment to see Mike smiling at him. "Craig! I am very happy to see you! I wasn't sure I was ever going to see you again after that last meeting."

Craig was taken aback slightly. "Really? To be honest I don't remember any of it. I didn't even know my car was here until a few minutes ago."

Mike held up his mug. "Would you like some tea?"

Craig waved his hand. "No, thank you. A friend of mine, Becky, is waiting for me, we're going to get coffee in a few minutes. I just wanted to come in and check on you and ask if you knew why I left my car here? Better question. What happened when I was here last?"

Mike squinted at Craig. "You don't remember any of it?"

Craig's eyes got a little wide. "No. I woke up in my bed this morning after having another really creepy dream and found my satchel out on the front porch, my car missing and no memory of where I was yesterday."

Mike walked to his chair and set his mug down before collapsing into his recliner. "Well, you were here Wednesday afternoon. You seemed a little shook up and not quite yourself. Not that you've been much of yourself lately anyway. I didn't get to talk to you. I heard you and that Reaper fella you call Glen having an argument. I stepped out into the hall and from what I gathered, Glen didn't like how much time you were spending here at the home. He felt that you were trying to do some recruiting in his territory. Glen got heated during the discussion when you were trying to explain that you were only here to visit me. I was concerned at first when you pointed at me from down the hall that Glen was going to come after me but it was like a train wreck, I couldn't look away."

Craig was jaw dropped, not remembering any of this confrontation. "I had a run in with Glen a while back where he told me never to come back. I guess he decided enough was enough. Did Glen see you standing there watching?"

Mike thought about it for a few seconds. "Yeah, he glanced my way, pretty sure he saw me watching but he went right back to yelling at you. He did bring up the fact that he's upset that I won't give in to him and let him reap my soul." Mike sat back and thought about that for a moment. "I just remembered that he brought that up. Anyway, as the yelling got pretty loud I noticed that your eyes turned black and the temperature in the building dropped considerably. I could see your breath coming out of your mouth as you were telling him you had no interest in the residents of this home. Then I noticed that it got dark outside all of a sudden. The windows down the hall went dark and I looked back in my room and noticed that it was dark out my window as well. I got a little spooked by that but, again, I couldn't look away."

Craig moved over to the sofa and sat down. "What happened then? Was that it?"

Mike sipped his tea. "Oh, no, that wasn't it at all. It was like a storm blew into the building! Fog and clouds blew down the hall and made it a little hard to see, Glen was getting into your face then put his hands around your neck. He was trying to choke you out! It was like something out of a science fiction movie. I don't know what either of you were trying to do to one another but it seemed to be getting serious. About the time that Glen fella put his hand around your neck, another one of those Reapers appeared out of the darkness. He had glowing red eyes and a booming voice. He seemed to know both of you. He grabbed onto each of you by the back of the neck like you were little kids and went straight up through the ceiling. Shortly after that the fog cleared out and it got light again and started warming back up. I thought for sure that was the last time I would ever see you. I stood in the hallway for at least ten minutes just wondering what had happened."

Craig realized his mouth was hanging open and closed it. He blinked hard, trying to take it all in and process what Mike had recounted as happening. "Did anyone else see what you saw?"

Mike nodded. "I noticed Jim, my neighbor, standing in his doorway a couple minutes after you all had disappeared. I didn't say anything to him right away and he went back into his room."

Craig raised an eyebrow. "You both have seen Glen around here pretty often right?"

Mike nodded. "Yes, we see that old ghost a couple times a day. He says something to us once in a while, but we both tell him we're not interested."

Mike paused but Craig could tell he wasn't done. "What is it? Did you think of something else?"

275

Mike pointed at the door. "I haven't seen that guy since you went up through the ceiling with him."

Craig looked at the door where Mike was pointing, then back at him. "Which guy? Jim, Your neighbor? Or the Reaper?"

Mike was looking Craig in the eyes. "That Reaper, I haven't seen him at all, yesterday or today. That's unusual. I usually see him every day."

Craig got a thoughtful look on his face. "What did I come over to talk to you about? I don't remember any of that stuff so I don't know why I was here."

Mike furrowed his brow. "I have no idea, we never got to speak to each other. Did you want to talk to me about that woman you've been seeing?"

Craig cringed. "Oh shoot! She's waiting outside. I totally forgot! She brought me here looking for my car."

Mike smiled and laughed at him. "So you think she wouldn't be into you if she knew about this Reaper stuff?"

Craig looked at the floor for a moment, then back at Mike. "I'm thinking probably not. But I should go out and tell her everything is fine."

Mike raised his hand and waved goodbye as Craig got to the door. "I'll let you know if I see the Reaper guy again."

Craig paused before stepping out the door. "Thank you. If you do see him, try not to interact with him. He knows I come here to see you, it might aggravate the situation."

Craig went out the front doors into the heat of the day. Becky was sitting in her car with the AC on high. Becky stepped out as Craig approached the drivers side door. "Is everything okay?"

Craig nodded. "It is. Dad's fine. He said I was here the other day just visiting but he didn't know what happened after I left. He didn't know that my car was still here. I wonder if I got nabbed in the parking lot and whoever took me realized they had the wrong person and dropped me off at my house?" Craig had a sideways smile on his face as he made up a scenario, trying to explain his short disappearance.

Becky didn't notice his sarcasm at first. "Well, why would they take you to your house? And how would they know where you live?" She looked up at Craig's face noticing his smirk. "Oh! You're joking! Okay, not funny. You had me there for a moment." Becky gave him a playful punch on the shoulder. "Since we found your car, I should be going back to work, I don't have time for coffee now, I have a showing this afternoon and this took a little longer than I thought it would." Becky stepped closer and gave Craig an unexpected hug. Craig almost didn't know how to react. Becky stepped back and looked at Craig's face. "Will I see you again soon?"

Craig blushed a little. "Yes. I almost forgot! You should take the paperwork with you." Craig went to the passenger side of Becky's car and retrieved his satchel. He handed Becky the envelope with the financial documents. "When you've had a chance to review we can make plans to get them signed and make it official." He could tell that wasn't what she meant by the look on her face. He quickly blurted out, "Then we can go out to dinner to celebrate?"

Becky's face lit up. "Yes, that sounds wonderful. I'll let you know when I'm ready."

31

Devil in the Details

Three days had passed since Craig had seen Becky. She texted him every day to say hello and ask how his day was. She sent every message with a kissy face emoji. Craig was surprised every time, but he sort of liked it. Not knowing if he should reciprocate, he would only send smiley faces in return.

Finally, Becky let him know her lawyer had finished his review of the documents. "He has made a few adjustments., one of the texts read.

Craig's palms got sweaty when he read it. *'Oh no. Was he able to see some of the Grimm language and remove it?'* He sent an inquiring text back. "Is it anything that will hold up the contract?" Craig watched his phone anxiously as three dots appeared, then disappeared several times, as Becky typed out her response. The dots finally went away as Craig waited for several minutes. No text came through. *'Whats happening?'* He gave up and set his phone on his desk. *'This is too much pressure.'* He closed his eyes, leaning back in his chair he took a few deep breaths, trying to let the anxious feelings go. Just after he let out the third breath, the phone vibrated on the desk. Craig lunged forward, grabbing it in a rush, frantically stabbing at the notification from Becky, realizing his fingers were too cold to get a reaction from the screen. He rubbed his hand on his leg, trying to warm it up. Finally, he was able to get the message to open.

"It should be fine. He said it was just some minor payment terms he wanted to update. He already contacted Rick and got them approved. When can we meet to sign? The sooner the better!" Followed by another kissy face.

Craig let out a sigh and felt some relief from his worry. "I'm available tomorrow afternoon, I will contact Rick to set it up, unless you want to take care of that part. Then we can meet at his office." Craig's anxious feelings weren't completely gone but he felt better that progress had been made.

Becky replied right away. "Pick me up? Then an early dinner afterward to celebrate?"

Craig felt a twinge of guilt. His feelings for Becky had been growing stronger, but he was leading her into darkness, down the same miserable existence he was stuck in. He had thought on a very selfish level that it would be nice to have someone to go through the dark time with, but would she feel the same after she found out that he was the one that put her in this position? His instincts told him no, that would not go ever well.

After all these thoughts clouded his brain, Craig typed out his response. "I would be happy to pick you up. I will let you know what time we need to be at the lenders office, just let me know where to pick you up, I will be there." Craig hit send and set his phone on his desk. He turned back to the stack of essays that he had to get through but had lost motivation for it. He started reading the one he had in front of him, thinking it was terrible and that this student wasn't getting anything out of his class. He wrote on the top of the paper in red ink. "Consider finding another class that is more interesting to you."

Craig's phone vibrated on the desk. This time he picked it up at a much more leisurely pace. Becky had sent her address. "I've already contacted Rick, pick me up at 3, I'll be ready." Two kissy faces followed the message.

Craig smiled and sent a smiley face in return. "See you then."

Craig struggled through the remainder of student essays in front of him. When he was done, he reviewed some of his notes on each paper. *I wasn't very nice to them today. I think the stress is affecting my work.'* Craig loaded his satchel and left the office. When he got to the parking lot he saw Jake unloading his music equipment from his car.

"Jake!" He called from across the lot as he walked over to greet him. "How are you? It's been a couple days since I've seen you."

Jake spun around and extended his hand. "I'm doing great! How are you? Where did you go the other day? I was enjoying the listening room and when I opened my eyes you were gone. It was just me and Mr. Miles."

Craig's eyes got wide. "I decided to let you two take the tour on your own. You both seemed to be in the same head space so I left you to it. How did it go?"

Jake smiled as big as ever. "It was awesome! The studios there are top of the line. We are going to be able to make some great music with all that equipment."

Craig was noticing Jake's skin seemed a little darker than the last time he saw him. *'That must be from the heat of the eruption coming from under the studio.'* He really wanted to ask if Jake saw anything unusual, but refrained. "So the tour went well? Was the rest of the building as nice as the listening room?"

Jake looked surprised. "You should have stayed for the tour! It's amazing, though that smoke smell seemed stronger when I left. Even Mr. Miles noticed it. I suggested he update the carpet in the lobby."

Craig smiled "Yes, I think that would go a long way in removing that smell. I've got to get going. It was good to see you. Let me know when your next show is, I'll come prepared next time."

Jake reached out to shake hands, then changed his mind and went in for a hug. "Thank you very much for helping me. The next show is on me. It's the least I can do."

Craig stiffly allowed the hug to happen. "I'll take you up on that."

* * *

Craig rung the bell next to the front door of Becky's home. He had expected he would be picking her up from her office. *'I suppose this makes sense since we're going to dinner afterward.'* Becky opened the door wearing a white one piece suit, looking rather stunning.

Craig was speechless for a moment, then finally managed to stammer out a few words. "You look amazing."

Becky smiled, showing her bright white teeth. "You look very handsome yourself."

Craig felt like it was merely a polite compliment, he was

wearing a dark suit but it wasn't much different from what he wore every day to work. "Thank you, are you ready to go?"

Beck closed the door as she stepped outside. "I am. Lets go make a deal with the Devil!" Becky laughed but Craig got a full body chill and froze in place. Becky saw the look on his face and noticed Craig's face had gone completely pale. "Are you okay?" Becky stood in front of him, reaching out to hold his arms in case he passed out. She stared at his face for a few seconds before Craig regained his composure.

"Yeah, I'm fine. Just a funny saying I guess."

Becky held Craig's arms for a few seconds more, then helped him turn toward the car. "Okay, let's go then."

Craig shook it off on the way to the car, opened the door for Becky, then drove them to Rick's office.

The paperwork took almost two hours to go through. Becky signed her name or initials in hundreds of places. Craig stood behind Becky, watching over her shoulder as Rick explained each section of paperwork to her. Craig saw Grimm's section of paperwork in the middle of the stack, under some other heading about direct deposit. She signed it without hesitation. Craig was sweating profusely, so much so that he was getting self conscious about it. Once Becky was done signing, Craig excused himself to the restroom to dry off his forehead and freshen up. When he returned, Becky and Rick were chatting politely.

"Are we all set?"

Becky looked at Craig and smiled. "Yes, I think we are ready to go."

They chose a nice Italian restaurant for an early dinner. Becky gave directions as they drove. "They have a wonderful wine selection, I'm in the mood to celebrate!"

Craig glanced at her and smirked. *'I wonder what that means.'* "You've started a new chapter, you should celebrate."

Once inside the restaurant, Becky excused herself to the restroom as Craig waited for a table. He stood in the lobby looking at the patrons. *'Surprisingly busy for 4:30 in the afternoon.'* Craig caught a chill in the air and glanced around the room, then to the ceiling to look for an air duct. He didn't see anything that should be causing the cold. *'Grimm, why? What now? I'm doing what I should be doing. Just leave me alone.'* Craig was instantly on edge, glancing again around the room and behind him. No sign of the Demon Reaper just yet.

Becky returned just in time to be led to their table placed squarely in the middle of the room. Craig played the gentleman and pulled the chair out for Becky before seating himself. Before letting the server go, "Could we get a wine list please?"

Becky smiled. "Wonderful, thank you for asking for that."

Craig was feeling awkward. "Do you have a plan?"

Becky cocked her head sideways. "What do you mean? For tonight?"

Craig's eyes got wide, that wasn't what he meant at all but now the thought was in his head. "Oh! No, not really. What I meant was, now that the financing is in order for your project, do you have a plan on moving forward. It's a massive undertaking that will require a huge amount of coordination and planning. Do you have a plan about what the next steps are?"

Becky smiled sheepishly. "I was rather hoping it was about tonight. But to answer your question, yes, I have a plan. I have gathered information about what I would do if this day ever came true for years. Now it's time to put the wheels in motion. I have reached out to my contracting partners and gotten on schedules for sight walks and quote updates. I know exactly what the next steps are."

Craig had stopped listening after she said she hoped it was about tonight. His mind raced, wondering what that meant. He was sure she had this whole evening planned out but wasn't sure if he wanted to know, or if he should just go with it and let the night unfold.

As Craig was lost in his thoughts about what the evening might bring, he felt a cold blast hit him in the face. It was stronger than the one he'd felt while standing at the front of the restaurant. Craig looked up to check the room. He didn't have to look far, seeing Grimm hovering 20 feet or so behind Becky. The temperature was dropping fast. It seemed Grimm wasn't pleased that Craig was having dinner with a client. His eyes were glowing a fierce red under the cloak.

Craig could see that the cold was effecting Becky as well as she rubbed her arms, feeling the goose bumps build up as the chill got into her skin. "It just got super cold in here didn't it?"

Craig pulled his attention back to Becky quickly. "You felt that too? I guess the AC kicked on high just now. Maybe it will even out in a few minutes."

Becky went back to looking over the wine menu as Craig looked back at Grimm over her shoulder. The area near Grimm seemed to be getting darker, as if his presence not only pulled all the heat from the area, but was also pulling the light from the room, into his dark cloak, like a black hole that nothing could escape from. A fog started to form at the floor Grimm was floating above, making the scene all the more creepy and hard for Craig to look away from.

Becky had asked Craig if he thought he wanted a Bordeaux or a Cabernet but Craig didn't hear what she said. Becky sat staring at him for a few moments, waiting for a reply, noticing he was lost somewhere else. She looked behind her to see what he was staring at, then back at Craig. "It looks a little darker back there doesn't it? Is that smoke in the room?"

Craig still didn't respond.

"Craig!"

He snapped his attention back. "Sorry, what did you say?"

Becky squinted at him. "What happened? Where are you?"

Craig shook his head quickly side to side. "Oh, I thought I saw someone I know over there and got a little distracted."

Becky turned around again and looked across the room. "Is it a little darker over there than it was when we came in? It seems smoky or something."

Craig focused his eyes on Becky. *'Is she seeing part of Grimm's presence already?'* "It does seem darker back there, and a little foggy. Maybe that's what is making it feel colder."

The server came back to the table, Becky ordered two glasses of Cabernet without asking Craig again what he preferred. Craig's face and ears were getting cold, so much that they were turning red.

Becky glanced behind her again after noticing Craig couldn't stop looking over her shoulder. "What is it? What are you looking at?"

Craig tried to pull his attention back to Becky. "It's just getting cold, I was trying to see where it's coming from."

Craig glanced at Grimm again. He hovered motionless behind Becky. Craig could see the red glow of his eyes under the cloak, pulsing brighter, then dimmer, then brighter again. The glow was distracting. Craig heard Grimm's voice in his head. *"She isn't the right one Craig. Don't get involved."* Craig reacted visibly, pulling his head back in surprise.

Becky saw him move suddenly. "What happened? Where are you?" She asked again.

Craig refocused quickly. "I'm right here, sorry, everything's fine. Did you find something on the menu?"

Becky paused, looking Craig in the eyes. "Yes, I think I have, how about you?"

Craig hadn't even looked at the menu yet. "No, I suppose I should figure that out."

As Craig stared at the menu purposely not looking up, but not reading anything, his mind was on Grimm hovering 20 feet behind Becky. He could hear Becky talking but he wasn't listening. Grimm spoke in his head again. *"Why are you here with her? The deal is complete, leave it at that and move on."*

Craig thought about why he was here. *'I think she's interested in me. I would like a relationship, a friendship with a woman.'*

Grimm received his thoughts and replied. *"Don't let your human emotions get in the way of your duty. You don't have the capability to have a relationship at this time."*

Craig slumped slightly. *'You said I could live a normal life.'* Grimm's eyes shot bright red beams at Craig. *"You can lead a somewhat normal life Craig, this is not part of it."*

Craig looked at Becky. She was looking back at him, knowing that something wasn't right. "Craig, how many relationships have you been in?"

Craig heard that question and recoiled. "What? Why do you ask?"

Becky leaned back in her seat. "Because you're terrible at being on a date."

Craig's face went pale. "Is this a date? I wasn't sure. I wanted it to be a date but I'm not good at picking up on clues."

Becky nodded slowly. "Yes, I can see that. But even so, if

we were just here as friends or colleagues, you're not keeping good company."

Craig's color slowly came back. He glanced at Grimm over her shoulder again and heard him in his head. *"End it."*

Craig looked into Becky's eyes. "You're right, I thought I wanted to be on a date with you and I had thought of a relationship. But I can't do it. I enjoy your company and would like to remain friends but I am not in a space in my personal life that I can pursue a relationship. I am too easily distracted and couldn't give you the attention you deserve."

Becky sipped her wine looking into Craig's eyes. "That's okay, I would like to be friends with you as well Craig. I wasn't completely sure I wanted a relationship. More like I wanted a romantic companion."

Craig's brows went up. "Really? I'm flattered that you would think of me that way." He looked at Grimm again. "I can't though, it would feel wrong."

Becky seemed surprised. "That's fine, we can have a nice celebratory dinner as friends. I appreciate that you can be honest with me about your feelings and not lead me on."

Craig felt a sheepish embarrassment but managed a smile. "Thank you for understanding. I really do hope that we can remain friendly, I am very interested in how your new venture works out."

Craig looked past Becky in time to see Grimm dissipate into nothing. The fog and chill in the air went away and they chatted and had a nice dinner. Craig dropped Becky at her house just before 8 PM and called it a night, returning home feeling a little sad and disappointed that he was convinced not to pursue a relationship, even though deep inside he knew it was the right thing to do.

32

Coliseum of Souls

Craig was getting ready for bed, washing his face, trying to put the day behind him. His mind was on Becky. He couldn't get the evening out of his head, it was too fresh. She didn't seem too disappointed but he sensed it a little bit. The thoughts of romance were hard to let go.

Grimm had made it clear that he shouldn't pursue Becky. *'Is it just Becky? Or should I not pursue any relationship?'* That was a sobering thought. *'It's probably best not to have any type of personal relationship given this situation. It would surely just lead to heartbreak.'*

He knew that if he continued to see Becky and the relationship grew into something deep, he would eventually break her heart having to pull away to fulfill his contract with the Evil One. Craig took a deep breath, feeling the need to let the thoughts of a potential romance go, knowing he was bound eternally to darkness. Craig stopped thinking about his eventual end for a moment, staring at himself in the mirror, noticing that the gray at his temples and on his face seemed much more pronounced than it had just a month ago. He turned away from the mirror and stepped toward the door. His foot caught on the rug and he stumbled forward. As he tried to step quickly and catch himself, his opposite foot slipped away from him and he lunged forward even harder. Craig's head slammed against the edge of the bathtub. Everything went black. He laid awkwardly on the bathroom floor, bleeding from a gash above his right eyebrow. A large goose egg formed over his eye. Several minutes went by as blood pooled on the floor near his head. Craig's eyes started twitching behind his closed eyelids, moving frantically back and forth.

Craig found himself walking into darkness, through a long corridor. His bare feet softly echoed off the stone walls only four feet to each side of him. The floor was cool and felt damp underfoot. He could smell the damp, dank air of wet earth, old and stale like wet dust, as he moved forward. Visibility was low, just enough light from ahead and behind kept the path visible. Everything looked gray, the walls of stone, the path, and the light coming from an unknown source. He felt like he was in an old time black and white movie, nothing had color. Craig kept walking, strangely drawn forward, not knowing where he was, how he got there, or why he was there. He felt calm, looking side to side at the stone walls, smooth and damp. Step after step.

Craig's eye caught sight of something ahead, something in the middle of the path. He tried to slow his pace but it didn't seem to change. His heart rate rose slightly, he couldn't make out what it was, ahead in the gray light. As he got closer, he could see there were more objects past the first one. Then he realized the first object was a stalagmite growing out of the floor of stone. The object was tall and thin, protruding from the floor like a stone spike, a natural formation from centuries of water dripping from the ceiling. *I'm in a cave? This is bizarre, I didn't know there were these types of caves in New Mexico.'*

Craig squinted his eyes, trying to see the objects ahead. They looked much bigger than the stalagmite he was standing next to. Some of them had points at the tops, while others were much bulkier. Craig continued moving farther into the tunnel. The stone hall started to open up into a cavernous chamber. Craig came to an opening to a space that looked like a cathedral made of rock, long forgotten, covered in stone statues of all shapes and sizes. *'What is this place?'*

Craig was able to overcome his forward motion and stop where the hallway opened into the massive, coliseum sized chamber. He stood in awe of the sheer size of the area, looking out over thousands of stone figures. At the ceiling, great scroll-works of stone and balconies overlooked the center stage an amphitheater where great leaders of the past would have held court or shows that would attract hundreds, if not thousands, to view. The statues covered every square foot as far as Craig could see in every direction.

He moved farther into the theater, this time with great curiosity. As he approached the first statue nearest him, he noticed the expression on the face. Surprised, he looked to another and yet another. The expressions were each different in their own way, but they all had something in common. Each statue seemed to be in fear of something. Some had their hands covering their faces, some had their arms outstretched to fend off an unknown attacker. Terror struck their faces. *'What happened that someone would make so many statues of people with fear in their eyes, terrified of something? The years this must have taken to complete is unthinkable.'*

Craig continued to walk his way carefully through the maze of statues, looking at each as he passed by. He stopped at the edge of the stage and looked up at the balconies filled with stone figures, all terrified and running from something. Craig noticed many of the balconies had stalactites hanging from their edges with corresponding stalagmites on the floor below. *'This place has been here for hundreds, maybe thousands of years! Has it been untouched all this time? Wait! that's not even possible, there weren't theaters like this in New Mexico that long ago!'* Craig's mind was blown. *'How could this be? Am I still in New Mexico? Could I have been transported to ancient Rome?'* Craig's thoughts started to race, thinking about how this could be possible. He stepped up onto the stage, moving through the statues, looking at the faces with his deepest curiosity. He had completely forgotten that he was in an unknown cave and wasn't sure how he got there. The statues and faces intrigued him so deeply that he lost track of time. Craig examined some of the statues closer than others, making note that some of the stone was darker and more aged than others. He also noted that there were cracks in some of the stone faces, as if the stone wasn't solid all the way through.

Craig stopped again under the edge of a balcony where dripping water filled with calcium had been landing on one of the statues. The calcium deposits had encased the statue from head to toe, its arms were protruding from the center of the stalagmite, as well as one leg from the knee to the foot. *'This one has been here thousands of years! Stalagmites take eons to form.'*

Some of the statue formations appeared to be trying to run in fear, as if being chased by a viscous attacker. Craig turned a slow circle, taking in the sheer amount of statues in the coliseum, as far as he could see in the gray light, heads and arms stood shoulder to shoulder. Craig wandered through to the opposite side of the massive stage, glancing at the faces, some with cracks, some almost new. He reached out and touched them as he passed, running his fingers over the faces, feeling the stone drag under his fingertips. Stone flaked off some of the older looking statues as he touched them, revealing a deeper level of rock under the surface.

He jumped down from the edge of the stage and landed face to face with a statue, it's lifeless gaze stopped him cold. *'I recognize that face!'* Craig gasped out loud and herd it echo off the stone walls. He stood frozen, as if he were one of the stone figures, staring into the blank eyes of James Lucky, the very person that had given Craig the contract which signed him into service of the Most Evil One without his knowledge. The very person that had gone missing years prior while working at NMSU. *'How is this possible?'* Craig looked him up and down, front to back. It was for certain James' face.

"How? How is this possible?" He heard the words echo off the stone walls, taking several seconds to dissipate back into silence.

Craig's heart rate spiked to panic level as he spun around and looked at the faces surrounding him. Each face nearby looked like new rock, freshly minted stone. *'Could I know more of them?'*

He started moving through more of the figures, checking each face as he passed, this time inspecting them and running through his memory to see if there was a match to the face. The gray light washed out some features, making it difficult to see who was behind the stone until he came to a figure Craig recognized instantly. He stopped with a gasp that almost turned to a shriek. He clasped his hand over his mouth to keep from screaming, only letting out a sharp piercing tone before muffling it silent. Craig again froze in the face of who he was seeing. The slender figure, smaller than himself, the features of her face unmistakable, her hair flowing back as if she were hit by a gust of wind just before being frozen in stone. The fear on her face made Craig break into tears, seeing Becky fearing for her life, frozen in time, broke Craig's heart. Tears streaming from his eyes, he reached out to touch her face, then, embracing her, he sobbed in disbelief. Craig tried to shake Becky awake, as if he could bring her back from her tragic demise.

Craig sobbed and wailed in pain, yelling, "No! This can't be! Bring her back!" Craig's legs gave out as he succumbed to the pain of loss.

He fell to the floor, banging his head on something on the way down. He jolted, his arm raising his hand to his head in physical pain. He felt the warm wet feeling of blood on his head and drug his arm through the wet sticky blood on the floor. Confused, he opened his eyes, blinking away tears, trying to focus in the blaring white light reflecting off the bathroom floor. Craig was confused and dizzy, his head hurt terribly. The red of the blood on the white tile floor was a stark contrast to the mono tone gray light of the coliseum and the gray statues that had stared back at him. Craig tried to sit up but the pain made him more dizzy, so he laid back down, rolling onto his back, covering his eyes with his forearm, touching the giant lump on his head, causing a wince in pain. Craig lay there catching his breath, wondering if what he just experienced were real.

"Damn it Grimm! What are you doing to me?"

33

Stone Army

Craig hadn't heard from Becky in three days. He texted and called her several times after his dream about the stone statues. He kept telling himself, *'It couldn't have been real. I was just upset about not being able to have a relationship.'* Yet he was scared something had happened to her since she hadn't gotten back to him. *'Maybe she is just upset with me for telling her we couldn't date.'*

Craig walked the stairs in the Great Hall to his office. He was struggling to find the drive to go to work every day. The darkness and the bad dreams that seemed real were having an effect on his health. The lump on his head was getting smaller but the bruise was looking worse. Dark purple and shades of green that ran down his forehead and pooled above his eyebrow. He had to explain it to people no less than three times per day. He felt tired every day and dreaded going to bed, fearing another dream would have him surrounded by something evil and inescapable. *'At least I've completed my recruiting quota for now. Hopefully the next round won't feel as difficult since I'll have more time.'*

Craig opened his office door in time to see Grimm descend through the ceiling in a dark cloud of smoke and materialize in front of him, hovering several inches above the floor. Craig stood in the doorway looking at Grimm, in admiration of his grace. He was always stunned at how elegant Grimm could look in the flowing black cloak. The room was bitter cold now, a hint of fog forming at the floor.

"Come in Craig, please get comfortable."

Craig gently closed the door behind himself and went to his desk to sit. "Hello, Grimm, I'm almost glad that you're here. I have a question for you."

Grimm turned and hovered in front of the desk. "You don't look well Craig. Have you been taking care of yourself?"

Craig cracked a sarcastic smile. "Grimm, are you showing a hint of care?"

Grimm didn't flinch. "Not at all, I need you to be healthy enough to follow through with your contract. That is my main concern. If you aren't taking care of yourself, you won't be able to recruit. If you don't recruit, then I must fill the gaps. I have other things to attend to and don't need your responsibilities on my plate as well."

Craig leaned back in his chair. *'Of course it is about you, not about caring about those that work for you.'*

Grimm's eyes brightened, glowing hot red. "Might I remind you who is standing in front of you. I know what you're thinking."

Craig's face burned hot even in the icy temperature of the room. "Yes of course, please excuse my inconsiderate thoughts. I am worn down, the dreams and anxiety I have had lately are taking their toll. I have had a couple of accidents causing some injury, I am still recovering." Craig stopped, noticing the glow of Grimm's eyes softening. "I need to know something."

Grimm stood motionless as the fog deepened in the room. "Proceed with your question."

Craig sat upright, leaning his arms on the desk in front of him. "A few days ago when I hit my head, I was unconscious for a while. Not really sure how long, but judging from the amount of blood on the bathroom floor, it was a long time. I had a vision, a dream possibly." Craig paused, looking up into Grimm's dark hood, only seeing a shadow of his ash white jaw line. Grimm waited for him to continue. Craig wasn't sure if Grimm already knew what he was going to say but continued anyway. "I was in a cavern or a coliseum type room. It was underground I think. It was all made of stone and had stalagmites and stalactites throughout. There were thousands of human statues filling the coliseum, or maybe it was a cathedral, I can't be sure. Have you ever seen such a place?"

Grimm was silent for an uncomfortable minute. Craig sat waiting to hear a response, but was concerned that he might have said something that he shouldn't have. Grimm put his hands behind his back. Click click click. His fingers rubbed together. The hair on the back of Craig's neck stood on end and goose bumps formed on his arms.

"Yes, I am aware of the coliseum that you speak of."

Craig drew a breath, realizing he hadn't been breathing. "Why would I see that in a dream?"

Grimm stopped clicking his fingers together. "You are being prepared for what may come. All the visions that you have seen are to get you ready for your future as a Reaper."

Craig looked away, staring at the papers on his desk and

blew out a plume of air visible in the frigid room. "What are all the statues for? What is that preparing me for?"

Grimm backed away from the desk slightly. "That is not what you really want to ask, is it Craig?"

Craig looked back into the hood. Grimm's eyes glowing red, but not very bright. "Not exactly, but I was working up to it."

Grimm held his hands out in front of himself. Craig looked at his hands, the bones looked warn and abused, with cracks in many of them and edges worn off. A few moments went by before an image appeared above Grimm's hands. It was the cavern, with all the statues visible. The image was holographic and rotated slowly in front of Craig so he could see all angles of the coliseum with thousands of statues in all positions, fear on their faces, leaving them contorted for eternity.

"Yes, that's the place I saw. What is it?"

Grimm held the image as it rotated and moved throughout the coliseum. "This is the Stone Army. They stand in wait for the dark days, when the Evil One will come to conquer humanity, when he decides to finish his wrath and take control of everything and everyone on earth. This is one of thousands of armys waiting." Grimm's voice was nearly happy, his tone changed as if the dark times were what he was looking forward to. He wanted to rejoice in the end when the dark days fell and evil ruled.

Craig was enthralled by the image, he couldn't take his eyes away from it. Craig jumped back into reality with a jolt. "How do people end up here?"

Grimm stood with the spinning holograph in front of him, not moving, as if he was enjoying it too much to want to. "This is where they go while they wait for the Emperor of

Darkness to call them into action before they serve their torturous eternity. They are frozen in stone with only their tortured thoughts to keep them company."

Craig stood motionless as he let that sink in for a few seconds and watched the image rotate in front of Grimm. "So if I fail, this is where I would go before being tortured for eternity?"

Grimm let the image fade and put his hands behind his back once more. "To put it simply, yes. Trust me when I tell you, this is the beginning of the torture, being trapped in stone with your thoughts still in tact is not a joyous occasion."

Craig thought of what that might be like. "There were statues down there that had to have been thousands of years old. Many of them were covered in calcium deposits that had dripped from the ceiling. Those people are still in there with their thoughts?"

Grimm clicked his fingers. "Yes they are, now imagine what your thoughts would be like after all that time."

Craig's eyes got wide. *'I don't like my thoughts after a few hours of no sleep, I can't imagine what that would be like.'* "They're going crazy in their heads."

Grimm stood waiting for Craig to put the rest of it together, he knew what Craig ultimately wanted to ask. "It is part of the process."

Craig stared off to the side of the room, not focusing on anything in particular, but the visions in his head were moving fast. "Wait! Becky was there! So was James Lucky! I just saw Becky and she just signed the contract, why would she be a statue? What did she do to get sent away?"

Grimm nodded slightly. "There it is, that is what you wanted to ask about all along. Do you recall your meeting with Becky?

I told you not to get involved. I applaud you for taking my advice. In short, Becky got greedy."

Craig furrowed his brow. "Isn't that what this entire empire, this pyramid scheme, is built on? It's all about greed! Find what someone wants more than keeping their morals in tact, and exploit it!"

Grimm let out a booming laugh. "Yes, Craig, it is. But even the One Most Evil has limits to what he will provide to the greedy. It is part of the contract, you know, fine print. You're not allowed to sign a second contract with the Darkness, it is grounds for immediate removal. She is now serving the beginning of her eternal sentence. Imagine what her thoughts were when she saw you in front of her stone being, staring at you, knowing that you were the reason she was frozen in stone because you tricked her into signing another deal with the Evil Emperor. That will torture her mind forever." Grimm sounded evil now, his words cutting into Craig's mind. His words would torture Craig, knowing that Becky would be thinking about what he did to her for eternity.

"She didn't know it was happening. Shouldn't she have gotten a warning?"

Grimm leaned into Craig's face and spoke in a low, menacing tone. "She should have read the contracts." Grimm stood up again as Craig processed his words. "I am not done with you. I will return, there are things I must discuss with you, but not now."

Grimm backed away and disintegrated before he got to the door. Craig sat stunned at the outcome of the conversation. The heat returned to the room but Craig was cold through his core and needed to go outside into the sun to think, trying to make sense of his new knowledge of how this all worked.

34

Fiery Depths

Craig tried to force himself not to think about anything having to do with Grimm but every once in a while it would bubble to the surface. Becky's face would pop into his mind and Craig would break into tears or be incapacitated by shortness of breath. He wasn't sure if it was the loss of Becky that struck him so hard, or if it was knowing that he might ultimately end up in the coliseum of souls too, unable to move but tortured by his own thoughts until the Darkness came calling.

Craig was going through the motions of everyday life but couldn't recount what he did yesterday or the day before. He had lost his sense of being. At the beginning, he hadn't thought that it would come to this, he had tried to stay positive, thinking that he would just do what he had to in order to survive and everything would work itself out.

Craig needed to visit his father, it had been over a week. *'Maybe he can help me look forward to something.'* Craig left his office a few minutes early and went straight to Winding Tree. He walked into the home and right to Mike's room. Craig tapped on the door and opened it without waiting for an answer. "Hello, Dad. Hope this is a good time."

Mike jolted a little bit, sitting up in his favorite chair and looking startled at Craig as he tried to gather his sleepy thoughts. "Oh! You scared me. I must have dozed off watching the television."

Craig broke a slight smile as he came into the room and sat on the sofa. "Sorry for the intrusion, I was just feeling the need to see you and catch up a bit."

Mike shuffled himself around in his seat, trying to gather himself together. "It's fine. How have you been this last week?"

Craig stared blankly at the floor in front of him, searching for the words. "It's been a rough week. Do you recall Becky? I mentioned that I was interested in her?"

Mike could tell from Craig's tone that this wasn't good news. "I do, she was the real estate lady right?"

Craig nodded. "She was, yes. She signed the contract. I had some hard feelings about that because I was growing to like her quite a bit. Well, it didn't matter. Grimm warned me that I should just stay in my lane and not get attached."

Mike cleared his throat. "I take it something has happened?"

Craig nodded slightly, turning his head to look at Mike with tears starting to well in his eyes. "Grimm took her."

Mike recoiled with a pained look on his face. "Oh, no! Why would he do that?"

Craig dabbed his sleeve to his eyes. "Apparently she had already signed a different contract with someone selling her soul to the Evil One before I got there. That's against the rules and she paid the price."

Mike shook his head. "Do you know what happened to her?"

Craig went pale. "Yes. She was sent to be tortured in hell. I

302

saw her. I had a dream about it, but it was real according to Grimm."

Mike was squinting at Craig. "What do you mean it was real? Your dream?"

Craig had gone into a day dream state and snapped back quickly. "Sorry, yes, I was dreaming, but it was a real place that I went to. I asked Grimm about a dream that I had. There were thousands of stone statues in an underground cathedral. Many of them had been there for a thousand of years but the Reapers keep adding to the collection if someone doesn't fulfill their contract or breaks the contract in some way. That's what happened to Becky. They are sent there until the Dark One pulls them back into service. Grimm said it was the start of their torture. Each soul lives inside a stone statue with nothing but their thoughts to keep them company. Basically they go crazy in there with nothing but their own thoughts in their heads forever."

Mike had a disgusted look on his face. "Oh, my. That sounds hideous."

Craig nodded agreement. "It does, and Becky is there now, knowing that I was the reason she got sent away to start her eternal torture."

Mike shook his head. "No. You aren't the reason she's there. She's there because of her own greed. She wanted things the simple way. She didn't want to put in the time to earn it herself. You just supplied the shortcut."

Craig looked Mike in the eyes blankly. "But she wont see it that way. She will be thinking I did it to her, for eternity. That will be going through her mind as she goes crazy."

Mike looked away in silence for a few moments. "Maybe so. It's not for you to worry about now. You said she already had signed another deal with the Devil, She was already down a bad path. I don't think this is something you should beat yourself up over."

Craig followed Mike's gaze over to the television droning on in the background. "I know that you're right but I don't like the feeling of how this happened."

Mike looked back at Craig with a calm expression. "What do you need to do now to move on?"

Craig drew in a deep breath. "Well, holiday break at school starts at the end of this week. I will need to start recruiting again after break."

Mike thought for a moment. "You've made your quota then? Congratulations."

Craig broke a weak smile. "I did. Even after Grimm added to it halfway through. No rest for the wicked though, I've got to try and get ahead of next year."

Craig's phone vibrated in his pocket. Craig stood up and pulled it out. "My neighbor Tom. Poor guy. Wants to meet and talk about his situation."

Mike watched Craig standing, sending a message to Tom. "You've got a lot going. I hope you can find some rest so you can think clearly about what you need to do."

Craig sent his reply to Tom and looked at his father. "Thank you. It hasn't been easy to sleep. I'm always afraid I'll have another one of those disturbing dreams. I'm going to head out now. I hope you have a nice evening. Thanks again for listening to me rant."

Mike stood and gave Craig a hug. "Anytime. Hope to see you again soon."

* * *

Tom had questions about what he was supposed to do now. He had texted Craig, asking to meet with him. They agreed to meet mid morning for a cup of coffee and have a talk at a local cafe, not far from Tom's and Craig's homes.

The streets were somewhat busy for a midweek day at 9 AM. People walking through the cute town, visiting the shops, some doing business, others more casual like they might be on vacation. The sun was warm on Craig's back as he walked toward the cafe but Craig rarely enjoyed the little things in life that used to make him smile anymore.

Craig entered the cafe, looking around the shop. He saw Tom sitting near the corner window, already with a coffee in front of him. Craig went to the counter and ordered himself coffee and a muffin, then went and sat across from Tom.

"Good morning, Tom. I hope you have been coping well with the situation."

Tom looked a bit sullen and paused before responding. "I've been trying to deal with it mentally. I don't think I'm doing well with it. I really don't know what to think or do. I feel like I am just waiting for the end of my life now and can't move forward."

Craig picked at his muffin and glanced at Tom's eyes as he heard the crack in Tom's voice leading him to believe Tom was about to break. "When I signed my contract, I didn't know it was happening so, unlike you, I didn't have to deal with knowing what was coming. It hit me out of the blue when the Reaper came to find me and tell me it was time to pay the toll. I tell you that because I don't really know what to tell you to do now. I suppose I should just tell you to live your life and make the best of it. Try not to dwell on the future, but I know that is much easier said than done."

Tom stared blankly into his cup of coffee, hoping he would see the answer floating in front of him. "I don't know how to get it out of my head. I feel like maybe I should just give in and start serving my sentence now. I really don't think I can just live a normal life knowing what I will have to do down the road."

Craig sipped at his hot coffee and let the silence hang for a few minutes. *'I wonder if there is anything I can do to help him forget what is coming.'* Craig pondered if he would need Grimm's help to erase some of the memory of this situation for Tom. "I don't think you want to start the recruiting job just yet. I know this is really overwhelming and terrible to think about, but take it from me, since I am right in the middle of it. You don't want to start this until you absolutely have to. Maybe the difficult thoughts will subside over time. You really need to try and live a normal life for the years that you have before, you know, the Reaper comes calling."

Tom cringed at the last statement. He didn't like to think about the Reaper coming calling for him but when it popped into his mind or when Craig brought it up, it made his chest get tight and his vision go dark, like he was going to black out. "I hear what you're telling me. Maybe this is all too fresh and I need to give it more time. I might be overthinking everything and that doesn't help, however, this is such an unimaginable situation that I'm not sure I will ever be able to let it go enough to live normally."

Craig again let the silence settle over their conversation and pondered what Tom was telling him. As Craig ate the last of his muffin, he glanced at someone coming through the door of the cafe. He recognized him right away, Richard from Adaptive. Craig looked away quickly, not wanting to engage given the delicate nature of his current conversation with Tom.

Richard walked to the counter and started to place his order. Craig glanced at Tom and noticed he had a glassy eyed look on his face. "Tom? Tom."

Tom wasn't responding. Craig waved his hand in front of Tom's face, still not responding. He looked around the room and noticed that everyone in the cafe had gone silent, no one was moving. They had all frozen mid sentence, mid motion, mid whatever they were doing in that moment, like someone had pushed a pause button.

Craig looked at Richard standing at the counter. He was moving, but slowly, somewhat unnaturally. At that moment, Tom got up from the table, startling Craig. The restaurant got savagely cold, Craig felt the presence of darkness at that moment. Craig knew what was happening this time. He watched Tom and Richard walk to the door and go outside. They walked stiffly like zombies from the movies, going out to the street in the mid morning sun.

Craig stood and walked to the front of the cafe as the earth started to rumble. Craig was almost unfazed by it, knowing he was just about to see a show of amazing power and unworldly transformation. Craig moved to the sidewalk, not wanting to be stuck in the building in case things got out of control. As he moved down the sidewalk, away from Tom and Richard, the street started to bend and ripple like waves from the ocean rolling across the beach. As the waves of pavement moved away from the center of the street in front of Tom and Richard, the power poles bent and leaned with the motion of the rolling street. The rumbling got louder as the waves in the street got stronger, until the pavement in front of the cafe broke open, splitting down the middle, the crack running a full block in either direction. Craig stepped farther to the side of the building, watching as Richard and Tom stood motionless, with no expressions on their faces. Craig didn't want to stick around, he knew Grimm would be nearby, but he was drawn to the sight. Each transformation had been spectacular in its own way.

Smoke and steam started streaming from below the pavement. Heat rose as flames jumped from deep within the earth, a crack as loud as nearby lightning echoed off the buildings. The waves of rolling earth continued making the buildings all down the street crack and break, glass shattering, awnings falling to the ground, beams on store fronts breaking off and crashing to the sidewalk. The earth opened up in front of the two men to be transformed, as a cloaked Reaper rose from the center of the earth, smoke billowing from the deep gash in the street, surrounding the Reaper in a dark cloud, obscuring everything else in the area as he rose out of the hot fiery depths of molten Hell. He was much larger than any human, more like a giant statue towering 50 feet tall. The Reaper faced Tom and Richard, raising his arms, summoning all the heat and power from within the earth, bringing himself more power than a small town would use in a year. The area went dark around them.

Craig looked to the sky, wondering if the smoke from the entrance to Hell had blocked the sun or if the Reaper had enough control to dim the sun at his will. He couldn't see the cause of the darkening, everything appeared gray and cast an ominous view of all the colors changing to black and white. Craig hadn't thought the transformation would be like this. The others he had witnessed were amazing but this one was on another level all together. The air was shockingly cold as the being seemed to grow even larger in front of them, his arms still outstretched, flames jumping from within the earth to touch the sky.

Another massive crack shook the area and lit up the face of the Reaper. It was lightning this time, Craig saw it. The bones of the Reapers face contorted as if his skull had been broken and the jagged edges of the bones had been laid into place like puzzle pieces that didn't fit together.

Tom and Richard stood motionless, literally frozen. Craig thought he could make out ice crystals on their hair and skin, reflecting the orange tinted flames from the crack in the earth. An explosion shook the ground, throwing molten rock into the air. Craig was ready to run for cover, watching the sky to spot where the glowing balls of goo would land. He was safe for now, he watched the red hot projectiles splatter into pieces when they hit the ground, some of it popped and sizzled as it came to rest nearby. Lightning cracked and split the sky near the giant being, again, giving Craig a view of the broken skull under the giant hood.

A breeze picked up from behind Craig, he spun around, wondering if some other torment was about to befall the area. He didn't immediately see what was happening but heard a voice in his head. *"Are you enjoying the show?"*

Craig bristled when he realized it was Grimm. "Yes, it is quite fantastic. Much more than the others I have seen."

Grimm moved silently next to Craig and spoke directly into his mind in a low, almost friendly, tone. *"You have something on your mind. Tell me what it is."*

Craig had to think back for a moment, glancing across the destruction surrounding the area. He looked at Richard and Tom and it came to him. "I was wondering if there was anything that could be done for Tom as he waits out his remaining years before becoming a Recruiter. Something to help him forget what is in store?" There was a long pause, Craig felt he hadn't been clear in his request. "Since he wasn't fully the recipient of the deal that was set forth and received nothing in return, maybe we could help him forget what has happened."

Grimm still said nothing. Craig waited silently, trying to calm his thoughts, knowing that Grimm could hear what he was thinking. "Yes, I understand what you are saying. I am not usually one for giving in to human feelings or taking pity on emotions. He did, however, agree to the deal without receiving a return payment." Grimm went silent again. Craig stood still, watching the fiery display in front of him. It seemed to be subsiding slightly. Craig glanced at Grimm, the flames reflecting off the ash bone under his cloaked skull. "It is done." Grimm spoke quickly, then retreated a few feet and disappeared into the ashy colored air.

Craig was shocked. *He took care of Tom? Wow, I didn't really think that would happen.* Craig could tell now that the show was about over and decided that he would leave the area so that he wouldn't be in front of Tom when he snapped out of his trance. He took one more look around as the giant Reaper descended back into the fiery earth, then turned and walked away.

35

Judgment Day

Craig was curious about Main Street when he left his house for work the next day. He drove down to the cafe where he had met Tom the day before. *'The transformation was the most elaborate I've seen yet. There's got to be left over destruction from that.'* Craig neared the end of the street that the crevasse had split. He inspected the street as closely as he could while driving. There were some cracks down the center of the pavement but he couldn't be sure they weren't there before the transformation. Craig turned his attention to the buildings. *'There was so much broken glass and the fronts of the buildings were falling apart. There has to be signs of the destruction.'* Craig came to a stop in front of the cafe where he and Tom met. It was in perfect condition, each store front down the way looked as good as before.

Someone honked at Craig from behind, causing him to snap out of his uneasy trance. *'Unbelievable! How does that much destruction just disappear?'* Craig slowly released the brake pedal and drove on, making his way to work. *'I just don't know if it was all another elaborate dream or if it really happened.'*

* * *

Grimm hovered in front of Craig Newman's desk, arms behind his back. The pitch black robe draped from his shoulders, hiding the contours of his skeletal body. Grimm rubbed his fingers together, clicking over the joints. Craig had grown to dislike that sounds, it grated at his nerves.

Craig was sure this would be a quick visit today, he had signed the last of his required contracts two days prior to his deadline. The next year would be much easier to accomplish as he was now in a groove, he knew how to find people that wanted something and discovered a relatively easy way to get it to them.

Grimm's right arm smoothly moved from behind his back, reaching into his cloak he pulled a list from within. He gracefully let the paper float in between himself and Craig and dropped his arm to his side.

"I see that you have achieved your six soul recruitment goal. It is almost impressive." His voice was nearly dripping with sarcasm and a smile.

Craig gave a sideways look into the hooded head of Grimm's cloak. "Almost impressive? Well, it doesn't need to be impressive, I am just happy that I accomplished it. I have already started working on the next quota."

Grimm put his right hand behind his back once again and started rubbing his fingers together, making Craig cringe at the sound of the bones clicking together. "About that," Grimm said slowly, "It was almost impressive, because you almost made it."

Craig's jaw went slack and his eyes got wide. "What do you mean? I got the six souls that you asked for!"

Grimm floated backward a few feet away from Craig's desk. The afternoon sun was shining through the window but the room was icy cold. "I beg to differ, your first contract was signed one day too late." He reached into his cloak once again and produced the three pages of the contract that Haley had signed and tossed it onto the desk in front of Craig.

Craig watched it float down in front of him but was frozen, he didn't want to touch it. The papers slid silently to the edge of the desk. "No! She signed the contract the Thursday after we met, that was exactly one week!"

Grimm was silent except for his finger bones clicking. Click, click, click. He watched as Craig began to panic. "What is the date next to her name?"

Craig grabbed at the paper, lifting it up to inspect the date written after Haley's name. 10/13/2017. Craig scrambled for his phone, opening the calendar app, swiping until he was in October. His body went limp for a moment. "She dated it wrong! She signed it on Thursday, I am absolutely positive!"

Grimm straightened up, as if his perfect posture weren't enough. "It matters not! The date on the contract is binding. You missed the deadline and there is no forgiveness for missing a contract deadline."

Craig started to shiver uncontrollably with the freezing air in the room and his panicked condition. "This isn't right, I didn't miss the deadline, I got the signature on the day I needed to. I can go ask Haley to confirm! I can even go to the admissions office, I am sure Janine will confirm the day that I turned it in!"

Grimm had heard enough. "It is written on the contract and the contract is final! I will not hear any more of this complaining. You missed the deadline and now you will pay the final price!" Grimm started to back farther away from Craig, floating toward the door, crossing the path of the sun shining through the window but not casting a shadow.

Craig started to move from behind his desk. "No! Don't leave, we need to work this out!" Craig was holding his hands out, reaching toward Grimm as if he could grab at the robe and stop him from leaving. "What can I do?! There must be something that I can do to remedy this mistake!"

Grimm stopped abruptly, Craig was closing in on him and brushed his arms through Grimm's cloak but didn't feel anything. Grimm looked down at him as if he were offended. "Again, you failed to read the contract. You should have noticed the date was incorrect and fixed it at the time of the signature. It is too late. Your soul will be reaped."

Craig dropped to his knees, nearly in tears. "NO! I have worked so hard to make it this far. I am not ready!"

Grimm backed through the door and started to hover down the hall. Craig scrambled to his feet and rushed out the door after him, flinging the door open, letting it crash against the wall of the office, this time breaking the glass as it bounced back, shattering it all over the office floor.

Craig ran down the hall, his dress shoes slapping against the tile floor, echoing ahead of him into the open Great Hall. "Wait! Give me a chance! I can do more, I can get even more souls next year!" Craig reached the end of the hall, sliding to a stop and turning left at the corner at the top of the stairs. He could see Grimm hovering at the lower landing, looking back at him with interest. "I can get double next year!" Craig exclaimed, then looked around the hall, noticing that there were groups of people looking at him. He was in a panic and didn't have time to explain why he was yelling at no one.

Craig could see that Grimm might be interested in his offer. He started running hurriedly down the curved tile stairs to get closer, in hopes of making a deal. At the mid way point down the stairs he lost his footing, his left foot slid out, his right knee jabbed onto the edge of one of the steps, sending a shooting pain from his knee to his brain, jamming his hip, dislocating it from its socket. His right hand reached out to brace himself instinctively but he missed the next step, his hand slid through the slats of the banister, breaking his arm sharply in two, the bone jabbing through the skin, spraying blood across the stair instantly as he fell. Craig shrieked in pain but was still trying to brace himself from the fall. He saw it happening in his mind as if he were floating ten feet above himself, looking down over this train wreck that was unfolding on the stairway. His head bashed against the sharp edge of the stone step, cracking his skull, his body went limp and floppy, rag doll rolling down the stairs, bones breaking, his head hitting multiple more times on the way to the bottom, each time sounding like a melon being slapped, hollow and grotesque, finally coming to a stop at Grimm's feet.

Grimm looked down at him and waited a few moments, he didn't move as the people that heard Craig yell and watched him fall came to Craig's side to see if he was okay. Craig was laying with his body twisted and his face on the stone floor, blood flowing slowly from his head. Grimm reached down to Craig's neck, sliding his long fingers into his body, clinching them around his vertebrae just below his skull. With a quick jerk, Grimm pulled Craig's skeletal soul from his body and moved away from the crowd. Quickly, Grimm rose up 40 feet above the Great Hall floor where he paused, holding the soul in the air like a trophy above his head. The stone floor of the Great Hall began to crack and open up in the center, shaking the building so hard the students paused, thinking they were having an earthquake, they looked at the ceiling, wondering if at any moment the roof would collapse. Flames and smoke rose from the molten earth below the floor, flames and sparks jumped from within, crackling as they split the air, heating the in between universe to incinerator temperatures. As the opening got wider, a stream of flame that looked like afterburners from a jet engine, shot out from under the Great Hall. Grimm rushed from high above the floor toward the opening with Craig's soul screaming in agony in his hand. Slamming into the fiery abyss, they disappeared in an explosion of molten earth and a cloud of smoke toward the Center of All That is Evil, causing the building to shake violently once again. Lightning flashed, striking the split open floor, rattling the building, causing chunks of the floor to cave in and erupt into searing flames.

The lightning concussion was so violent that even mortal students felt the building tremble—though they couldn't see the jagged opening to Hell yawning at the center of the Great Hall nor did they witness Grimm take Craig's soul into the evil depths. The structure groaned and rattled as the gash in the lobby floor slammed shut behind Grimm, sealing without a trace. For a moment, everyone froze. The silence was absolute, broken only by the soft, sickening drip of Craig's blood cascading down the stairs.

Then, as if triggered by that sound, panic erupted. Students bolted for cover; many fled through the doors into the sunlight, leaving behind Craig's mangled remains—a mushy pile of body parts leaking every imaginable fluid onto the steps.

Minutes passed. When the building didn't shake again, a few students crept back to the scene. Craig's body had spread further, blood pooling beneath his lifeless shell.

Haley descended the stairs carefully, skirting the blood splattered across each step—evidence of where Craig's fall had begun. At first, she didn't know who had fallen, only that the aftermath looked horrific. As she neared the bottom, a bystander rolled the body onto its back, revealing a face so battered it barely resembled a person.

Haley stopped several steps above, her breath catching. Something about the way the body moved wasn't right. She gasped, hand flying to her mouth, stunned to realize she knew the victim.

The student who had turned Craig over reached for his neck to check for a pulse. Haley watched as his fingers pressed into Craig's flesh—there was no resistance. It was mush. He couldn't even find where to check. Craig's body was spongy and limp, like a skin shell filled with pudding.

The student recoiled, gagging, stumbling back as he fought not to add his lunch to the mess on the floor. Around them, the crowd began to disperse. The scene was too much to take in. Several students were already on their phones, calling for help.

* * *

Craig found himself staring motionless at thousands of stone figures—souls he'd seen before in one of his many dreams. Each one waited to be called into action, condemned to live out a torturous nightmare for eternity. He could glance around the coliseum of souls he had visited before, but he couldn't move. Trapped within his stone encasement, he struggled slightly, desperate to be freed from his statue.

Panic set in quickly.

'This is it?! This is where I have to wait?! I'll go insane here for sure.'

His mind raced. Eyes darted back and forth. Then a realization struck him.

'If I can see these other statues...'

Craig stared straight ahead, his gaze blank as it passed over the countless figures before him. His thoughts slowed. The panic dulled slightly. He wondered how long some of these souls had been here. The calcium deposits dripping from the ceiling had taken eons to form, crusting over the tops of each statue—while inside, a soul waited to be summoned by the Dark Lord to carry out his evil work.

Craig could hear water dripping nearby.

'Is that dripping onto someone else's head? That would be an extra level of torture.'

He couldn't un-hear it now. Each drop landed with a soft splat on the stone—almost rhythmic, but not quite. He began anticipating the sound before it came, trying not to, but failing. Sometimes the drips slowed, stretching seconds between them. Then, without warning, the pace would quicken again.

'I've only been here a short time and already the sound is getting to me. This is what Hell is like—trapped with nothing but my thoughts and a leaky faucet to drive me insane.'

Craig tried closing his eyes for the first time.

'Oh no.'

He tried again. Nothing changed. There was no darkness—

only the same dim, gray room. His soul strained for release from its stone prison, but it was no use. Eyes still open. Mind racing. Panic rising at the thought of never being able to rest again.

He wanted to take a deep, calming breath. To relax. To meditate. But there was no breath to take. He wasn't breathing—just existing in pure consciousness. Sleep evaded him. Only his recurring nightmares passed before his mind's eye as he stared blankly ahead.

His gaze darted around the cavern, searching side to side for something—anything—though he wasn't sure what. At the edge of his peripheral vision, a sudden flash blinded him. White spots lingered in his sight before the gray light returned.

Craig scanned the cavern again. He hadn't yet taken mental inventory of the statues around him, but he was fairly certain that to his right, a few rows forward, there was a new figure. He watched it for what felt like an hour, half-expecting it to move.

'Did anyone else see that?'

He began counting the heads he could see, taking mental inventory—trying to occupy his mind, knowing that eventually, he would go completely mad.